W9-AOQ-901

TARGETS COMING DOWNSTREAM FAST!

Upstream 400 meters, Commander Ben Mount could see the two American destroyers poised for an attack. . . .

The U-boats gliding down the river seemed determined to try to run for it—to break through the destroyer defense. They were playing against enormous odds, hoping that one or two of them could break through.

Why were they so desperate?

Were these the boats with the loads of loot— and the top Nazi brass?

As if in reply, Ben saw the destroyers wheel into action. It was time for a . . .

DEEPWATER SHOWDOWN

DEEPWATER SHOWDOWN

Halsey Clark

A DELL/JAMES A. BRYANS BOOK

Published by
Dell Publishing Co., Inc.
1 Dag Hammarskjold Plaza
New York, New York 10017

Dell ® TM 681510, Dell Publishing Co., Inc.

ISBN: 0-440-01840-4

Printed in the United States of America

First printing—May 1983

Chapter 1

The HMS *Seashell* sliced gracefully through the Atlantic's light swell at twelve knots while on special patrol off Gibraltar. Lieutenant Commander Benjamin Mount, United States Navy, stood on the bridge with his elbows on the rail and binoculars to his eyes, scanning the cold waters. It had been a quiet patrol. They had been on station six days and had not sighted a single enemy ship. Tomorrow they would go back to port.

The patrol had been sent out to support the Allied beachhead on Anzio, just below Rome. Having landed on January 22, the troops had been bottled up, and the Allied command wanted to guard against any reinforcements.

Lieutenant Commander Mount had been working with the British on and off for five years. He had been assigned to England even before that country was at war. However, this was the first time that he had been put in command of a British submarine on patrol. It seemed very irregular. He was told that there was a serious lack of experienced skippers for the Gibraltar squadron, and when this special patrol came up he was drafted. Ben was delighted. He was sure his command wouldn't last long, but he was determined to make the most of it.

His eyes swept the constantly moving sea, stopped, and returned to look again. It was an hour to dusk, and soon the best hunting time would be over. There was little action around Gibraltar from the Axis side. Dozens of Allied convoys ploughed through the seas and past the famous rock, but Germany was reinforcing its troops in Italy through the overland route.

Ben's eyes again found the smudge. It wasn't on the horizon but closer. Maybe five thousand meters out. Something sat low on the water, not moving. He watched it until it came out of a trough and crested a swell. Then he was sure. The smudge was a submarine on the surface. Ours or theirs?

Ben spoke softly through the voice pipe and changed course, He moved his British submarine toward the silent craft. He would investigate. Instantly the crew below was at battle stations. They had been alerted as much by his tone of voice as his words. Ben reduced speed to half forward and moved quietly toward the unidentified craft. His second in command, Sublieutenant Lester Malcolm, came up through the hatch, stood by him, and put his own glasses up to his eyes.

"All stop," Ben commanded. The boat immediately lost speed and glided more slowly through the darkening waters.

"You're right," Malcolm said. "She's a Jerry U-boat. Must be charging her batteries."

"What happened to their famous snorkel devices?" Ben asked. "Those new gadgets that let them recharge their batteries without surfacing that we've been hearing about?"

Before Malcolm could answer Ben pointed below. "Let's take her down and have a look."

"Prepare to dive, battle stations," Malcolm said as he and Ben dropped through the hatch. "Clear the bridge."

He pushed the button sounding the Klaxon three times before he pulled down the hatch, heard it click, and spun the steel wheel on its center to dog it securely.

From the control room Ben heard the familiar sounds of the air venting. There was a slight surge of pressure on his ears, then a quick report from one of the men.

"We have pressure in the boat, sir."

Ben felt the old tightness in his throat and the sudden surge of acid in his stomach, but he tightened his jaw and pushed it down. He had it beaten. His claustrophobia was gone. There was just a gentle reminder every time he dived. He heard the bow and stern planes working and air venting from a negative tank as the ship went down. An internal vent opened and the pressure clogged their ears.

"Take her to periscope depth," Ben said.

Shortly they were in position.

"Periscope depth, Skipper."

"Up periscope."

There was a sharp clank as the brake on the hoist motor was released. Ben heard the whirring of the cable and sheaves as the big eye of the scope surfaced. He caught the tube and flipped out the handles. He followed it up with his eyes glued to the lens as he watched foam and bubbles clear the mirror. He turned to where the target should be and she was still there— a dark, long blob at rest.

"Range and bearing!" Ben shouted.

"Four-three-double-zero," he paused. "Three-five-zero."

"Come to a heading of three-five-zero."

"Aye, sir, three-five-zero."

Ben turned to the ASDIC operator. "Any changes? Is she moving?"

"No, sir, dead in the water."

He turned around 360 degrees with the periscope

and checked for other craft in the area, but found nothing. He slapped the handles up.

"Down periscope."

"Aye, sir, down scope."

Ben stepped back as the instrument slid down into the well. For two minutes they moved slowly toward the enemy, then he ordered the periscope up long enough to check on bearing and range. They were at a range of twelve hundred meters with no change in bearing. A minute after Ben had checked with the periscope, the U-boat spotted them. She was getting underway.

Ben could see men running for the aft hatch and dropping down the conning tower.

"Prepare forward tubes," he said, his voice calm and deliberate.

Sublieutenant Malcolm already had the "fruit machine" working. It was a glass-faced display with a large, complex dial and a crude shape of a ship indicating direction. A smaller dial was positioned below. The two were operated with a celluloid, donut-shaped disc of calculations to match the bearings to target with the submarine's own course. With the target's estimated speed, range and course, the "fruit machine" calculated the torpedo depth and course to intercept the enemy.

In U.S. submarines there was a similar gadget called the Is-Was board. Ben looked at the fruit machine.

"Come to bearing three-five-five," he commanded. He could feel the slight correction in direction without looking at the instruments. "Prepare to fire."

The telephone man repeated the command to the torpedo room.

Ben watched the target a few seconds. He wiped sweat from his forehead and looked again. "Fire one!" he barked.

"Fire two," the man spoke sharply into his phone.

Ben felt the rumble forward. A short blast of compressed air had shot the twenty-two-foot bullet from a long rifle tube. *Seashell*'s bow rose slightly, then eased back down as water gushed into the empty space and more seawater fed into the external tanks to keep the boat in trim.

"One fired, sir."

Ben counted off six seconds. "Fire two!"

"Fire two," he man spoke sharply into his phone.

Again the boat convulsed slightly as the lethal dart shot from its womb. Ben watched through the periscope. The U-boat was starting to dive and was picking up speed, but there wasn't enough time. Two men raced to the aft hatch. It closed before they got there. They pounded on the hatch as seawater swirled around their feet. They ran screaming forward and held onto the gun mount. Their mouths were still open as the boat slid lower and lower into the Atlantic. They were still struggling, fighting, screaming when Ben saw them torn away from the gun mount.

"Two is fired, sir."

The German pigboat made a sluggish turn to port, but it was far too slow for the torpedos. The crewmen below in *Seashell* were counting the seconds. Ben felt perspiration beading on his forehead as he waited.

"It has been too long!" he thought. "No, not too long for the range."

Then he saw a flash in the fading winter light and the aft end of the U-boat lifted out of the water. He could see the smoking, steaming mass of open cross section where the torpedo had blasted the boat in two. Then water cascaded into the opening, quickly filling the *untersee-boot*. It listed forty-five degrees to starboard, then went down suddenly, bow first. Ben never saw the piece of the stern that had been sheared off. A moment later there was nothing showing but the dark, gentle waves.

The *Seashell*'s crew cheered. They had heard the explosion through the water. They laughed and joked and shook hands, but Ben hung over the periscope. He worked it slowly around in a circle, looking for figures in the water. He saw none.

Death.

Ben never thought a lot about death. He was a military man. A girl at Annapolis had called him a professional killer. She said he was trained to kill, his only reason for existence was to kill. He told her she was wrong. It had been a short romance. Ben knew he was more than a killer. He knew that. Yet he had killed. If this German VII-C submarine had a full crew, forty-four men had just met their deaths. Forty-four German sailors.

He stepped back, signaled for Malcolm to put down the scope.

"Mister Malcolm, take us up for surface running. We shall continue our patrol."

"Aye, sir." Malcolm's eyes met Ben's for a moment. Ben turned away. "Secure from battle stations, stand by to surface," Malcolm ordered and watched the men jump to their jobs.

A few moments later Malcolm reported. "Ship is ready to surface."

Ben pushed the diving alarm button and sounded the Klaxon three times.

"Blow safety," Malcolm ordered. Air gushed into tanks and was shut off at Sublieutenant Malcolm's signal. The bow planesman pushed his bow plane up to the full rise position. The *Seashell* tilted slightly upward at the bow and the depth gauge needles began to drop.

As he felt the ship lift toward the surface, Ben moved to the rungs of the ladder in the conning tower. He felt the upward move stop suddenly as the boat broached.

Surfacing wasn't as complicated or dangerous as submerging, Ben knew, but the final moment of breaking the surface always gave him a tight feeling of danger. Every man stayed at his station. The boat was ready for an instant dive if necessary, and that was Ben's responsibility. He went up the ladder and put his hands on the hatch.

"Eighteen feet and holding," Sublieutenant Malcolm called up. The conning tower was out of the water.

"Cracking the hatch, Mr. Malcolm," Ben said as he spun the handle on the hatch several times, and listened to the familiar whistling sound of the slightly increased air pressure vented through the opening hatch.

"Set up low-pressure pumps on the main, shut the Kingstons. Line up the ballast tanks for pumping and trim the ship. Switch to diesel power." The surfacing routine went on below as two lookout men came into the bridge and Ben threw open the hatch.

The seas were calm for a change, which was unusual off Gibraltar in almost any season. They were on radio silence for sending, but they hoisted their radar scanner and began searching through the heavy dusk for those ghostly blips that might mean an enemy ship or another U-boat.

Ben shivered. The heat of the control room had seemed comfortable when he was there, and now the outside air chilled him.

"All ahead one half, Sublieutenant Malcolm," Ben said. He felt the diesels throbbing as they steadied and propelled the *Seashell* through the water. They would continue patrolling on the surface at eight knots, scanning with the ASDIC listening for any ships, and lookouts watching for lights. In the morning they would complete their assigned patrol and return to Gibraltar.

Sublieutenant Malcolm came up to the bridge and held out his hand. "Congratulations, Skipper, on your first kill. Excellent work."

Ben took his hand. "You know this is my first real command, Malcolm. I've been playing advisor to half the ships in Her Majesty's navy and haven't been able to get orders to send me to the Pacific where I could have my own boat. I'd get one of the Fleet-class boats. Have you ever seen one of those submarines? They're three hundred and eleven feet long, almost a hundred feet longer than the *Seashell*. They can do twenty knots on the surface and nine submerged. They have a cruising range of fifteen thousand miles without re-fueling. There are four diesel engines, and ten torpedo tubes with twenty-four fish in the nest. Some of them have two five-inch guns and antiaircraft guns as well. I'd give half a year's pay to be in Australia right now with my own boat."

"You've done a fine job here, Skipper. I've heard about some of the things you've accomplished. Like those first anti-sub nets you engineered up at Firth of Forth. Then you did a lot on radar development and your anti-submarine work with the surface boys in destroyers. We bloody well couldn't have gotten on without you."

"Thanks, Malcolm. But you can see how pleased I am to have command of the *Seashell*, even for just a week-long patrol."

"Yes, sir. Certainly. I understand."

"Take over the watch, Sublieutenant Malcolm. I'm going below and catch up on my log."

"Aye, aye, sir."

In his cabin, Ben realized his feat with a surge of pleasure. He sat at the small table fastened to the bulk-head and wrote in the official log what had happened on the patrol. He indicated that he had seen no designation number on the submarine when he filled in the log. He wrote in the best military report style, then closed the book and put it away.

Lately he had been doing a lot of thinking about the cost of anti-submarine efforts by the Allied forces. It was tremendously out of proportion to the cost of putting the U-boats into the sea. He thought it strange that more effort hadn't been made to bottle up the boats in their harbors, to stop them before they got into the Atlantic. Ben knew of dozens of bays along the French coast where U-boats could be based. Perhaps it was an impossible job, but still the idea haunted him.

"Why not knock out the U-boat pens they were building in France and Germany or wherever?" he wondered aloud.

He thought about it for another half hour, put down some thoughts in a spiral-bound notebook he carried in his seabag, and decided that he was going to pursue the idea. First he would see what he could find in print on it, and then he would start asking a lot of questions.

"Why hunt down a U-boat at sea when you could wait for it at the sub base and blast it into hell?" Ben was sure someone had thought of it before, maybe even tried it. Such a plan might not work. The fortifications were too massive. Or perhaps the war simply shifted in emphasis and charged off in another direction. If he concentrated on the problem, perhaps he could find some way to solve it.

A half hour after the sinking, Ben had called for a ration of rum for the troops, one of his prerogatives as captain. Now he sipped his own glass, but it would be a long time before rum became his favorite drink.

He had been lucky tonight: lucky to find a sub on the surface, and lucky that it had so many crewmen and so much equipment on deck that it took so long to dive. For a moment Ben remembered the silent screaming faces of those two German seamen trapped on deck when the boat began to dive. He would never forget the terror, the agony, the stark reality of death on the men's faces.

For a minute, his mind went back to the *Sebago* disaster. Jack McCrary, a former Academy classmate of his, had been assigned to the newly fitted *Sebago*, whose main induction valve failed to close when it made its first dive. McCrary had survived, but the invading ocean had brought swift death to all the men in the engine room—including Jack's younger brother, Edward.

Jack had blamed Ben, as one of the primary architects of *Sebago*, for the tragedy. His bitter—and undignified—accusations against Ben had eventually been rejected by a board of inquiry, but it had caused Ben a great deal of anxiety, and left Jack's own future seriously in doubt. Ben knew that the two-year desk job in Washington had been severe punishment for Jack, and had to admire him for sticking it out. McCrary was rewarded for his patience with command of *Stickleback*, and later *Manta*, a fine *Gato*-class submarine assigned to the Pacific. In spite of the enmity that had existed between the two men, Ben Mount had been shocked and dismayed when, in June of 1944, *Manta*, with Commander Jack McCrary and the entire crew aboard, was posted Overdue—Presumed Lost.

Ben took a sip of rum and tried to think of other things. Betsy Kirkland. Now there was something to think about. He hadn't seen Betsy in a year, maybe longer. She was still in England. Betsy said since she had lived through the London blitz there was no sense in going back to the States. Betsy was the daughter of Admiral Gar Kirkland, the U.S. Navy's best submariner, now working with the sub fleet in the Pacific. Ben grinned as he remembered how angry Kirkland had been about his relationship with Betsy. Kirkland would have preferred Jack McCrary—or, for that matter, anyone other than a Jew—as his daughter's betrothed. The old man had pulled some strings and arranged to have Ben ordered as far from his daughter as possible. He had Ben offered a post in England with the British submarine forces. Ben leaped at the chance. He sailed on the *Queen Mary*, and Betsy Kirkland decided on a sudden visit to her aunt in London. She sailed with him and it had been a wonderful crossing.

With war so close in England, they decided to live together while they could, and after a while they talked seriously of marriage. But something always came up, got in the way, or sent them spinning off in opposite directions. Then Betsy's former fiancé came to London and complicated the situation even further.

Ben lay on his bunk and turned out the lights, but sleep would not come. The silent screaming faces of the two German youths came smashing back at him.

He turned over. He wondered if he would ever get into the Pacific theater and skipper a submarine of his own. It was the greatest dream of his life. He had joined the Navy because he figured his Jewish faith would have the least hindering effect on him. The Army of 1939 had black units and blacks could move up in the enlisted ranks, but never into command. They had only white officers, and never a Jew. In the Navy there was only one billet open for blacks, as stewards, and they could aspire to nothing higher. The Navy also had barriers to Jews, but they were more subtle.

Ben had worked hard and at last had won an appointment to Annapolis, the U.S. Naval Academy. He had gone through extreme pressures, harassments and discrimination there, but he had anticipated as much. Consequently he had to do everything twice as well as anyone else. He had to excel in the classroom, in sports, and in organizations. He did and graduated high in his class. Then he went into the submarine service. He knew he would never become an admiral. The best he could hope for would be commander— even if the United States did get into the big war everyone said was coming.

Now he was a lieutenant commander, and still on detached service with the British Royal Navy.

"Someday, maybe . . . someday."

He turned over and went to sleep. He dreamed twice. The first was of Betsy Kirkland and their wonderful days together. Her lips were red and inviting and her smile so sweet, and her arms were reaching for him.

In the second dream he was in the middle of a huge Nazi U-boat pen and he was destroying it with his bare hands. Everyone was shooting at him but no one could hurt him.

Chapter 2

A hundred kilometers due west of Brest, France, a German U-boat rode on the surface in a light chop, her lookouts on the control tower sectioning the sea. They were watching for the next convoy from the United States heading to England. The boat was also a hundred kilometers from Land's End, England, the first bit of English soil a convoy lookout would see if he were heading toward Portsmouth or London. The time was 1600 hours. It would soon be dark in the Atlantic.

Below in his kapitan quarters, Commander Wilhelm Fricke of the *untersee-boot U-89*, checked his reports. There had been a radio message to all boats that the Focke-Wulf Condor 200 long-range planes had reported no enemy convoys in sight over this part of the Atlantic Ocean.

Fricke hoped this would not be a wasted night, not another one. He paced the small cabin, then studied his code words for the various coordinates on his map. He had nine U-boats under his command, spread ten to fifteen kilometers apart, forming a fence across the line of travel covering ninety percent of the Allied convoys' routes to England. If anything came through they would find it. On the surface they could see for a little over seven miles each way before the curve of the earth defeated them. Their underwater hydrophones and sonarlike listening devices could cover several miles.

Fricke smiled through his beard. Sometimes over-anxious American escorts or screening vessels gave a convoy away. Some captains had the habit of drop-ping random depth charges as they came into the zones with high U-boat activity, on the off chance of hitting one. Fricke had never heard of a German sub being damaged by these random drops, but countless times the exploding depth charges had sent sound and shock waves through the water to distant hydrophones and had alerted the submarines of a possible convoy.

For more than four years the Germans had worked a perfect system with their wolf pack submarine tactics. One sub against a defended convoy could sink one, maybe two ships. But eight or nine subs attacking in a coordinated move could sink three or even more, and the safety factor was much greater for each U-boat.

The happy days of 1941 to 1943 were not over as far as Fricke was concerned. The wolf pack principle was still valid; they simply needed more aggressive kapitans to do the job. Fricke loved the submarine service. Twice he had refused promotions because they would have taken him out of the underwater duty.

He was one of the few who could refuse. His first kill, the dramatic sinking of the English aircraft carrier *Courage* in 1939, had made him a hero of the Third Reich. He had gained much more than his iron cross. He had gained the reputation of being the boy who could do no wrong, and he had proved to his superiors that the British did have sensitive hydrophone equip-ment, which made underwater attacks obsolete. A surface attack at night was more effective.

In the years since Fricke had skippered three differ-ent U-boats, had sunk forty-three ships including three men-of-war and a carrier. He had once been depth charged so severely by some aggressive U.S. destroyers that he had limped back to port with two watertight compartments flooded, ten men dead, and the boat in danger of foundering. Yet he pulled the boat back, saw her repaired, and watched her go back to sea under another skipper.

Fricke had grown a thick black beard since the days of his first command. His detractors had fallen by the wayside, and his champions were in control. He could have almost any post in the German Naval Forces that he wanted. That's why he was here in this two hundred and twenty foot long coffin, chugging along on the surface at seventeen knots, looking for Allied convoys. He was ready to pit his death wish against the best the Allies could throw at him.

He had helped develop the wolf pack techniques. Admiral Doenitz had worked with him, and they had laid down the general principles of group attacks. Then they worked out methods, tried and changed them until at last they knew the ideal size of packs, and the best way to deploy them in search patterns. These patterns were as wide as possible yet allowed for a reasonable amount of time for the boats to converge and attack under cover of night.

They worked out coordinates on maps and gave them code names. They crisscrossed the Atlantic with hundreds of special words that meant something to every German U-boat commander. Now, when the search aircraft or a U-boat spotted a convoy, the information was radioed immediately to Paris, where Admiral Doenitz as *Befehlshaber der Untersee-boot* had his headquarters at 18 Boulevard Suchet. There the information was charted, and all submarines within that zone or in that wolf pack were notified by radio to converge on a coordinate position that would be used as an intercept target zone.

The system had worked remarkably well. Over eight

hundred thousand tons of Allied shipping were sent to the bottom every month for many months.

"The Allies couldn't afford losses like these," Fricke thought with a frown. But still the convoys came. "Where did they get all the ships?"

He bent over his charts, memorizing the change in code words that had been programmed for that day—sunfish, dolphin, salmon, skipjack, shark, mackerel, tuna. He put the code book away and went back to the bridge. The radio operator handed him a message.

"It just went out to Paris, Kapitan."

Fricke read it. "Shark. Shark. Shark." The three repetitions indicated it was wolf pack three, Fricke's own. Shark was a ten-kilometer-square sector at the far side of their search area. No wonder the Condor aircraft had not seen anything. The convoy was just now steaming into range.

Fricke looked at the charts. His second in command already had plotted their route and had estimated the time to target. Fricke glanced up at him.

"Kapitan, we are fifty-six kilometers from the area shark. We should intercept in two hours and forty-five minutes of surface running. Our intercept bearing is three-zero-one."

"Proceed. Let me know if there is any change, Oberleutnant."

"Aye, aye."

The radio man came up with another message. It was the instructions from Paris. Fricke read them, knowing almost to the word what they would say. "All starfish area *untersee-booten* converge shark 14."

Fricke knew some commanders who would take a nap while charging toward an intercept like this. He would not. He could not. Since his early days he had pushed himself further and harder than anyone else. He had to be first, to be the leader, to be Germany's first U-boat ace, then to keep the lead with the most kills, the most tonnage.

He spent an hour in the forward torpedo room, inspecting the equipment and talking with the crew. He told them what was happening. The forward crew had ten torpedos, four in the tubes, and six ready to reload. In the aft torpedo room, the tube was loaded and ready. There were three more fish ready to swim. He had his full load of fourteen torpedos and he would not even think of using his deck gun with a convoy as there would be too many support ships. He wondered how many destroyers would attack them.

Back in the control room, Fricke watched the sub's progress. He then went back topside and relaxed as the daylight failed and the moon came out. It would be a good night for an attack, a perfect night. He smiled and watched the water as it went rushing past.

When they were an estimated seven miles from intercept, the German U-boat slid easily under the water and positioned itself in the path of the oncoming Allied convoy. It rigged for silent operation, and the men made no unnecessary noise.

They could not run all the way to the intercept zone on the surface as the escort ships would spot them on radar, but radar operated along a line of sight and would not work past the seven-mile curvature of the earth. Inside that limit, the U-boat submerged and lay silent, escaping detection by the hydrophones on the convoy ships. When they were next to or even inside the convoy, the submarines attacked. They surfaced and fired, often at point blank range. Sometimes they would aim the submarines from the bridge like a rifle, and fire torpedoes at every target they could find.

There was no safe way to contact other members of the wolf pack. The basic direction from Paris held one number at the end of the message. This was usually in code, but occasionally in the clear and doubled. That day the code number was fourteen. By dividing it in half, the target attack time became seven. At seven P.M. or 1900 hours, the attack would begin. Paris calculated where each sub should be by that time. This prearrangement prevented the convoy from hearing any radio transmissions from the wolf pack.

The attack point had been coded "converge," which meant the attack should be at the point where the shark zone ended and the next zone square began. It was a little rough for a rendezvous point, but it usually worked well as the route of the convoy remained constant.

Deep in the *U-89* the soundman was the first alerted that the convoy was near. He had picked up the sound of the enemy propellers. He held the phones tightly to his ears for a moment, then called out his report.

"Propellers, Kapitan. Twenty to thirty ships."

Fricke nodded. "Closest range?"

"Six-eight-zero-zero meters."

"Bearing?"

"Three-zero-one."

"Maintain total silence," Fricke said. "We'll wait for them to come. Bring her up to periscope depth and hold."

The ship nosed upward.

"Periscope depth," the chief said.

"Up periscope."

Fricke hung onto the scope astride the saddle in the narrow space between the periscope shaft and the tower wall. His face was tight against the rubber shell and his thighs were spread wide. He held his feet on the pedals so he could spin the great column and his saddle around 360 degrees without making a sound. Fricke hit a button to lower the scope slightly, and kept it just above the surface of the water. He could see little in the darkness.

"Targets changing course, sir," the hydrophone operator said. "Zigging to the left forty-five degrees."

"All ahead one quarter, prepare to surface. Take her up."

Commander Fricke was the first one to the tower and up the ladder. When the word came that the tower was out of the water, he opened the hatch and leapt onto the bridge. The moon was still out, a half crescent in the western sky. Fricke quickly focused his binoculars and stared toward the target spot. At last he could make out the plumes of smoke trailing from the transports. He saw one, then another, then more than a dozen.

"All stop," he said into the voice tube. A moment later the craft slowed. Fricke watched the gray and black shapes come closer. Within ten minutes the convoy would be steaming almost alongside them at about two thousand meters. He swung around and looked for the escort craft, the destroyers, corvettes and the sweepers. He'd much rather see one and avoid it then have it appear unexpectedly.

"Range, two-eight-zero-zero," the hydrophone man's word was passed topside.

The first watch officer came up onto the bridge.

"Battle stations. Flood forward tubes. Floor rear tube. Stand by." The officer watched his commander.

Fricke had been waiting for the targets to come closer. He waited five minutes. It was three minutes past seven. There should be other U-boat commanders ready to attack. "Full speed ahead!" he shouted through the hatch. "Hard to port. Commence attack. Open all torpedo doors!"

Repetitions of the orders were shouted below as men surged into action. Quickly the bow swung toward the black hulks.

"Hold her steady as she goes," the captain shouted. "Hold on eighty-five degrees." The *U-89* was racing now, ploughing straight ahead at the broad sides of a dozen Allied merchantmen.

The bow of the *U-89* sliced through the dark sea, slashing aside a foaming, churning mass of angry water. The swell showed ahead and glinted in the pale moonlight. The boat rose with it then dropped. Surging seawater swept over the bow, spraying the bridge and soaking everyone. The water dripped down the bridge hatch.

"Pick your targets, First!" Commander Fricke shouted.

Already the first watch officer had bent over his sight, straining through the blackness of the sky at the blacker outlines of the merchantmen. "The big tanker just to the left. Put two in her both amidships, then one each for the freighters just in back of her."

"Clear doors on all torpedos," the commander called into the voice tube.

The first watch officer stayed on his sights. He was giving instructions quietly now—setting the torpedoes, revising the point of attack. He moved his right hand to the firing lever.

"Connect tubes one and two. Angle seventy-three . . . follow changing angle."

"Angle requested," a voice came back sharply.

"Angle seventy-five . . . no eighty."

Commander Fricke listened, watched the targets, then spoke. "Tubes one and two, permission to fire!"

The first watch officer immediately repeated the order. "Tubes one and two, fire!"

There seemed to be no difference in the boat as the torpedoes slammed out of the tubes but four thousand pounds of weight were gone. The sub rose slightly and the first watch officer compensated on his sights.

"Connect tube three."

"Tube three . . . fire!" the first shouted.

"To port five degrees," Commander Fricke said with a calm voice.

The bow inched around, as if it were a giant shark searching for a new meal.

"Connect tube four," the first watch officer said. He checked the sights, waited until the hairline centered on a freighter, then called, "Tube four, fire!"

Fricke saw the flash first—a brilliant, towering plume of orange-red flame that created a burst of daylight—then before it died, there was a second flash. The fire, which began at once, soon lit up the sea for a quarter of a mile. A third torpedo blasted into the freighter, but before the last "fish" found a home, Fricke saw a gray shadow leave the blackness of the freighter.

The shadow erupted with a dozen bursts of brilliant orange flashes. Then something burst and Fricke screamed orders to dive the boat. He hit the alarm as he and the first watch officer dropped through the bridge hatch. Fricke slammed the hatch down and dogged it closed, shouting, "Dive! Dive! damnit, he's right down our throat!"

"Flood tanks. Hard to starboard. Both engines ahead full. Dive! Dive! Dive!"

"Close torpedo doors," the first watch officer shouted. He looked at the skipper. "What depth, sir?"

"Two hundred feet, fast. We've got a corvette slamming down on us. I didn't think she saw us. Then that damned tanker went off like a giant flare. It was daylight."

"Our friends from the pack are here, Skipper," the first watch officer said. "I saw two other ships torpedoed somewhere ahead of us."

"At least the escort ships won't be able to gang up on one of us."

"Hold hard down on both plates," the boat chief yelled. "Both engines full ahead. All hands forward!"

Every man not performing a diving task rushed through the compartments, down the slanting deck and into the forward part of the boat. They needed to get as much weight there as possible to help push the sub deeper into the safety of the sea. Men slipped and slid through the tilted deck of the control room as if it were a playground slide. They fell, cursed, jumped up, and hurried on. Weight forward, that was the whole idea.

Fricke had a preset timetable in his head, manufactured from long experience. "We'll be taking depth charges soon, so get ready."

Nothing happened for another ten seconds.

"Coming up on two hundred feet, sir. Shall I level out?" the chief asked.

"Right. Maintain two hundred."

The chief gave orders to start leveling the boat.

"All hands, man diving stations," he barked, and the men who had run, slid, and fallen forward now struggled back up the still slanted deck to their stations.

Kapitan Fricke looked at the first watch officer. "About now I would guess," he said, but before he finished, the boat took a sledgehammer blow and a *karrumph, karrumph, karrumph.* Fricke braced for the depth charge and the resulting triple impact as the water smashed back together filling up the void that had been created by the massive explosion.

"Right full rudder, both engines half speed," Kapitan Fricke said in the quiet after the first explosion. However, before the move could be made, two more pounding, roaring blasts came from outside as the five-hundred-pound bombs detonated.

"That one was well astern," Fricke said. "Maintain course."

They heard two more explosions farther away, then nothing for several seconds.

"Full speed both sides," Fricke shouted. The boat kept ahead again on its E-motor power.

"Let's head for two-fifty, Chief," the captain said as the bow tilted downward.

The next explosion knocked out the lights. Immediately, pocket flashlight beams sliced holes in the darkness.

"Damage report!" the chief called.

Voice reports drifted back from the various compartments, repeated even when not needed.

"Engine room, no damage."

"Main motor room, all right. No leaks."

"Aft torpedo room, tight. No damage."

The lights flickered and came back on. The small flashlights vanished into pockets.

"Pump out forward torpedo tubes as soon as we get another barrage of charges," the chief ordered.

Fricke nodded. The chief was a good man, he thought. By pumping the seawater out of the tubes, it would give them better control of the boat; and by doing it during the sounds of the depth charges, the hydrophones above couldn't hear it happening.

Three more explosions sounded to one side and in front of them. The pumps worked quickly, exhausting the water from the four forward tubes. The chief brought the boat back into trim at two hundred and fifty feet and they waited.

Nothing happened for five minutes. They stayed on course at half speed two hundred and fifty feet below surface.

"The game has begun, gentlemen," Fricke announced. "From now on, it's a psychological battle to see who can stand the most pressure. But I know you men. I know my crew. We've played this game before. The important point is that we always win."

He had just looked back at the first officer when three more charges went off. Again, the lights flickered, but stayed on. The floor plates danced a tune, then quieted.

"That's fifteen charges at us," the bow plate man said.

"Let's go down again," the kapitan ordered.

Another explosion rattled the pipes and brought a gasp from a man who grabbed the chart table to keep from falling.

"That one was a bit closer. Take her down to three hundred."

"Aye, aye," the chief answered.

Fricke seemed to be plotting both his course and that of the corvette three hundred feet above him. What was the skipper up there thinking about? How did his mind work? What would his next move be?

"Take the helm hard to starboard!" Fricke ordered suddenly.

"Aye, sir. Hard to starboard."

Fricke was plotting again, judging the maneuvering on the surface and the tactics they might use. The sub leveled off at three hundred feet and the kapitan was notified. His job was to find a path that would allow him to sneak away from the devil ship over him.

Every man on board the *U-89* knew that a depth charge did not have to hit the boat to kill it. The five hundred pound charges were set to explode at a given depth by means of a pressure fuse. When the bomb goes off, the pressure wave jolts out in all directions. It can be lethal to a submarine if the wave starts within three hundred feet and three hundred and fifty feet of water. Below that depth, the lethal zone of the charge is smaller as there is increased water pressure.

The soundman looked out of his small enclosed area.

"Screw sounds about the same, sir, no increase in sound level. They're staying with us."

"All ahead full, go down to three seventy-five."

Again the boat jumped ahead through the silent waters.

"Hard to port!" the kapitan called sharply. He let it run on that course for thirty seconds. "Hard to starboard! Keep it moving down to four hundred, then level off."

At the end of the maneuver the kapitan called for the engines to come to a full stop.

"Now, gentlemen, if we only knew if we had a current, we could slip out from under our friend up there. Sometimes I wish we could put out an underwater sail and let the current drag us along without a whisper of a propeller."

As he was speaking, they heard what sounded like someone throwing small pebbles against the hull. The newer men looked up in alarm. They had never heard such a noise.

"ASDIC," the first watch officer said with a cringing respect in his voice. "Anti-Submarine Development Investigation Committee," he continued. "An electronic beam is sent out and bounced off an object and it returns to the sending device. It doesn't care if we make any noise or not, it's concerned only with the mass of our boat, the bulk, the size of it."

Fricke frowned. More and more ships were using ASDIC. It made his job twice as dangerous. With ASDIC it didn't matter how quiet they were. The directional beam slamming against the side of the pressure hull would find them, and make a rattling noise at the same time. From what he could tell, there were thirty seconds between the beam pulses.

The lights dimmed again after the next explosion. Then there was another. Two more followed on the other side, flicking off the lights for five seconds, but again they came back on.

Kapitan Fricke looked at the soundman. "Bearing?"

"Two hundred forty degrees, sir. Coming closer."

"Thirty-four," the historian counted, listing the last bomb hurled at them.

"Keep reading the bearing," Fricke called. He was scowling, thinking again. "Hard to starboard . . . mark!"

The boat turned and the sound operator leaned into the passageway. "It's getting louder, sir, and the bearing is changing to two-three-zero."

"He's attacking again. Turn out all nonessential lights. Conserve batteries."

They waited for ten seconds, then the kapitan bellowed his order. "Full ahead, both engines!"

They were moving again. Fricke paced the control room. This was the hardest part. You couldn't stand and fight. You were helpless. Even with torpedoes in the five tubes, he was as impotent as a newborn babe. He would love to be on the surface and sending two fish at the corvette, watching it squirm and try to evade. He glanced at the arrow on the manometer. It read four hundred and twenty-five. He remembered when they first got the shipyards to guarantee the hulls down to three hundred feet. He wouldn't think about that. He'd been deeper than this, but not on purpose.

After ten minutes of full power running, Fricke had the engines turned off, and the boat sat in deep water, trimmed, ready to move, to sneak away—ready for anything but death. The lethal zone was reduced at that depth and the corvette would need to have better marksmen or luckier ones to hit them.

The ASDIC pebbles pounded into the hull again, and Fricke knew that within seconds the corvette would again have their exact position and depth.

"Full ahead, both engines!" he shouted. Just as the propellers bit into the sea two blasts hit them. The first jolted Fricke down to his spine and blurred his eyes.

"That's nothing," he said after the second charge had shaken them like a rabbit in a dog's mouth. "They'll have to do a lot better than that. I've never seen such rotten gunners."

"That's forty-eight and forty-nine," the counter called.

"That's a lot of money those British are wasting," Fricke replied with a note of pleasure in his voice.

The depth charges came again, three to the left, two on the right, then two more. Fricke squinted. For a moment he couldn't tell how many charges they were throwing at them. He pushed himself up beside the sound shack.

"The sound. Is it coming at us or receding?"

"Still coming, louder, sir."

"A hundred and eighty to port. We'll go back under him."

The boat was sluggish as it turned. The pinging came again, and Fricke knew this maneuver wouldn't fool the corvette commander. Still, it might throw him off the track for a brief moment and help lead some depth charges astray.

Another explosion aft and the floor plates rattled and hummed as they danced through the vibrations. Fricke wondered how many more shocks the hull could take. He'd had some patches he wasn't pleased about, and this kind of pounding could mean trouble if it kept up. He checked the manometer. It read six hundred and five feet. That would give him more time to maneuver before the bombs could reach the boat. He looked at the soundman. "Tell me when he's starting to make another attack, when the bearing closes down."

"Aye, aye."

"What's the ash can count?" Fricke asked.

"Fifty-eight, sir, give or take a pair. They came hot and heavy there for a while."

"Good work, close enough."

Five minutes crawled by in the deepwater pressure.

"He's coming again, sir," the soundman said calmly.

"All ahead full!"

"All ahead full, sir," the chief called.

A depth charge exploded well over them. Another blasted to their rear. Then two more. They didn't seem as close.

"Bearing, soundman."

"He turned to two hundred and seventy. He thought we would turn, sir."

Fricke smiled. "The sound, is it coming or going away?"

There was a hush in the control room, then slowly the man in the sound room spoke.

"It's going away. Fainter . . . he's heading away!"

"Reduce to half forward, both sides, ease it up to three hundred feet. He's moving away, all right. He threw more than half of his depth charges at us and it took him two hours. He must be mad as hell. Probably saving a few depth charges for some sure kill."

Fricke looked at the first watch officer. "Take us back toward our own patrol square. I'll be in my cabin catching up on the battle log."

"Aye, sir. Shall we go up and have a look around soon? Our batteries are low."

"Take her up slowly. Let's have a look on the surface. If there's no contact, we'll run back on top and you can charge batteries with one engine."

"Aye, sir, moving up to periscope depth."

Commander Kapitan Fricke nodded. If the war lasted long enough, his first watch officer would have his own boat. Right then, that was a big if. He'd heard rumors about the enemy planning a landing on the

French coast. It was almost certain now that they
would as there was a huge buildup of men and arms
in England. The question was where and when. Fricke
sighed. It had been a long war, a terribly long war.
He went into his small cabin and stretched out on the
bunk. A minute later he was sleeping. Kapitan Fricke
did not dream.

Chapter 3

Lieutenant Commander Ben Mount had brought the *Seashell* into dockside at the Gibraltar British sub base precisely on schedule. There was a request that he report to the base commander. Once there, Ben gave a quick rundown of his patrol and turned in his written summary. He watched the British Royal navy captain skim it.

"I see you put down a U-boat! Good show. Did you get the identification number on the tower?"

"No, sir. There was none that I could see."

"Excellent, excellent. And it's a confirmed sinking?"

"Yes, sir. She broke in half and went down within thirty seconds."

"I say, that is good news! Now I have some new orders for you. Sorry to lose you, but you knew all along that this command of the *Seashell* was a temporary billet. Well, now, you'll be going back to England, at least. Portsmouth, I believe, if what I've heard is correct."

The British captain sat down after having paced to the window and back. He was a short, fat man—a submariner who commanded a sub base. His hair was thinning outwardly from a bald spot on top of his head, his face was ruddy from the long years of staring into ocean winds.

"At least this time it's from your own Navy Department. So I'd say you'll be having something to do with the joint command. You know the big invasion is coming up soon. Lord knows where, but this could have something to do with that. At least it might. Now, there will be transport for you at the airdrome in a little over an hour. Sorry to speed you on your way, but you know how the Admiralty can be when it gets a wild hair up its nose."

The captain handed Ben an envelope. Ben broke the seal and quickly read the first line.

". . . to proceed to Portsmouth and to the submarine base there at Fort Blockhouse. . . ." He skipped over more of the usual service mumbo-jumbo. ". . . and to report to Rear Admiral Joseph Graves, USN, coordinator of Project Smash."

Ben stood. "Well, sir. Then if there's nothing more . . ."

"Quite. Yes, you'll have to rush. I've phoned your boat, and the first has stowed your gear in your seabag. It will be dockside and I have a jeep I'm bringing around for you."

The captain held out his hand.

"Good luck, old man. And all that sort of thing. You've helped us out here and we appreciate it. Oh, give a big hello for me to Skip Graves. We've hoisted a few pints together in our time."

Ben mumbled that he would, snapped a salute, which the captain waved off, and went out the door. His seabag was at the dock, and he paused to take one last look at his first, and maybe his last, submarine command. Then he waved the jeep forward.

When he stepped out of the converted De Haviland at the airdrome in England, he was aware at once of the change in the weather. It had changed from warm-pleasant to cool-cold-miserable. An hour later he reached the outer office of Rear Admiral "Skip" Joseph Graves, USN. It was in a large building that was part of the Fort Blockhouse complex. The complex housed a number of different Navy functions. The sign outside read Joint Naval Command Headquarters, Allied Forces, Europe.

For a moment Ben was agitated with all of this high-level bureaucracy that kept him out of a combat submarine. He wanted to go on patrol and fire some torpedoes, or at least put some spies into foreign nations, or run courier trips, or pick up some commandos, or any damn thing he could do that would contribute to the fight. Four years in the European theater and only during this last week had he been in any offensive action.

"What is a sub commander for, damnit!" he muttered to himself.

A WREN, with two rockers on her sleeve, jiggled up to him. She made no secret of the fact that her regulation blouse was at least a size too small and that it failed in its gallant effort to contain her thrusting bosom.

"Commander, your meeting with the admiral has been set back an hour. However, there is another officer here who would like to talk to you."

Ben was so caught up in debating whether the center button of the blue blouse would stand up to the strain or pop off that he didn't notice that someone had come up behind the girl. He looked up.

"Moxie! Moxie Mulford! What in hell are you doing here?"

Moxie grinned, and shook Ben's hand. "Doing? The same bloody thing you're doing here." The WREN went back to her desk.

"Same thing? You're assigned here too?"

"You don't know what's going on here, do you? Time you had a briefing. Come with me, mon. Time it is for old Moxie to set your spinnaker straight and adjust your top gallants."

"That sounds like an offer for a drink. Where?"

Five minutes later they were at a little pub with little light and a swirl of Yank music blasting from a player in the corner. It was officer country.

"So nobody's told you, mon? They brought you over in the dark? Well, must be security. Aye, security."

Ben sipped at the pint of ale, which he had learned to halfway like after several years with the British.

"Give, buddy. What the hell is going on?"

"R and D, my friend. Research and Development, but for us mostly development and application. Somebody came up with the wild idea that since you and I worked together on some other things, we might as well team up again and do our final bit of fluff here and rid the North Sea of the rest of Jerry's battered U-boat fleet. Do you realize he's been losing as many as forty pig boats a month? And still we're getting pushed around by the *untersee-boot*. Ah, yes, lad. Joint effort. You saw the sign outside the bloody building." Moxie sipped his ale and chuckled.

"Don't be too impressed by the sign. We found we have so bloody many Jerry spies over here that we put up contradictory signs all over the place. This damn well isn't the joint naval command headquarters for all of Europe. That place is buried in a bunker under London somewhere. You've got to be at least an admiral of the fleet to know where the bleeding place is."

"Development? What are you talking about?" Ben asked.

"What do you think? Anti-submarine development, weapons, my boy, to give some more hell for U-boat commanders. That radar you rigged for our boats is standard equipment now, as you know. It's been improved some, but the same basic design you worked out is still there. Now they want a committee, you and me mostly, mate, to take a look at the rest of the

secret weapons the bright-eyed designers have come up
with on both sides of the Atlantic. Sort them out, see
if there is anything worthwhile developing that we can
get into combat before it's too damn late to do any
good."

"So we find something almost ready to go, adapt it,
and demand a three-month total in-field time, then
get it on the boats or the destroyers before the war in
Europe is over."

Moxie drained his pint and motioned to the bar-
maid for another. When she brought it she bent low,
showing off the long line of cleavage between her
large breasts. She winked at Ben.

" 'Ow is it goin', luv?"

"Fine, fine," he said, staring directly at her breasts.
"I'd say both of them are going just fine."

She screeched with laughter, slapped him on the
back and went on to the next table.

"You have a way with the birds, now, don't you,
Ben? So you know what the assignment is. We'll get
more details later on today. We're billeted here at the
base where we'll do most of the preliminary work. I've
got a boat now, my own sub and she'll be on temporary
duty as a guinea pig if we need one. But no more
damn nets. I won't try to ram through any of your
anti-sub nets across some firth."

Both were quiet for a moment, remembering the
first great experiment with U-boat nets that Ben had
developed back in 1939. Moxie's test submarine had
been trapped trying to break through them, and all
escape hatches fouled. The crew was saved at the last
moment by cranes and cables hoisting the conning
tower out of the water. Ben had jumped aboard
through the rough water to throw open the hatch.

"I won't let you be the target for any more tests,"
Ben said, shaking his head at the thought. "We'll go
on a cruise in a destroyer and find a Jerry U-boat for

our test run. I've kept you alive for five years of this war, and I'm not going to let you croak on me now. Especially not from friendly fire."

They drank and remembered old times. Then Moxie looked at his official Royal Navy watch.

"We better get cracking, Yank, or the old man will be chewing ass for our being late."

They went back to the headquarters building and Moxie led the way to the conference room. Six other officers, three with the U.S.N. blue, were already waiting. Ben didn't know any of them, but he was relieved to see that Admiral Kirkland wasn't there. He figured Gar must have been running the sub show in the Pacific, and for a moment the thought of Betsy's father made him think of her. He wondered if she were still in England, and if so, where. Moxie might know.

Before he could ask, the men stood and Admiral Joseph Graves of the United States Navy marched through the door.

Admiral Graves nodded at the men and asked them to sit down. He was a large man with a bristling mustache, a full head of red hair, and a body trim and fit for his over fifty years. He looked around the room, and when he saw Ben he spoke.

"Commander Mount?"

Ben stood at once. "Aye, sir."

"I hear you're to be congratulated on your first U-boat kill. I get word from Gibraltar that you filled in on a patrol in the Atlantic and bagged a boat. Our congratulations."

The admiral looked at the other men as Ben sat down. "I bring this up to let you know that Commander Mount is not only a top-flight submarine engineering expert, but a seasoned combat veteran of British underseas craft as well. We're glad he's here rather than in the Pacific where Admiral Nimitz and

Lockwood could certainly use him. It fact they asked to have Commander Mount back, but I've talked them out of it."

He turned to a chart on the stand behind him. "Gentlemen, our latest count on German U-boats that have been sunk. You'll see the rising curve up through November of 1943, then the curve moves down. Forty-two U-boats were sent to the bottom in November. That may be the monthly high. One reason is the Germans are not building as many of the VII-C boats. They have switched to a new class which is larger, stronger, faster, and with much greater hitting power. We think this is the boat they refer to as the XXI, the Twenty-one-class boat. Our people who collect data say this boat may never make it to the sea. It has massive problems with the hydraulic power. Instead of using electric motors, much of the boat's machinery is operated with hydraulics. In short it's a giant boondoggle.

"Which means we still have to fight against the VII-C-class boats. As most of you know, the sub war in the Atlantic is virtually over. Germany has recalled most of her wolf packs from that area, to concentrate them in a more defensive posture in the North Sea. We need weapons to handle the U-boats wherever we can find them. That's the purpose of this meeting.

"We have both United States Navy research people here and those from the Royal Navy. In this cooperative effort we want all potential weapons presented to the board, and with the aid of our two experts in combat, Commander Mount and Commander Mulford, we hope for some rapidly perfected new equipment for our anti-sub boats."

The admiral stopped speaking and looked around. "Are there any questions?"

Ben smiled. He had learned long ago never to ask a superior officer a question in a situation like this. It only pointed out an error, problem or ineffectiveness in the officer's speech, and nobody appreciated it.

Admiral Graves motioned to another man. "I'll turn this operation over to Captain White-Johnson. He'll be my liaison with your team. Incidentally, this project has an AA-1 priority. So let's see some results. Thank you, gentlemen."

Captain White-Johnson called the officers to attention as the admiral left the room with an aide. Then the men got down to business. They moved to a conference table, and the captain sat in the head chair.

"Gentlemen, it's late in the day, and I suggest we exchange whatever paperwork we have and check over the available designs to be presented tomorrow. We want to weed out as many of the impractical designs and ideas as we can before we get them into the hands of our combat experts. Let's meet back here at 1000 hours tomorrow. Any questions?"

Ben felt Moxie grow tense. When the meeting broke up, the other officers exchanged papers but Ben and Moxie went up to the captain. They double-checked with him that they were to have no part in the paper shuffling yet. When this was confirmed, they saluted and left.

"Now, my tall, lean, and lanky Yank buddy, I thought we both could use a bit of relaxation. How about a bottle of champagne at my digs? I could hustle up a pair of birds, if you like. By the way, you almost bit that serving wench's titties. I think it's time you have a go at one of our local lassies."

Ben laughed and slapped Moxie on the shoulder. "Hell, Moxie, I'm so glad to see you that I'll even put up with one of those sad-eyed, flat-chested little Scottish lassies of yours. But I'm not promising how much good I can do her. I'm making no guarantees. I'm half ready for twenty hours of solid sleep, to help me get back my land legs."

"I've got faith in you, mon," Moxie said, doubling up on his brogue accent so Ben could barely understand him. "Let's stop by at the greengrocer and then be off to my digs. I've been on call here for two weeks, so I'm pretty well set up. Even got a staff car for us, not the best, an old Austin, but she runs and we get petrol on the base."

Moxie came out of the grocery store a few minutes later with two sacks of supplies. They drove through the streets of Portsmouth until they were in the country and headed north on a back road toward Guildford. They turned into a lane with two cottages and parked in front of the first one. Moxie bounced out, grabbed the groceries, and motioned.

"Well, come on, mon. You can't do any good out here in the creeping fog."

Ben stepped out of the small car and took one of the sacks. He was a little sorry he had come, but decided he would play the game. Lord knew he deserved a bit of a rest and recuperation. What the hell, he hadn't even seen this bird Moxie had lined up for him. Moxie had known about the assignment early, and had put this holiday together. Knowing the Scot, the bird probably wouldn't be too bad.

Moxie was ahead of him and at the door. He knocked once and the door opened. A pretty dark-haired girl stood smiling at him. Ben could see she was young, slender and had eyes only for Moxie.

"Pru, this is my Yank buddy, Ben Mount. Ben, Pru, and she's mine so push your eyeballs back in their sockets, mate. This other bird is for you, over here."

Ben had been vaguely aware of someone else, but she was shielded by Moxie. Now the canny Scot made a little flourish and stepped away just as he said the girl's name.

"Mr. Benjamin Mount, I'd like to introduce you to a pretty little bird. Her name is Betsy Kirkland!"

Chapter 4

Ben's eyes bounced out of their sockets. He looked past the grinning Moxie and saw her. It was Betsy Kirkland. Over and over he had remembered how she had looked that night on board the *Queen Mary* when she had decided to sail to England with him. It was suddenly no longer just a memory. He saw her oval, lovely face smiling at him, her pointed chin and her highlighted, full red lips. He stared at her uniquely tilted nose and uncertain eyes.

"Betsy!" was all he could say as he rushed across the room and held her in his arms, crushing her against him, her light brown hair streaming around his face. Suddenly he realized he never wanted to let her go. As they moved apart, he reached down and kissed her so gently that their lips barely made contact.

Then the questions tumbled out. "How did Moxie find you? Where are you living now? How long have you been in this area? What are you doing now?" He picked up her left hand, saw that it held no rings and kissed it. "And I'm as glad as hell that you aren't married. What ever happened to . . ."

She shook her pretty head. "No I won't even talk about him, or think about him. That's past. I just don't know how I ever let you get away from me the last time. What was it, some dumb little thing like a global war going on? Some stupid admiral in the

Mediterranean needing a consultant on anti-sub warfare?" She put her arms around his neck and pulled his head down and kissed him, her lips hard against his, her slender, enticing body pressing fully against him.

Moxie cheered and so did his girl, Pru.

Betsy watched Ben. "I hope you aren't too surprised, or disappointed. I'm sure that Moxie promised you a riotous night of drink and wild, wild women."

Ben laughed and kissed her cheek, then her nose. "I'm not very good with those wild women, they always keep getting away from me." He caught her hand and angled her to a couch where they sat down, so close together that their shoulders, thighs, and legs touched. He kissed her lips again, and then shook his head in delighted impatience. "Now, for God's sakes, tell me how all this came about. How Moxie found you, and how you two plotted behind my back to set this up."

She patted her hair back into place. "I cut it again," she said. "It takes less time to fix it, less water to wash it, and less heat to curl it." She stopped speaking, caught his hand, pulled it to her lap, and she held it tightly with both of hers. Her large, happy eyes glistened with a touch of wetness as she looked at him.

"Ben Mount, I'm so happy to see you that I think I'm going to cry. It's been a year, six months, and three days since you went to the Mediterranean. And letters are such a damn poor substitute. Then even they stopped." She took a deep breath and brushed at her eyes. "I work just outside of Portsmouth a ways, and I hoped that if you came back to England you would be stationed here. I work in a war plant."

She laughed. "No, I can't possibly give away any war secrets, because I don't have the slightest idea what I'm making. I put one little thing together with another little gadget and then test it to be sure it's right and works. Somebody said they were artillery shell fuses. Somebody else said they were parts of an airplane. I really don't know."

"And then . . ." Ben interrupted.

"Oh, well . . . I've been working most of the time, and driving an ambulance at night when it's needed. We've been lucky lately. Then one day at work I got a note from my supervisor. It was from Moxie giving his phone number at the base and asking me to call him. He went through the war production agency to find out where I was working. It was a lot of work for him."

"I'll stand him a pint the next time I get him in a pub." Ben couldn't turn his eyes away from her. "You're a little thinner than you were. I like you this way."

She smiled. "I bet Moxie a pound note that you would notice right off," she said as she squeezed his hand. "Do you think it would be too forward if I asked you to kiss me again?"

Ben grinned and kissed her, hard at first and then softer. His tongue touched her lips and felt them part. He quickly pulled away from her, pecked at her cheek, and sat back.

"Maybe we better wait a little bit for those kind of kisses."

"Damn," she said and laughed softly, her eyes crinkling at the corners. "I guess I can wait for a while."

"Remember that cottage we had up in Scotland?" he asked. "You were driving for somebody, and I'd come home from the base and it would be almost like we were married."

She kissed his cheek and ran her fingers down his sideburns. She couldn't keep her hands away from him.

"Those two months were the happiest in my life,

I really do think," she said, "except maybe for right now." She smoothed his hand. "You certainly do bring back a lot of good memories for a girl."

"Where are you living?" he asked.

"Here."

"This is your cottage?"

"Yes. I'm sharing it with Pru. When Moxie first met her a week ago, I thought he was going to seduce her right in the hallway. She really knocked him out, and Pru couldn't be more pleased." She watched Ben a moment, then giggled. "Yes, silly, we have two bedrooms, and I wouldn't dream of making you go back to the base on a cold, foggy old night like this."

Ben kissed her again, hard, insistent, but again pulled away.

"Now that we've got that settled, let's see how Moxie is messing up that good food we bought."

"We better. Pru is good at boiling water and frying eggs, but that's about it."

Betsy surveyed the stack of food, tins, and packages on the kitchen table in her characteristic take-charge style. She had the whole meal arranged and underway within five minutes. Ben watched her from a turned around chair, marveling at her mannerisms that he'd forgotten, She used the back of her hand to push away strands of brown hair, and narrowed her eyes as she measured a cup of flour. She glanced up and caught him watching.

"Am I doing it right?" she asked.

Ben grinned and continued peeling the potatoes she had handed him.

"I'll let you know when I see the finished product," he answered.

Moxie came in from the back door with an armful of wood, and together he and Pru built a fire. When it had settled down to eating a crescent from a ten-inch-thick oak log, Moxie sat down near the flames and called Ben over.

"We've got two months of good duty coming up, mate."

"It should be. I'm just pissed that I didn't know about that request from Nimitz for me to report to the Pacific. If I'd known about it I might have been able to get it approved."

"You're good at fighting an admiral, are you? Face it, bucko, if Graves wants to keep you here, nothing you or anyone else says will talk him out of it. Hell, don't fight it. Best duty in the world. So you don't get on board one of those new Fleet-class U.S. subs. You'll have lots of time to skipper a sub after people stop shooting at us. You're a lifer, aren't you, like me? We'll have lots of time. For now, we just do what they bloody well tell us and try to get this war over with before we get our asses shot off, or blown up or crushed a hundred fathoms down with nothing to breathe but saltwater."

Ben pushed the wood around with an iron poker, and nodded. "Yeah, I know you're right, Moxie. But I'm a submariner. I've got the dolphins and I'm not really using them. I went back to the States and got my board out of the way, so I'm qualified to command a boat. Now I want to. You've had lots of sea time in your sub. How much sea time do you have?"

"Over a year."

"And you've fired a few fish in anger, right? And sunk some ships or U-boats or some damn missions?"

"Yes, but what we're doing now is more important than that. You'll realize it some day."

"What I'd really like to do is figure out some way to blast those Nazi U-boat pens, the ones the bombers can't get to. If we could take care of them, we wouldn't have to put in all the effort of tracking down and sinking the U-boats out in the North Sea and the Atlantic."

Moxie threw a small stick into the fire and watched it blaze up, burn fiercely, and fizzle out. "The Navy has given a lot of thought to that problem. But so far it's been shunted aside somewhere."

"Maybe this is the time then, to put together some plans for a real knockout raid on some of the pens," Ben suggested.

"How?"

"Damned if I know, haven't done that much research on them. Must be something in the files. Intelligence must have lots on them. It wouldn't take much digging and it should be easy enough to get cleared."

Moxie nodded. "I'll just tell them it's your show and they'll clear the Queen herself. God, but you've got a lot of clout with the brass."

"It's just because I know you, Moxie Mulford," Ben said, laughing. "Damn, but it still seems like a good idea. I'm going to start digging into some sources and see what I can learn about the U-boat pens. Maybe they aren't worth blasting, but if the rumors are true and there is going to be an invasion of the continent, then the high command sure as hell should want to get rid of as many of the U-boats as possible."

"Logic, old man. You're starting to use logic again, and you know from long experience that logic has nothing to do with military planning or thought. Brass and logic don't mix, you know the old saying."

"Blimey, mate. I'm still going to give it a go," Ben said.

Moxie laughed. "You're starting to sound more British than a duke." He paused and hooded his eyes. "But I'll be damned if it doesn't sound like some fun. Let's have a go at Jerry's U-boat pens. Might do some looking around myself on that score. Why don't we work together on it?"

"You're on, mate. Now where is the food? I'm starving."

They moved back to the small kitchen and worried the cooks by peeking in pots, looking in the oven, and making a nuisance of themselves until Betsy chased them out with a wooden spoon.

The men were halfway through a game of darts when Betsy called that dinner was ready. Ben sat down and enjoyed the home-cooked meal, but for the life of him he couldn't remember what he had eaten ten minutes after the dishes were put away.

They went into the tiny living room, and Pru turned on the radio and found the U.S. Armed Forces station. Tunes they were singing back in the States were being played. "Praise the Lord and Pass the Ammunition," was one, and "There'll Be Bluebirds over the White Cliffs of Dover Tomorrow Just You Wait and See" was another. The third one, "When the Lights Go on Again, All Over the World," was new to Ben.

Others came on, but the four friends talked over them. Moxie had figured out a way he could get copies of any information the Navy had on the German sub pens.

"I Left My Heart at the Stage Door Canteen" flowed out of the wireless, followed by "You'd be So Nice To Come Home To."

Moxie kissed Pru seriously, and then whispered to her. They stood up.

"Pru is going to show me some of the pictures in her photo album," Moxie said. Pru blushed just enough to make it interesting, and they went through one of the doors that hadn't been opened.

Betsy glanced up at Ben. "Prudence does not have

a photo album. I wondered how Moxie was going to get things started. I warned Pru that Moxie could be a pill. I told her he has four hands and isn't a bit bashful."

"Pru is gone on him I'd guess. She wasn't exactly screaming and fighting him off."

"But we don't have to pretend, or play games, do we, Ben? I want you to stay here tonight with me."

Ben reached over and kissed her lips and she slid down next to him on the braided rug in front of the fireplace. She sat close and was ready when he kissed her again.

"I want to stay, and I was hoping you wanted me to. I know it's been a long time, but somehow, it seems so much the same, the best part of it all."

"The cottage," she said. "That was the good times."

"Let's make it that way again," he said. He held her close. They leaned back against a chair. He put his arm around her and she lay her hand on his thigh. He kissed her lips again and her mouth was open. She sighed as his tongue explored hers for a moment.

"I've often wondered why we didn't get married that first two months up in Scotland," he said. "We talked about it, then things just slipped away, went to pieces, and that damn problem came up."

"Please don't mention that problem. I keep seeing her name in the papers, some benefit for the boys, some reception, an open house for the officers. Let's not talk about her."

"How is your Aunt Sabrina? Is she still in the old family manor house in London?"

"Oh, no. During the worst of the Blitz I talked her into going into the country. She had a small vacation house up in the lake country somewhere, and she's still there. It's so much nicer, and she can raise a few vegetables. She wrote that the London house had some bomb damage. A small bomb hit just outside one of the wings, and smashed in one wall, but it didn't burn. Neighbors helped patch up the worst of it for her, so the wet wouldn't seep in. I should run up there and check it for her. Two of the servants are still living there as caretakers."

Ben kissed her and she clung to him. He moved his hand so it covered one of her breasts. He could feel it throbbing through her blouse. She looked at him, then down at his hand. She kissed his hand.

"Darling, I was hoping you would do that."

He kissed her again. Her mouth opened and her tongue slid into his mouth. He found her hand and pulled it to his crotch where the bulge was growing. When the kiss ended, he opened the buttons down the front of her white blouse and she smiled, waiting for him. Then his hands went around her, under the cloth to the hook of her bra. After a moment, he found the magic formula and it loosened. His hands came back and captured one of her pulsating, warm breasts. Ben touched her nipple and played with it, and soon it stood up higher and hardened.

She worked at the buttons on his trousers until at last her hand crept inside.

"Oh, my, he's so anxious, so eager!"

"A year and a half eager," Ben said. He looked at Pru's door. "Will they be coming out?"

Betsy shook her head. "No. Only in the direst of emergencies. We agreed the first one to go into a bedroom stayed there. So we've got the fire and the rug and the whole big living room to ourselves."

Ben sat up and pushed the white blouse from her shoulders, then pulled the bra straps down her arms. Betsy sat with her shoulders back, and her modest-sized breasts pushed forward. Her breasts were slightly up-tipped—pink circles glowing now with hot blood and the nipples both erect, hard. Ben bent and kissed each one.

She made a soft groaning sound in her throat.

"You can do that half the night if you want to," she said as she stroked his hair. He kissed them again and ran his tongue around a vibrating nipple.

"My God, Ben. You certainly do remember how to get me excited, don't you? I can hardly talk from the panting." She helped him take off his shirt and his white T-shirt, then she pushed down his pants. Ben slid out of them and took off his shoes at the same time.

"God, but you're beautiful," she said. "A man ready to make love is God's most beautiful creature. Did you know that, pretty man?"

He kissed her lips one time more, then unzipped the side of her skirt and pulled it down. A moment later they both sat watching the fire and holding each other.

Betsy leaned back and smiled at him. "Are you in any hurry? We've got all night. Shall we make the first time slow and easy and relaxed?"

He nodded, put more wood on the fire so it would blaze up, then stood and turned out the light. As he moved beside her, he saw that she had slipped out of her panties, so he pushed down his regulation boxer shorts. He cupped one breast, as he knew she liked him to do, and she smoothed the soft hair on his chest.

"I've been thinking a lot about you, Commander Benjamin Mount, ever since Moxie told me you were coming. I know you're going to be here for a while, and I think what I'm going to do is work up my courage and ask you to marry me. Would you be old-fashioned and not like that, or would it be all right if I asked you?"

He smiled and caressed her gently. "Strange that you should ask that. You remember my one unbreakable rule. That is that I never argue with a naked lady, because she has all the advantages and I always lose."

"Good," she said, and her hand caught his erection.

"Remember," he said. "We're going to have a long discussion on the highest intellectual level."

An hour later they left the fire and the rug and ran into her bedroom where they slid between cold sheets and clung together.

"Once more?" he asked, putting his head under the covers and chewing on her breasts.

She pulled his head up for air and frowned at him.

"One more time? No, don't be ridiculous. Two or three or four more times, depending on how long our strength holds out."

Ben Mount laughed softly and covered her mouth with his. He knew that he wasn't going to get any sleep at all that night and he didn't mind.

Chapter 5

At 0945 hours the next morning, both Ben and Moxie were on hand at Fort Blockhouse. The other participants were there early as well. For an hour the group sat and listened as fifteen different new weapons were sketched, briefed, and detailed by representatives from both the United States and Britain.

Six ideas were discarded at once because technology had not advanced far enough to support the hardware. One was a torpedo with a sonic homing system that could listen for the target ship's propeller, home in on it, hit the ship and explode. The lead time was estimated at eighteen months for design and a year after that for the first prototype.

"Two months, maximum," Captain White-Johnson reminded them. "We need something in the fleet that can be adapted, retrofitted, or reslanted now."

The group went through another series of suggestions. One was for sub nets to be strung along the ports the U-boats used. They had connective contact depth charges that would swing in, strike the U-boat when it tried to penetrate the net, and blow it out of the water.

At last the team selected six ideas for possible development. No one was happy with any of them. They had an idea for a magnetic depth charge that would not bounce off or slide past a submarine, but would be magnetically pulled to it and set off by the contact.

Another one was for a new radar picket aircraft that could fly at twenty thousand feet with an exceptionally strong radar system. Submarines could be spotted and checked out as far away as two hundred miles. Again, the problem was the technology, but they had hopes for it.

Captain White-Johnson broke his wooden pencil in half and stood.

"Gentlemen, I'm afraid I don't see many good chances here for giving Admiral Graves what he wants, what we need. How about a good old bull session? Any ideas, any suggestions? Commander Mount, any comments? Ideas that we could boot around?"

Ben stood and walked to the window. It was raining. He came back and put one foot on the chair and leaned on his knee. "As you gentlemen know, one of the best tools an anti-sub fighter has is ASDIC or sonar, as the Americans call it. It's great, but when a destroyer is charging up on a deep-running sub, there is a problem.

"The ASDIC gives out an accurate range and depth on a prowling sub, but the device simply can't keep contact with a target close aboard, especially if the target is running deep, say four hundred to six hundred feet.

"I've been on a lot of destroyers that are gunning in on a U-boat, charging along, say three hundred yards behind it and closing quickly. Then at three hundred feet, we lose the sonar signal. What can we do then? All that is left is to estimate where the U-boat is going to be, charge forward to our estimated point of release, and put out six or eight charges in a pattern. And hope. This is a guesstimation, and it usually is wrong. We've all heard Tin Can Commanders weep and moan about solving that little problem."

Ben moved from the chair to the blackboard. "So we came up with the Hedgehog, and it works. It puts something out there with a chance of hitting the boat before it changes course in that cone of silence. What I'm getting at is how about improving the Hedgehog? We don't have time to work the basic problem in ASDIC. But how about doing something with those twenty-four little rockets the destroyers fire in a pattern up to two hundred and fifty yards ahead of the tin can while they still have the correct sonar data?"

Captain White-Johnson looked up. "How would you improve them?"

"I don't know, Captain. Haven't done much thinking about it. They are contact weapons now, right? If they hit the sub, they go off with their thirty pounds of TNT and blow a hole right through the hull. What if they were fixed with pressure sensitive fuses, so if they didn't hit the sub they would still go off at a preset depth? I don't know if that would be practical, but it looks like something that could be done quickly and gotten into the field in a rush."

The captain nodded. "You work on that, Commander. The rest of you pick out one of those six other ones and let's do some high level brainstorming. See if there is any way that one or more of them could work out, if they are practical, and if they would come in under the time limit."

Ben grabbed Moxie and they headed for a telephone. It took them the rest of the day to find blueprints and schematics for the Hedgehog. When they finally had them in their hands, they herded the little Austin back to the Navy base and spread them out in the workroom the captain had reserved for them.

The two men studied the material. Two hours later they knew exactly how the Hedgehog was put together, why it went off, how much it weighed, and how much explosives each one carried.

"Impact detonator," Ben said. "It's insensitive enough that when it slams into the water at about forty miles per hour it won't detonate, but then when it sinks through the water for a hundred or two hundred feet it has to be sensitive enough to go off if it hits a submarine."

"That part works," Moxie said. "So we don't have to worry about how they did it. I heard about a destroyer forcing a U-boat to the surface in Skagerrak with the Hedgehog. Then the destroyer blew the U-boat out of the water with her guns."

"They work if they get a hit, but that's not a high enough percentage system. Trying to combine this with a depth charge could take a lot of changes." Ben tapped his finger on the tabletop. "It probably will take too long."

Moxie tossed a blueprint on the table. "These Hedgehogs are made here in England. Let's call up the people who make them. They might have done some advanced designs on their own, hoping for another sale. Maybe they've already got a prototype out. It's worth a try."

"A try? It's inspired."

They made four calls before reaching the design department at Sea Weapons Ltd. The chief design engineer remained cool and uninterested until Ben explained their project.

"Yes, as a matter of fact we did make some advanced designs and submitted them to the Royal Navy, but they shot us down before we got our mouths open."

"How advanced were the designs?" Ben asked sharply. "Could they fire from the same launcher the Hedgehog uses?"

"Of course. That was the whole thrust of our proposal. A quick retrofit and a better weapon."

Briefly Ben explained what his function was and the engineer, C. C. Phillips, warmed at once.

"I can have the prototype and design specifications

ready for you by tomorrow noon, if you can get up here to Croydon, it's just outside of London."

"Make it thirteen hundred hours tomorrow, one P.M." Ben said and took the address as he sat back smiling.

"This bloke of yours may already have solved our problem," he announced when he hung up the phone. "We find out tomorrow afternoon."

It was slightly after six and Moxie was in a rush to get moving. "You want to pick up a suitcase or a seabag? I'm going to be living in with my bird for a time, and I figured you might be, too."

Ben confirmed that he was moving in as well. The little cottage would bulge for a while, but with the continual housing shortage all over England, they were glad to have any kind of a roof over their heads.

The next morning, Ben and Moxie fired up the Austin and drove north toward London. As Moxie knew the area, they quickly found Croydon and the office of the arms maker. The building was small, obviously not a production plant. They introduced themselves to the chief engineer, a sales representative, and the vice president in charge of production and marketing.

"Gentlemen, we are happy with your product, but we're hoping that you have something even better in the works," Ben said.

Phillips, the chief engineer, showed Ben a blueprint.

"So, I see you use the same launcher, but the missile looks about twice the size. Yes, I like that. Any other changes?"

"The big change is in the size and weight of the charge, otherwise the fish is basically the same," Phillips said.

"Contact detonation?" Moxie asked.

"Yes, no change there."

Moxie took the blueprint and rolled it into a tube. "What we really need is a combination of this weapon and a depth charge. We want to throw a small depth charge ahead of our destroyers and DEs if we can, and have them drop down. If no contact is made, we want them to detonate like an ash can. How soon can you come up with a design like that with a variable depth setting?"

The engineer looked at his co-workers. The marketing man shrugged. "Engineering-wise you need to splice in a variable setting depth fuse and a dual triggering on the charge," he said. "Doesn't seem to be much of a problem."

"You want the same missile we now produce, only with a hydrostatic fuse on it?" Phillips asked.

Ben shook his head. "That would give us a thirty-one pound depth charge. Most of our regular depth charges weigh in at five hundred pounds. Can't we give the destroyers something heavier than the thirty-one pounds? Maybe sixty or seventy pounds?"

"And you want it fired from the same missile launcher we now use on the Hedgehog? There is no way it will work. What we can do is design the largest possible payload for the missile that we can pump two hundred and fifty yards through the same launcher. We'll get all the size we can out of it, but it's dependent on how much propellant we can ram into that tube to get the missiles out to range."

Ben smiled and extended his hand. "I'll buy that. Now, I can't offer you a contract, but as soon as you get the specs worked up and a production schedule, I'd almost bet that you'll get a contract. Speed is our problem. We must have this new missile in the field and in action within three months."

Mr. Phillips threw up both hands.

"And, Mr. Phillips," Ben continued, "I'll give you

all the engineering support that I can, starting as soon as you find me a good strong cup of black coffee."

Phillips took a deep breath. "You mean you'll be a free engineer for us?"

"Right, whatever I can do."

"And we stick to the use of the present launcher, no new tack on devices?"

"Right, that helps get them into the field and in use faster."

"True. Yes, all right. Let's get to work on the preliminary plans. I figure we have about three days to do six weeks' worth of engineering. Then another two or three days to fabricate our test prototypes and then two days to test them. That gives us two months for production and a week for shipping time. Goddamn, but you Yanks do get in a rush, don't you." He laughed and shook hands with Ben and Moxie.

"But I'm damn glad that you're on board. Now, follow me and we'll find a couple of desks for you gentlemen and get you to work. I'll bring in a couple of cots so we don't have to waste a lot of time finding a bed. I hope you don't mind working around the clock."

"War is hell," Ben said and everyone smiled and relaxed.

Moxie was at Ben's elbow for most of the next six days. He did the drafting work, ran errands, and called the girls to tell them he and Ben would be closeted in London for a while. He even found a radio and let it play softly as they worked.

Moxie got the go-ahead from Captain White-Johnson to work on the project. He promised to send blueprints on the suggested new design within a week.

The two men worked closely with Phillips, who turned out to be a talented engineer who knew how to cut through theory and get an idea into practical form. The third day he and Ben looked at Moxie's final drawings.

"Should work," Phillips said.

"I'm still worried about the range," Ben admitted.

"We've got some new juice to put in the propellant that should give us enough boost. The men in the plant will have three handmade missiles ready for us tomorrow morning. If they work, the hydrostatic fuses will be ready the next day for testing."

"How do we test them?"

"Put in a dummy charge, fuse it normally, and let the missile down on a rope in the ocean to a preset test level, say a hundred feet, and see if it detonates. Routine."

"If we can get enough range, we can fiddle with the hydrostatic fuse, I'm not worried about that."

The next morning they got to the test range, went through military security, and backed the truck up to a locked warehouse. Phillips rolled out a trailer with a Hedgehog launcher on it and they moved to the assigned testing area.

The launcher contained twenty-four missile launching brackets, Phillips and his crew loaded one of the new fatter missiles into place and made the proper connections for an electrical ignition.

The range ahead of them was marked with white fences one hundred, two hundred, and two hundred and fifty yards.

"We have a full charge of propellant in this test model," Phillips explained. "But there is no payload explosive or detonator. The weight is the same as we hope the completed missile will be. Shall we have a go at it?"

Moxie gave him a thumbs up signal and Ben nodded. They walked twenty yards to one side and saw

Phillips pick up a push button switch on a long wire lead. He handed it to Ben.

"You have the honors."

Ben looked around the range. There was no one in sight, so he pushed the button. A cracking roar shattered the foggy morning, and the missile popped fifteen feet into the air and fell to the ground. The Hedgehog launcher shattered as the propellant charge broke through the walled canister and instead of shooting the missile down range tore up the launcher metal as though it were cardboard.

Moxie groaned and went down on one knee. Blood spurted from a tear in his pants leg just below the knee. Ben quickly forced him down, sliced open the pants and found the two-inch gash. It didn't look serious but a black, jagged piece of metal showed through the blood of the wound. Ben wrapped his handkerchief around the leg to stop the bleeding.

Moxie ground his teeth and then looked up at Phillips. "I'd say we go back to the bloody drawing board."

Within moments an ambulance came racing to the scene. A young nurse unwrapped the handkerchief and checked the wound. She pressed the skin around it, then wiggled the metal fragment.

"You're lucky, it's just a scratch. See?" she asked as she pulled the metal out. Moxie winced.

"I'm ruined for life! They'll put me out to pasture! I'll get a medical discharge for sure!" he said, trying to ignore the pain.

"I've seen little old ladies during the Blitz walking around with five times that much metal in them. They were helping the less fortunate," she said as she sprinkled some sulfa powder into the wound, then wrapped it up and taped it securely.

"There you go. You'll be dancing in a week."

"No ambulance ride? No hospital? Not even a Military Cross decoration? What kind of a bloody war is this?"

"Off your arse and on your feet, Commander, I've got some important work to do this morning." She popped him a fast salute, got back into the ambulance and promptly sped away.

"Damn, two failures in a row," Moxie said. "Ah well, Pru is still at Portsmouth. Now there is one fine bird!"

The three of them walked out to the launcher. It was a twisted mass of unusable junk.

"So we'd better drop the weight by twenty percent and cut down on the propellant," Phillips said.

"Maybe we should eliminate that hot new explosive and go with what you used before, try to pack more of it into the casing," Ben suggested.

"Or both of the above," Phillips said. "Let's go see what the old slide rule says."

A week later Moxie stood at least a hundred yards away when he pushed the button on a long cord.

"You guarantee this won't splatter us all over this end of England?" Moxie asked.

Phillips snorted and motioned for him to fire it. Ben slapped Moxie's shoulder and scowled. "If you British submariners don't have enough guts for this experimental work, Mulford, let me do it."

"Hell no, you blew up the last one, Yank," Moxie answered as he pushed the button.

The explosion was more like those Ben had heard on the destroyers when the Hedgehogs went off. The missile sailed out and came down within five yards of the two hundred and fifty yard fence.

"Bravo!" Moxie shouted.

Phillips turned and ran for the jeep. Ben followed and Moxie limped along behind.

"Come on, no lagging. If that one works the other

two will fly too. We'll let the others test them. We've got to set up the next tests with the hydrostatic fuses."

The next day they took the three test missiles to Portsmouth. Phillips confirmed that the hydrostatic fuses were from the same firm that supplied most of the British depth charge fuses. They had already been scaled down and tested. The firm provided a dozen fuses and helped with the installation. They used a ready-made method of tying the fuse train in with the contact head. That way either one would set off the main charge.

Phillips stayed in a hotel that night in Portsmouth, but Moxie and Ben drove on to the sub base. They had received clearance from the captain to use Ben's sub, the *Seawitch,* for further testing. When they had finished, the two weary submariners headed for the cottage.

By the time they arrived, Pru and Betsy had finished dinner. Betsy reheated some stew. The men ate like they hadn't eaten in a pair of Tuesdays.

Pru sat with her arms folded, pouting.

"Two weeks. Two weeks and I ain't seen eye nor ear of you! Now you come steaming in like we was married or something."

Betsy put her arm around Pru and the two spoke quietly in the other room as the men finished the rest of the stew. When they returned, Pru was smiling again. She moved up beside Moxie and gave him a quick kiss on the cheek.

"I guess since you've been aworking so hard up there by London and all, that I won't be a spoilsport." Moxie looked at her, not quite sure what she was talking about, but he kissed her wetly on the mouth and pulled her into his lap as he finished a piece of apple pie.

"How about going to a dance?" Moxie asked. "How about the four of us going out to a dance somewhere?

There must be a dance for us gallant boys in blue."

"But, luv, you're wounded. Remember your leg?" Pru asked with concern.

"It's fine, fine, nothing more than a scratch, and I won't get a medal or anything. How about it?"

"Not me," Betsy said. "I've got to work tomorrow."

"You two run along if you want," Ben said. "I want to be up and ready to go at the crack of a fog bank in the morning."

"Hell," Moxie said and shrugged his shoulders. "I guess we could stay here and have a fire and maybe pop some corn. You folks like popped corn?"

Finally, they went to bed. Ben watched Betsy undress in their bedroom, and slip into a cotton flannel nightgown. She was not strip-teasing or being coy. She was natural. Suddenly he realized he was so bone weary that he couldn't be much use to Betsy anyway. She smiled and helped him out of his clothes. He rolled into bed in his shorts, kissed Betsy once and was sleeping before she could pull the covers over him.

Betsy kissed his cheek, then curled up beside him and reminded herself that there would be hundreds of nights to be with Ben, just hundreds and hundreds. She smiled and went to sleep.

Early the next morning Ben watched Mr. Phillips step on board the *Seawitch*. He knew immediately the man had never been on a submarine before. They stood quietly on the deck as the test missiles were carefully loaded through the forward hatch, then went to the bridge.

Ben and Moxie teased Mr. Phillips by telling salty, hair-raising tales of undersea terror. They described being crushed by the sea, and being depth charged just a dozen miles off the coast.

At last Phillips turned to them. "I know you chaps are having some fun at my expense, but it's a bit more than the natural worry with me. A motor launch would have worked just fine for the test."

Ben relented. "We won't even be diving, Mr. Phillips. Just a kind of initiation for a person new to subs."

"Why don't you come below for a quick tour while the hatches are open," Moxie suggested. "I understand your feeling. Once I had a close friend who had trouble with claustrophobia, and the crazy man insisted on being a submariner. We'll be running on the surface all the way, but we had better take the tour now as things get a little busy once we're underway."

Moxie and Phillips vanished down the conning tower ladder. Ben followed with only a twinge of the old fear, and that was mostly remembrances. For months, even years, he was frightened to death to go under the surface. Ben watched Phillips return from one of the quickest tours of the improved S-class British submarines on record. Sweat beaded Phillips's forehead.

"A bit tight down there, isn't it, Mr. Phillips? That was me Moxie was talking about, but I've got it beaten now."

Phillips gasped in a lungful of fresh air. He closed his eyes, and a look of relief swept over his face. When he opened them, he stared at the dock, and Ben knew the man was debating whether to ask to be put ashore. At last he was calm and by the time Moxie cast off the lines, he was almost his old self.

The HMS *Seawitch* slid away from the greasy piles at Fort Blockhouse, Portsmouth. She swam easily with the flood tide into Hasler creek and moved away from the sub base into the harbor. They went two miles offshore and east of the Isle of Wight.

No surprises were encountered on the run out to their prearranged test site. Moxie brought the sub to a full stop, and Phillips directed his crew to lower the first test missile over the side. The missile had been set to detonate at one hundred feet below the surface, and when the test crew came to the first knot in the line, one of them called out the depth and stopped lowering.

"Down, sir. But I don't hear anything."

They pulled the test round back up and found that the nose cone had been blown out. Success number one.

The other two tests worked equally as well, one going off at two hundred feet and the next at three hundred feet. The test equipment was recovered, and they moved back toward Portsmouth.

Phillips, who had stayed rooted on the bridge, was now all smiles. He held a cup of tea from the galley and talked loudly about what a good design the missile was and how well it had functioned.

"Now who do we talk to about a contract?" he asked.

"Give me your cost figures and we'll submit them tomorrow," Ben said. "We can't guarantee anything, but the captain said you have a good chance of getting an order. If not, the Navy will compensate you at a cost plus basis for your development work."

"I'd rather have an order for about fifty thousand missiles," Phillips said. "Oh, since this is a new size, new type, we've given it a new name. It's the Squid, that sounds a lot more maritime than Hedgehog."

Ben and Moxie both agreed.

Back at the base Moxie came storming into their office holding a notice he had found on the officers' bulletin board.

"Look at this, will you? A special ball. An officers' ball and it's being held tonight right here near town. I'm going to run out and get Pru, have her put on her fancy dancing dress and come charging back to the dance. How about you, old buddy?"

Ben shook his head. "Tonight I'm going to take off

my shoes, push my feet up toward the fire, and try to remember how normal folks live."

"Come on, the four of us can make a night of it," Moxie urged. "I bet Betsy would love to go."

Ben shook his head. "Nope, not this time."

"Then at least rustle your bones so you can ride home with me. That way Pru and I can get ready and get back to the dance before the buffet and the drinks are gone. It's supposed to be held at some swanky lord's estate outside of town."

Ben pushed some papers into a drawer, and the two men headed out the door.

Chapter 6

Moxie knew the dance was to be held at Lord some-body's estate, but he raised his eyebrows when he saw the district it was in. He had followed the map, and they were out of Portsmouth about ten miles. The area had become gentle countryside with hedges and fences and lots of horses. There were also some fancy wood-lands that had been planted to screen the impressive mansions. This was landed gentry country, and one of the lords was rolling out an upper-class welcome for the boys in the service. Nothing was too good for the Royal Naval officers fighting for God and Country.

Moxie saw the gate and gatehouse along a macadam roadway just in time to turn in the driveway. The gatehouse was larger than any house Moxie had ever lived in. The light was failing as they drove along the winding lane to Rolling Hills Estate. Pru sat stiffly beside him, well aware that they were going to a mansion that they never would have been invited to had Moxie not been wearing a Navy officer's uniform during a war.

"Maybe we should go back," Pru said. "I'm starting to feel like we shouldn't even drive in here."

"Generations of conditioning, my girl. Hold your chin up and smile. Push your chest out and you'll have the men drooling out of their upper-class lips."

"Oh, Moxie!"

"True, we're just as good as anybody who's going to be there tonight. So make them believe it."

"But he's a lord you said."

"So what? With this monkey suit on I'm just as important as they are, and they better snap to and remember it. Their blood runs just as red as ours, and flows just as fast, and some of them are at last beginning to realize it."

They drove around a curve a quarter of a mile from the road, and headed toward a pair of ancient oaks that fronted a parking lot half the size of an airdrome. In front of the lot were Rolls-Royces, Bentleys, Jaguars, and Mercedeses. Moxie saw even a few Cadillacs. There were also some Austins, Morris Minors, and MGs, and some French and Italian prewar cars.

The car ahead of them had rolled into a circular drive and had stopped under an awning-covered walkway. Moxie pulled in behind it, then ahead when the other car moved. The mansion beyond the walkway took Moxie's breath away. It was spread out on each side halfway across the landscape. Muted lights showed a dim outline of a two-story manor house.

"My God, it must have thirty rooms!" Pru exclaimed.

A liveried man opened the door. Pru looked at Moxie, who nodded, and she stepped out. The man came around and opened the door for Moxie.

"I'll park it for you, sir. Leave the keys in the ignition."

"Thank you."

Pru clutched at Moxie's hand, and for a moment he put his arm around her to steady her.

"Eyes up, chest out, luv, and you'll wow them all, let's have at them."

They strolled up the long walk and climbed a dozen marble steps to the front door. A costumed servant took their light wraps, and pointed to the left.

"The ballroom is down that way, sir," the servant said.

Moxie nodded, took Pru's hand, and marched away.

"Moxie, it's magnificent!" Pru said. "Look at the drapes, the floor, the paintings!"

"Yes, a few castoffs from my country place," Moxie said. Pru couldn't help breaking into a nervous giggle.

Another couple walked past them. Moxie didn't recognize the man's uniform. He expected there would be a lot of different uniforms there tonight, and he was right.

At the ballroom door they paused. There were thirty or forty couples dancing, another twenty standing around a bar and buffet table, and dozens more sitting around the room.

The room was at least sixty feet long, and almost as wide. At the far end a band played on a raised platform, pounding out both American and British tunes. The chandelier in the center would be magnificent, Moxie thought, if it were completely lighted. However, it held only a few lights as everyone was conserving electricity for the war effort.

Ninety percent of the men wore uniforms, and for a moment Moxie thought he saw a familiar face at the punch bowl, but he decided he'd been mistaken.

There seemed to be no official hostess, so Moxie and Pru danced a pair of numbers, then worked their way toward the punch bowl. One of the commanders on the sub development team at the base spotted Moxie. They talked for a moment, then changed partners and danced. The commander's girl was tall and thin, and Moxie wondered if she had any breasts. She was, however, a good dancer, and soon the set of three tunes was over.

"Was he a good dancer?" Moxie asked Pru. She shook her head.

"No, he was a crusher. I think he was trying to feel what size bra I wear."

Moxie squeezed her hand. "He shows good judgement."

They stepped up to the punch bowl. As Moxie held out his cup, a hand grabbed his. He looked up, surprised.

The woman who held his hand had long, sleek black hair falling around her shoulders and cut straight across her forehead. She stared at him with aquamarine eyes set deep and wide over high cheekbones. Her richly red lips parted and the tip of her tongue moistened them.

"Now I remember. You're Commander Mulford, Moxie Mulford. You were a guest at our country place the day we declared war way back in 1939. You were with an American, yes, Ben Mount. Whatever happened to Lieutenant Mount, anyway, Commander?"

Moxie stared. Then he remembered her name.

"Well, Lady Clifford, this is a surprise. Oh, may I present Prudence Lafferty. Prudence this is Lady Clifford."

Pru said something she hoped was polite and took Moxie's arm, clinging desperately.

"Whatever did happen with that nice Ben Mount?" Lady Clifford asked. "Did he get called back to the States?"

"Yes he did," Moxie said. "Then he came back over to help us with the U-boat problem."

"Is he still here?" Lady Clifford asked.

Moxie hesitated. Lady Clifford's hard eyes bore into his and a lifetime of training and custom surged up. He almost bowed as he cleared his throat. She was upper class. She was to be deferred to, respected, obeyed.

"Yes, ma'am. He's here. But he doesn't want to see you."

Lady Clifford's eyes turned cold as blue snow. They glittered with anger. She poured punch, slopping it on his hand, down his sleeve.

"Well, now, Mr. Mulford. I doubt very much if he told you that. You made it up because you dislike me, but that is quite all right, because I have never liked you for an instant. Tell Ben Mount that I'll be in touch with him, soon."

"Sorry, ma'am, but I won't be able to do that."

She pulled him past the punch bowl with a chilly smile on her highbred face. "Mr. Mulford, it really doesn't matter to me one way or the other whether you tell him or not, because I am now determined to see him."

Moxie hurried Pru to the side of the room and dried off his cuff and uniform sleeve the best he could with his handkerchief. The pink punch made a dark stain on the deep blue fabric, but he was sure it would come out.

"Damn her!" Moxie said, sudden anger flooding through him.

"You knew that grand lady, then, Mox, didn't you?" Pru asked him.

"No, but I've met her once or twice before. She almost ruined Ben five years ago. She's a snotty, gold-plated bitch. Lady Clifford was the big reason Ben and Betsy didn't get married back in the fall of 1939. Anything she wants, she thinks she can get, just reaches out and takes it. Betsy knew from the moment she saw Lady Clifford she was trouble, but there wasn't a thing Betsy could do about it."

"She doesn't look so mean," Pru said, "and she certainly is pretty. Goodness, that white gown she's wearing must have cost a hundred quid at least. And it was cut so low. Why, if I wore that, half my boobs would be pushing right out into the room."

"Aye, lass. There's nothing to spoil an evening as much as the likes of that Lady Clifford. Damnation, I don't even feel like dancing now! Don't want to make the drive out here just to be insulted by that sweet bitch."

"We could go home," Pru said sincerely. "Truly, Mox, I wouldn't mind in the least. I still got prickles up and down me spine just being in this mansion."

"Let her run me out? Not by her ladyship's fancy arse I won't. Come on, we're going to dance and dance. Then I'll drink the rest of the punch and when we get home I'm gonna strip you naked and pop you three times in front of the fire before you know what time it is."

Moxie kept his word, but was barely awakened in time the next morning. He had made Pru swear on a stack of prayer books that she wouldn't mention a word about Lady Clifford. Pru made up her mind that she wouldn't breathe a syllable about it to Betsy. Betsy and Ben were so deliriously happy, and she didn't want to spoil that.

Over hot biscuits and tea Ben made plans for the day. "We've got only to check over Phillips's test report and his offer of sale and see what kind of a contract purchasing can give him. Then I'd say we should be free for a day or so. I'm going to put in for a test sample of twenty-four of the new Squids for an in-field test from a destroyer, just as soon as they can get them made. That will only be if the contract is awarded."

"Good, I'll go along with you on the tin can," Moxie said. "You planning on calling up a German U-boat to act as your target?"

"I plan to, but if we don't run into one by the

end of the second day, we'll have six barrels welded together end to end and half filled with water. They'll at least drop down to a hundred feet. We'll fly a flag buoy on the surface and use that as our underwater target. They can make practice runs, lobbing volleys of six at a time and see what happens below."

"Sure you don't want me in the barrels as an observer?"

Ben nodded. "Swell idea, but the Royal Navy might not like it. I was thinking you and the *Seawitch* could be riding alongside at periscope depth, say three hundred yards off and see if your ASDIC picked up the charges."

Moxie yawned, said it seemed like a good followup test idea and that he was sure Admiral Graves would approve it. Then he turned his head to the window and slept the rest of the way to Fort Blockhouse.

It took until almost noon to check over, approve, and give to Captain White-Johnson the test reports Phillips had prepared.

"Gentlemen, I'm pleased. And the admiral is delighted. There had been some talk of doing something like this at one time, but it got lost in the paperwork, or in some emergency. Now I've put my recommendation for approval on Squid, and I'm positive that Admiral Graves wants it. If the company can meet the schedule they set up, Squid should be operational on most of our destroyers well within the three-month deadline we were given."

"What about the sea trials from a destroyer?" Ben asked.

"I approved that too, Commander. But that will depend on the situation at the time. Things are starting to tighten up around here. I suppose you've heard the rumor about the continent. Everybody knows we're going to invade Europe, especially the Germans. Now it's just a matter of when, where, and with how many troops. The invasion might scrub a destroyer test, but I hope not. We want Squid to be fully operational so we can keep the U-boats on the run. We sure don't want a dozen wolf packs harassing our troop transports when they do head for Europe."

"France," Ben said. "It's got to be France. We've got France, Germany, and Belgium to choose from. Obviously not Germany if you want some partisan support. Belgium is too close to Germany so that leaves France."

"And still one hell of a long coastline," Captain White-Johnson said. He picked up some papers as if the meeting were over.

Moxie almost stood but Ben ignored the signal.

"Captain, have you ever considered some more direct action against the U-boats, like hitting the sub pens harder? Moxie and I have been doing some thinking about taking it to the Nazis in their own backyard. If we could knock out their nests, the U-boats would have no place to hide, to refuel, or to get repairs."

"Commander, we're not total idiots up here. Yes, we've thought about that, and we've put hundreds of bombers into the air to try it. But I'm sure you know that the roofs on those reinforced concrete sub pens are now eight meters thick. For your Yankee counting system that's over twenty-six feet thick. We don't have a bomb yet that will go through it. Any other ideas?"

Ben stood and walked around his chair. "Well, if this little project with Squid is over, how would it be if Moxie and I do some thinking about the sub pens? No expense account, no big program, just some digging into it?"

The captain sighed. "You damn Yanks do get to the point quickly, don't you? And you want me to get on the phone and ask Admiral Graves if it's all right with him?"

"It had occurred to me, sir," Ben said.

"I'll get back to you this afternoon. Now please get the hell out of here so I can get my other work caught up."

Ben chuckled as he and Moxie saluted smartly and walked out with their hats under their arms.

"What the hell you trying to do?" Moxie asked the moment the door closed behind them.

"Just nosing around. We have been working on it already. Haven't you got half a briefcase full of data on the U-boat pens? You showed me some dope about pens at Brest and Lorient in France, and in Hamburg in Germany."

"Sorry I did. No worry, the admiral would never give a pair of wild-eyed junior officers like us a go-ahead on something like this. I'm hungry, want to have lunch?"

As they ate, Ben asked about the dance.

"Not much to it. Saw one or two guys I knew. He was a Royal Navy commander on our project who had this bird I wasn't sure even was a bird. I mean she had no tits at all. I danced with her and she was a great dancer, but nothing up top."

"Not like Pru," Ben said.

"True, but Pru is a good kid. What if her bust size is twice that of her IQ? I still like her, and besides, she's great in bed."

"Glad I didn't go to your big dance," Ben said.

Moxie looked away and lifted his brows. "Yeah, it would have been a bloody waste of your time."

After lunch Ben headed for the Austin.

"Where to, mate?"

"Allied Naval Intelligence. They've got an office somewhere around here. I've got the address."

"What we going there for?" Moxie asked.

"See what they know about the sub pens."

"You out of your blithering mind? That sounds like work. We could go to the cinema, take the girls for a walk in the park, or go home and make passionate love. Allied Naval Intelligence! You've got to have a clearance even to get in the front door at that place."

"So they can't do any more than throw us out."

Moxie shook his head as he directed Ben toward the right street. "Somebody telling you no before hasn't even slowed you down, Mount, do you realize that?"

"Hadn't occurred to me. Good thing to remember though."

Twenty minutes later they entered a small, three-story building. Two U.S. Marines with side arms and automatic weapons slung over their shoulders stood beside a desk in the front hall.

A full commander in the Royal Navy looked up from the desk. He did not smile.

"What can I do for you gentlemen?" he asked curtly.

"Good afternoon, Commander. We're from Captain White-Johnson's office of special weapons from Fort Blockhouse. We're on a research project to learn as much as we can about the U-boat pens."

"Authorization?"

"I beg your pardon?" Ben asked.

"Who has authorized you to receive this information?"

"You don't understand. We're on your side. All we're . . ."

Moxie moved up. "Commander, you could give the

captain a call. He said he was going to check about
it this morning with Admiral Graves."

"Is that Admiral Joseph Graves, in Special Weapons?"

"Yes sir."

The commander's steely gray eyes melted, and he
grinned. "Well, that's different. How is old Joe,
anyway? He used to be my CO a few months back."

He wrote something on two passes and gave them
to Ben and Moxie. "Take these up to the second
floor to room fourteen. The girl can show you what
we have. None of that material is classified anymore.
They should have some good sketches from the French
underground and some aerial photos."

When he had finished giving directions, he nodded
toward Ben. "Is he really on our side?"

"Some of the time. Thanks, Commander."

Moxie laughed as they climbed the steps. "He had
the right idea; you Yanks just aren't to be trusted."

"Take your pick," a sloppy WREN said when they
showed their passes. "Please keep the folders in numerical order."

The first folder contained a photo of the sub pens
at Brest at surface water level. They looked like big
garages built on the bay. They were cement boxes,
wide enough for two subs to fit in each one, and
about forty feet high. The concrete roofs were about
fifteen feet thick.

"Look at that, no camouflage at all," Ben said.
"They're saying 'Here we are, blow us up if you
can.' That must be why they put the additional concrete on top to bring them up to the twenty-six-foot
thickness the captain was talking about."

"Look at all that water," Moxie said.

"Best way to get to them is by water."

"Sure, Yank. We sail the *Seawitch* right in the bay
and blast them with our torpedoes."

"Or we capture a U-boat and sail right in. Load it with TNT with a time fuse and blow it up in one of the doors."

"Hell yes, that's easy. Just go out and capture a German U-boat. Make sense, Ben. Any ideas we get have to be halfway possible."

They sorted through more of the photos. Some were aerial shots taken from so high that the pens showed only as a pancake of concrete beside a river or a bay.

They found photo after photo of the huge concrete pillboxes where the U-boats could nestle, safe from air attack, to be refitted and refueled.

After two hours of mulling over the material, they sat back and Ben pulled out a pad of yellow ruled paper.

"Let's get some ideas down," he said, writing as he spoke. "Purpose: to destroy one U-boat pen as a pattern to use on all such locations."

"Yeah, Yank, but how the hell do we accomplish that little task? That's the hard part."

"My tall, limey friend, that is why I've got a full-fledged submarine commander as a partner. So start coming up with those brilliant ideas of yours."

Chapter 7

Moxie waved at him and went to talk to the WREN clerk. A few minutes later he came back with two cups of coffee.

"You damn Yanks are destroying the very fabric of our English civilization. Nothing in the tea cabinet but coffee, can you bloody well imagine that?"

Ben snorted and grabbed a cup, then motioned to the list. He knew Moxie had been hooked on coffee while he was in the States and that he loved to gripe about it.

"So, give with the ideas, Moxie. Kilroy isn't going to come help you out on this one."

"Right-o! All right. First, we know there are pens at Brest, Cherbourg, and St. Nazaire in France. There must be others we don't know about yet, Le Havre, maybe Port-Louis. We know they have some in Hamburg and up in Norway at Trondheims Fjord. We only need one for our attack."

Ben sat back, made notes, and let Moxie go on talking.

"So, we want to set this up to prevent massive U-boat damage to an invasion fleet. I don't know how many German submarines there are left now, but it's way down from what it was in mid-1943. Let's say they massed U-boats at their pens, knowing about when the invasion was coming—and they jolly well must know that it is coming by now—and we get in and surprise a whole shit-pot full of Jerry U-boats in the pens or just outside them and we blow them all to hell. Agreed, so far, but how do we hit them? We can't burn down their barn because that fifteen-foot-thick concrete don't burn none too well."

"Let's pick our target," Ben suggested. "Why not make it Brest, France. It's close to the channel, at the far end of Brittany there, and looks like a prime point for U-boats to gather. They could sweep into the channel quickly to hit an invasion fleet. It's only a hundred miles or so from Le Havre."

Moxie shrugged. "Fine, so we go against the Brest pens. Let's find out everything we can about Brest and their operation there. We'll copy all the important data and put it into our think box. Hell, Graves is going to cut us off at the pockets anyway. I don't know why I'm going along with you on this."

"Why would he stop us? It's free brainstorming for him," Ben said.

"Ben, you're thinking like a peasant. Graves is a damned admiral. He can put a dozen experts on it if he wants to and it wouldn't cost him a farthing." Moxie put the folders back in the boxes. "You want to check back with the captain before we head out to the cottage?"

"Leave? It isn't even five o'clock yet."

"Yeah, Yank. Right, so let's get out of here."

Ben shrugged and they went back to the base to the captain's office. He was just coming out when they arrived.

"I was afraid you might come. I've got bad news. But it's probably bad news for the U-boat pens. Admiral Graves says to turn you two loose and see what you can do. See what ideas you can put together. You have a month to work out all the theories and plans you want to. He also wants that test by the destroyer before any Squid goes on board as regular issue. The contract is all set, so it looks like you two are employed again. Set up the production of those first twenty-five rounds as soon as you can, and I'll get a destroyer to run you out for a day or two for the test."

"Yes, sir," Moxie said. "Should we use the same office?"

"Yes. If there's anything you need just send me a memo. Or come in and we'll argue about it." He went to the door shaking his head. "I don't know how you two do it, but good luck anyway."

When the captain left, Ben tossed the car keys in the air. "Now we can go home," he said, and they did.

The girls had dinner ready, and that evening the war seemed far away. They sang songs around the fire, popped corn, and ate apples. Pru told them stories about the first early days of the war when she was only thirteen and didn't really understand what was going on.

Moxie leaned over and kissed her cheek. "Luv, most of us still don't understand what's happening. We just take it one day and one assignment at a time."

Pru pecked his cheek and turned to Ben with a radiant smile bursting across her round face. "Isn't this man about the smartest most wonderful bloke in the whole world?"

"Right, Pru. Right," Ben agreed quickly. "Whatever you say." He stood and caught Betsy's hand. "I think it's time we went to bed, woman. Not necessarily to sleep, but to bed."

Betsy laughed and pretended to be offended, then pulled up close beside him and they walked into the bedroom. Ben closed the door softly, reached for Betsy and kissed her gently on the mouth.

"Pretty lady, I would love to make love to you for the next thirty years or so, as a start."

Betsy smiled, then sobered. "Is that a proposal of marriage, or just for a long, sexy affair?"

"Both," he said and pulled her hard against him. He kissed her and she pulled him toward the bed.

"Let's lie down and talk about this," she said.

Ben put a pillow for their heads and lay down close beside her with his arm around her shoulder.

"Isn't it strange, this sex business?" she asked. "The physical act is so natural, so simple, yet the psychological aspect of it has people reeling all their lives. My mother spent hours lecturing me on purity and how to be a good girl. A good girl never kissed a boy, and if she ever did when she got older, it was never with her mouth open. A good girl never showed any bare breast under a dress. A good girl never crossed her legs with a skirt on. A good girl never let a boy touch her breasts and never, never, never her crotch. And of course there were no good boys. Boys always wanted to have sex, to get their *things* pushed inside girls. A good girl always fought off the boys."

Ben watched her as she talked, then nodded. "Mothers have a way of doing that," he said. "It preserves the family unit, the structure of Western society, they tell us."

Betsy snuggled closer against him. "Yes, I know. I had my sociology at Vassar. But it's strange how things change. Did you know that in that cottage up in Edinburgh you were my very first lover? My first ever?"

"I didn't know."

"I didn't want you to know. I was trying to be so ultrasophisticated, so worldly and experienced."

"It couldn't have been better," Ben said.

She leaned over and kissed his mouth and felt it

open. "I learned a lot driving that ambulance in London," she said, pulling away. "You see people at their worst and their best. One man I had in back kept yelling that he was dying. He was the only one in the ambulance and he kept yelling for me to stop. At last I did and went back, because we didn't have any attendants in the back. He was strapped into a stretcher and I could see he was injured badly. He was young, maybe twenty, a soldier who had been home on leave and caught in a bombing raid.

"When I went in back he looked at me and said please, he wanted to make love to a woman just once more before he died. He pleaded with me. I had learned quickly which ones would make it and the ones who probably would die in my ambulance. I saw he wouldn't make it another two or three kilometers. He looked at me and his glance went down to my breasts. Right there in the middle of an air raid I knew I had to help him somehow, maybe make his dying a little easier. So I opened my blouse and unhooked my bra and let it down. I moved beside him and his hands came up and touched my breasts so tenderly, so gently that I cried. He stroked my breasts and he smiled and thanked me and then his eyes came open and a moment later his hands fell away. He was dead."

Now, safe beside Ben on the bed, Betsy blinked back tears. "I sat there beside him, holding his hand for a while. Then I put it back on his chest and got my clothes back on and drove to the hospital. I parked outside and leaned over the wheel and blew the horn until somebody came out and carried him inside. I couldn't bear to look at that poor boy again."

Ben kissed her cheek. "I'm totally proud of you, Betsy. That was a fine, thoughtful, beautiful thing to do."

She sat up. "Remember when you and I were down

in that shelter during the Blitz? I was caught several times that way. Once I was sitting beside a pretty girl about my age and over the hours we were there, we began talking. The bombs were coming close, and this underground wouldn't be safe if it got a direct hit. People open up a little more in those situations.

"She was a little thin, with haunted eyes and a big bust. After about an hour she told me she was a prostitute. She watched me as she said it, and when I wasn't shocked, she relaxed a little. I'll never forget it. She reached out and held my hand as the bombs kept falling, and it helped both of us. She asked me if I were married or a virgin, and I told her neither. I told her about our weeks in the cottage, and she said we were lucky. Most young couples didn't have that much time together. She asked me if I liked making love, and I said I did. She said she did too, and she never charged the enlisted men. The officers could afford it.

"We talked for four hours, and I learned a lot about her. She said some folks looked down on her and called her bad names, but she didn't see it that way. She was filling a real need. With thousands of boys away from home, and away from their girls, they needed some company, even if just for an hour. She said if she could give somebody a little bit of pleasure, some relief, why not? It was such a simple thing to do. Nobody got hurt, nothing was damaged, used up, or broken. She said that after making love she felt wonderful, like she had helped someone just a little bit."

Betsy looked at Ben, then continued. "We had a long talk. I'd never talked with anyone about sex, but with her it was easy, seemed natural. I grew up a lot that night. Then the bombs started falling farther away, and by the time the air raid was over it was morning. We had hot chocolate and biscuits, at a little cafe. Then we hugged each other and said good-bye. I've never seen her since."

They lay there a moment and neither spoke. Then Ben raised himself up on one elbow. "What would your father say if you and I got married?"

Betsy smiled. "He'd roar, and swear and rave around for a while. Then he'd say at least you are Navy. Then he'd walk around puffing on that old pipe of his and admit that at least you were in the submarine force. In the end he'd blame himself for introducing us at that party. When he sees his first grandchild he will be totally on our side."

Ben nodded. "Then, pretty lady Betsy Kirkland, will you marry me?"

Her eyes closed for a moment, and she smiled and leaned forward and touched his chin. "Yes, Benjamin Mount, I most certainly will!"

Ben kissed her lips softly and they made love. They fell asleep in each other's arms.

Betsy was vaguely aware that something was missing, and only after Ben had left the next morning did she realize that they had not said anything about *when*. No date had been set. In wartime that was a risky move. Ben could be jerked away from her on a few hours' notice, and he might be gone for months, or a year or more. Worst of all, he might go on a mission and never return. She was determined to talk about setting a date as soon as he got home that night.

For the next two days Ben and Moxie stayed at the Allied Naval Intelligence headquarters learning everything they could about the Brest area and the harbor there. After hours of absorbing maps, sketches, and photos, Moxie put down his pen and sipped at his coffee.

"Looks like a piece of cake, mate," he said. "All we have to do is come in past Pointe de St. Mathieu out there, pick up on the dark lighthouse at Point Minou, then glide through the Goulet de Brest, which for you non-Frenchies is the small opening or channel between the mainland to the north and a big peninsula that juts out from the south protecting the bay with Point Spanish. We get past the guns along there and we should be looking right down the throats of those German U-boat pens."

Ben had been doing his homework too. "When we get in that close we should be able to see the French Naval College up on the hill and slightly to the north. But we can't expect any Free French or underground help from there since the Nazis took over the college as their headquarters for the First U-boat flotilla."

"They must have short batteries all over the place. Coming through that strait would be murder for even a pair of cruisers. How do we smash those pens without taking the commandos in there and capturing the whole damn place?"

The two men stared at each other for a while. Ben went to the coffee pot, brought it back, and filled both cups.

"Maybe what we're talking about is a raid on the subs in the pens, and not on the bloody pens themselves."

Moxie jumped up and saluted him. "*Mon capitaine,* I think you are finding the solution for zee problem." He rubbed his hands together. "Yeah, I like it. We go in with a strike force not to blow up the damn pens. Hell, no. We go with a force trained to blow up all the U-boats we catch inside."

They put away the files. Moxie surprised the little clerk with a kiss on the cheek, and they headed back to their office at Fort Blockhouse.

"Now all we have to do is design a striking force, then figure how to get in, do the job, and get out."

Ben lifted his brows in surprise. "Moxie, old man. I thought you would be leading a suicide raid on this one with a bully batch of rough and tough British commandos."

"You know I'm just in this war for the high sea pay, Yank. And while suicide pay is much better, there is no mention of a pension plan."

There were notes on their desks asking them to call Phillips at the plant near London. Moxie made the call. The twenty-four requested Squid missiles would be ready for field testing within a week. Moxie said he would let Phillips know where to send them.

He then told the captain to work out the logistics of the shipment and began trying to find a free destroyer for a few days of special duty.

Ben concentrated on some ideas about the U-boat pens. "I still say the best method of getting into the pens is with a captured U-boat. That way we sail right up to the gates home free. They won't even shoot at us."

"Sure, easy to say, old man, hard to do. You don't just go out and capture a German submarine. After five years of war we have captured only two operational U-boats. One of those sank because nobody on the destroyer knew how to blow the sub's tanks to keep her up. Those German crews are fanatical. You know most of them say that no English boots will ever step on a U-boat deck except as a prisoner of war."

"But, Moxie, wouldn't it be great sailing up to the pens at Brest on the surface, fire four torpedoes, load and fire four more, then hit them with two from the tail end and charge out the straits to the open sea?"

"Sure, sounds great. We'd get off one salvo, then they'd come down on us with everything they had. We'd get maybe three feet before they blew us out of the water. And those German U-boat folks aren't exactly a passel of sissies. You ever heard the German submariner's oath? I carry one in my billfold for reference. Here it is, folded up and dirty, but I can read it. Listen up. 'I swear this holy oath by God, that I shall obey the Führer of the German Reich and People, Adolph Hitler, the Highest Commander of the armed forces and that I am prepared to give my life as a brave soldier at any time for this oath."

"How about using the sub that you captured?" Ben asked. "Do they really take an oath like that? It makes them all prime suicide mission fodder, doesn't it? But what about that U-boat already in the British Navy? Let's try to use that one and we don't have to worry about capturing one."

"Forget it. That is their prize. There is no way the Royal Navy would throw their precious captured U-boat into a mission like this."

Ben took out his lined yellow pad and put down a number one and behind it the words: "Capture U-boat, use it."

"Okay, authority. Any more good ideas? How are we going to go in there and blow up twenty U-boats?"

"From what those pictures showed, we can forget about catching any boats outside the protective pens. Those pens are right on the banks of the bay, so they have no protection at all unless the boats are inside. They will be inside."

"I don't remember seeing any kind of doors on those pens," Ben said. "Why couldn't we fire torpedoes in each opening. We lay off and put one fish into each of the big doors and haul ass? We could do it while submerged, periscope depth. They see lots of periscopes off that place."

"Maybe," Moxie said. "Put it down on your list."

They were quiet for a moment. "Commandos. Your crack about commandos might not be so bad," Moxie exclaimed. "Why not go in with two or three subs full of commandos, land them right in the base and let them set charges on all the subs in the pens. They can do miracles with the new plastic explosives and shaped charges."

The idea was added to the list.

For the rest of the afternoon they brainstormed. They seemed to generate a creative fountain and they kept throwing out diabolical plans to destroy the U-boats in the pens.

By the end of the following day they had twenty plans laid out. They took the following afternoon off and went for a long walk through the woods with the girls. The four of them stopped by a small stream and ate sandwiches. Moxie and Pru wandered away and Betsy laughed. "We know what they're doing," she said.

"We certainly do," Ben said as he kissed her. "Does being out in the woods get you all excited?"

"No, but being near you sure does." She held up her hand. "But I'd be too chicken to try making love out here. Sure as we got mother naked, twenty-six schoolgirls would come by with a nun on a nature walk."

"Sounds a little wild."

"Too wild for me, Ben Mount." She paused and flicked some strands of hair off her face. "Commander, did you really mean what you said a few days back?"

"About wanting to marry you?"

"Yes. This is your one last chance in a nonpassionate moment to get out of it."

He bent and kissed her lips gently, then stared at her. "I meant it, and I want to marry you, Betsy Kirkland."

"Good," she said and kissed his nose. "When?"

"I know what you're worried about. We were close once before. I don't think there are any restrictions

on getting married for me, especially to an American
citizen. I'll talk to the chaplain at the American
destroyer base. I can call him tomorrow."

"Tomorrow morning," she said.

"Right."

"Ben, I think we better do it sudden, quick, before something else smashes in and ruins everything
again."

"It would take a hell of a lot to stop me now."

"We have lots of 'hell of a lot' of things around
these days that can do it. Like you could get sent
to the Pacific with four hours' notice. I could walk
in front of a truck. We both might just happen to
be under one of those lone German night bombers
that got shot down."

"Nobody would dare do that," he said.

She stretched out in the grass, and he lay beside
her.

"Just hold me, Ben. Hold me and talk to me and
tell me all the great things we're going to do when
this mess is all cleaned up over here and we can
go home again."

They talked for two hours, and when Moxie and
Pru didn't come back, they walked through the crisp
sunshine back toward the cottage.

"This has been a perfect day," Betsy said.

"And tomorrow I give that chaplain a call and see
what needs to be done. Some kind of a license, some
official notation I would guess, then a quiet ceremony
with the chaplain and you can cable your mother the
good news."

"Promise?" she said.

"Promise."

Chapter 8

The next morning at Fort Blockhouse, Ben called the chaplain. It took him almost ten minutes to get through to his office, but the chaplain had stepped out. Ben left a message with his assistant to call him back. By noon there had been no reply.

Just after lunch Captain White-Johnson called Ben and Moxie into his office.

"The schedule is down, gentlemen. The missiles arrived this morning. Phillips assured me that they are hand tooled, but to identical proportions, clearances, and with the exact amount of explosive and specifications that the ensuing missiles will have. We had asked him for all possible speed. The HMS *Bulldog* will be waiting for you at her berth at zero eight hundred hours tomorrow morning. She has had the Hedgehog before, so her crew is experienced in such firings. Here are your orders.

"Briefly you are instructed to take the *Bulldog* into the channel and head in a generally westerly direction where you will make your search for an enemy target U-boat. Search will be normal patrol search by the destroyer's crew. If, after two days, no target is found, you are to test the Squid on the dummy sub target made of six fifty-gallon drums welded together, weighted and secured with buoys and floats, so they will sink to one hundred feet. The target will be on board the destroyer. Test on the drums with four salvos of six missiles each on four runs. Are there any questions?"

"No sir," Moxie said.

Ben scrubbed his face with one hand.

"Commander?" Captain White-Johnson asked.

"Sir, we requested a submarine observer. I believe the boat was to be the *Seawitch*. Was she authorized, sir?"

"Yes, Mr. Mount. The *Seawitch*, under command of Captain Mulford, is to proceed as a shadow with the destroyer and observe any tests, except an actual attack on an enemy, and to return and report."

"Thank you, sir!" Ben said.

"How are the plans for ridding the sea of U-boats coming along?" the captain asked.

"Working on it, sir," Moxie said. "Some of our ideas you wouldn't believe."

"You're right," the captain said, and ushered the two submariners out the door.

Moxie hurried down to his charge, the *Seawitch*. Ben trailed along. Now with a sailing date Moxie would be anxious for the crew to get his sub in top shape. He didn't tell them what the mission was, but they were glad for a chance to get out of port. Time had been dragging for some of the men.

Sublieutenant John Barry gave Ben a tour of the boat while Moxie tended to some details. It was an improved S-class boat, and while similar to the S boat Ben had been on in Gibraltar, it had a few refinements.

When they got back to the wardroom, Ben found Moxie shaking his head and scowling at a seaman.

"Mr. Barry, come in here please," Moxie said sternly. Barry went inside and Ben followed him.

"Sublieutenant Barry, I thought we had this small problem all worked out the last time."

"We did, sir. Total and absolute agreement by all

hands. It would never, never happen again. That was the agreement."

"And then Mr. Leslie here must have won for himself another leave," Moxie said. "Let me see, three big windows, a chair, one large mirror, twelve broken bottles of whiskey and one lady of the evening who says you never paid her. The bill comes to a total of . . ." Moxie looked up at the seaman but Leslie stared straight ahead. He was over six-one, taller than most submariners, with sandy red hair, a touch of a mustache, and a bad bruise over one eye. There was a gouge out of his cheek and a lump on the side of his head. Both of his hands were bandaged.

"Mr. James Leslie, you owe more than three months' pay to this one pub. Do you realize that?"

"Yes, sir. Now I do, sir."

"But last night you were drunk and fighting mad about something. Do you remember what you were so angry about, Leslie?"

"No sir, I can't."

"What about your buddies, didn't they take care of you?"

"It was them I hit first, sir. That's what they tell me. I was blotto."

"And according to this note, you've got twelve more hours to meet the payment of the tab, or you'll be talking to the magistrate. The pub owner says *again* talking to the magistrate, Mr. Leslie. Have you been before the magistrate before?"

"Yes sir. Just before you took over the boat, sir."

Moxie scowled. "Have you any money, lad?"

"No sir, not a bob."

"The ship's fund, Mr. Barry?"

"Yes, sir, it will cover it, just."

"Mr. Leslie. This will go on your record. The company fund will settle your bill. You'll repay it with half your wages for the next six months. You'll go on no leave unless accompanied by a warrant or rated officer, and you'll pull extra duty whenever we're in port. No loss of pay, no reduction in rating."

Leslie's shoulders slumped for a moment, then braced stiffer than ever.

"Comments, Mr. Barry?"

"A more than fair settlement, Captain. Seaman Leslie is fortunate."

"Mr. Leslie?"

"Thank you, sir. Thank you."

"Mr. Leslie. We'll be at sea in two days. I'll expect that forward torpedo room to shine like a baby's bottom. Dismissed."

"Aye, sir!" Leslie shouted his recognition of the order, did an about face, and hurried out of the ward room.

Moxie shook his head, and when Leslie was gone, looked at Barry. "Keep better track of him next time, Mr. Barry. He's your personal responsibility."

"Yes sir. I thought he could handle it."

"He's an alcoholic. It's a disease with him. But he's also the best torpedo man we have; we can't afford to lose him. Set up the paperwork with the paymaster, Mr. Barry."

"Aye, sir."

Moxie then turned to Ben. "Is it a little cramped down here for you, mate?"

Ben glanced around and shook his head. "Not a twinge, not a bubble. That's all been worked out. Oh, I might get one little dig when the boat is at pressure and we're slipping under, but nothing more than that, just a twinge."

"You riding out with us?"

"No, I'll be on the *Bulldog*. I want to monitor those firings and see what happens. With that experienced crew, I don't see any problems. After the tests I want to ride back with you. We can work on that list of twenty, maybe prune it down a little and come up with five to show to the captain."

"You've got a date."

Ben tried three more times that afternoon and the next day, but he could not make contact with the chaplain at the American destroyer base. He promised Betsy that he would drive over to the base after the sea trials on the Squid and track down the chaplain in person.

HMS *Bulldog* was a battle-scarred veteran, her crew blooded, with six U-boat swastikas on her brag board. Her crew was well trained, quick, alert, and her young captain, a lieutenant commander, was as interested in the tests as Ben was. They talked as the destroyer moved out with the full tide and swept through the harbor into the channel. His name was Nelson but he was no relation to the great Admiral Nelson, a fact he quickly pointed out.

"We've used the Hedgehog, but usually you use just one salvo per sub. If that can slow him down or stop him, it's great. That circular pattern it throws out in front is as good as any. But now with the Squid, it will tremendously increase its effectiveness. When those charges go off, the sub commander is going to be confused. He thought we were three hundred yards behind him and now suddenly he's getting hit with charges. It may make him stop dead in the water or turn, and we can pick him up on the ASDIC again."

They prowled the Channel and out toward the Atlantic all morning. They used a grid pattern to search for sounds from underwater or blips from the radar antenna. There was nothing.

Time dragged. The first day passed with no sightings. The second day nothing changed so Moxie ran the sub up close to the destroyer and they shouted headings to avoid becoming separated in the darkness. By first light the *Seawitch* was right in the destroyer's wake, and the crew was glad the sub was one of theirs.

Shortly after eight A.M. the destroyer slowed to launch the dummy target. It sank with alarming speed, but the air buoys held and from all surface appearances the target had trimmed out a hundred feet down. Strong double cables held it in place. The *Bulldog* pulled away and then turned around for its first run at the target buoys.

Captain Nelson's fire control men brought the ship into position and launched a salvo of six Squid missiles. They smashed into the sea ten yards beyond the buoy in a roughly diamond-shaped pattern.

Ben ran to the bridge. It had been fitted with experimental VHF radio voice communications for contact with the sub. The signals traveled only a short distance and couldn't be picked up by ship-locating devices.

"Salvo fired on target. Swimmer, any reaction?"

"Floater One. Nothing yet. We're about three hundred yards out at ninety degrees off the target, on the surface. Nothing yet."

There was a moment of silence.

"Floater One, I have detonation. ASDIC says a strange sound, at least three small explosions and on the right bearing. We have a detonation. Swimmer One moving in to within a hundred yards of the buoy. So drop these babies right on target."

"Don't get any closer, Swimmer One. We might have a wild one or two here."

"Right-o. Carry on."

The second salvo of six hit about ten yards short of the buoys. The radio crackled into life.

"Floater One. Saw your hit, waiting."

Another pause. Ben looked at Captain Nelson.

"These must sink a lot slower than a five-hundred-pound depth charge," Nelson said.

"Bingo, Floater One. We have four distinct sounds as they went off. Request you set depth for four hundred feet on next salvo."

"Let's see if they will work at four hundred feet," Ben said.

They did. The last six missiles were set for one hundred feet, and the *Seawitch* moved closer to the target.

Having fired, the destroyer moved up on the buoys. The crew stood and stared at them in surprise. They were snagged. The twenty-four-foot-long target looked more like a sieve than a stack of oil drums. The last drum in the line was crushed sideways where a direct hit must have smashed it. The shrapnel from the Squid's metal cases had torn through the thin skin of the drums in dozens of places.

They called the *Seawitch* alongside, and Moxie came over in a dinghy.

"Christ, I'm glad that wasn't my boat," Moxie said. "That one on the end looks like a direct hit. That would have punched a hole in the average German sub and put it to the bottom."

They counted the shrapnel holes, and then Ben and Moxie talked briefly with Captain Nelson.

"I'd call the mission completed, Captain," Moxie said. "Let's head back for port. You can move at your regular search speed and we'll come trailing along behind you. Just hold that punctured target for us, it's the proof we need. Oh, and I'd like a written statement from you for my report."

Ben and Moxie were taken back to the sub. Moxie went below. Ben paused on the bridge to watch the destroyer turn and head back for Portsmouth. The ship would reach port long before the sub did, but they too could do some search patterns on the way back. The time was a little past 0930.

The sub cruised at fourteen knots on the surface while watching its radar and listening to ASDIC for any U-boats. They were well out in the Atlantic after their two-day cruise, and Moxie figured it might take them two days to return. He was in no rush. He felt good being at sea again with a fighting submarine in his command. To break up the monotony he had the crew run through a firing drill, then put them on standby. Without a little action a crew could get stale in a hurry.

Ben was on the bridge taking a watch, so Moxie joined him. It was about one o'clock when radar picked up something on a zero-six-zero bearing.

Moxie downplayed it. "Could be a lifeboat, some wreckage from a sinking, almost anything. This radar is so damn sensitive it will even pick up that big beer barrel snorkel the U-boats use now. Come around to a heading of zero-six-zero," he ordered. "We'll go have a look. Battle stations, battle stations."

The whole boat suddenly pulsed with activity.

"Do we have a range on that blip?"

"About four-five-zero-zero meters, sir. Way out. We're closing on it."

Both officers used their binoculars but they could see nothing. The radar antenna was well over their heads and had a longer angle. Still they watched.

"Three thousand meters, sir. She doesn't seem to be moving."

"Nothing from ASDIC, she must be dead in the water."

There was no smoke trail, no long streamer that so often gave away a tanker, freighter, or a convoy. No masts, no superstructure showed on the horizon. They should be able to see something soon.

"Must be a sub," Ben said.

"Charging up. But why dead in the water? It doesn't make sense," Moxie said as he shook his head and stared through the glasses.

"Fifteen hundred meters off, sir."

"There!" Moxie shouted. A plume of black smoke smudged the horizon. They could see the boat riding low in the water. A submarine, all right.

"A U-boat," Ben said.

"Damn right, and she's trying to get under way."

The black smoke suddenly stopped.

"Her diesels blew, they must have been working on the engines," Ben shouted.

"Make forward tubes ready to fire," Moxie said.

"Aye, sir."

"Bring her to zero-six-five."

"Zero-six-five, aye."

"Range!" Moxie barked.

"Five-zero-zero."

"Stand by to fire one."

"Standing by on one, sir."

"Moxie, look at her! She's dead in the water again. She has her forward hatch open. Look how she's tail heavy. I think she's in trouble. How about a gun crew?"

"Not waste a torpedo?"

"Maybe we can capture her."

"Capture?" Moxie looked through his glasses again. No one was on the bridge. Nobody manned the twin twenty-millimeter guns or the quad twenty-millimeter guns forward. He saw a head pop out of the forward hatch, then drop down.

"Why the hell not?" Moxie bellowed. "Gun crew on deck! Break out the small arms locker. Two rifles and ammo to the bridge, six riflemen on the aft deck. Move it!"

Men scrambled out the forward hatch, the gun

crew readied the three-inch gun just forward of the bridge.

"Fire when ready. Put six rounds into her control tower. Engines all stop."

The rifles and clips of ammunition were brought to the bridge and both officers loaded and sent five rounds each toward the sub. Both officers loaded again, and Ben heard the three-incher go off below. The round struck the lower part of the conning tower but apparently did little damage.

"Keep their heads down," Moxie yelled. "Engines ahead a quarter, let's crawl up on them."

Ben was watching the aft hatch of the sub, which was still open. A man's head emerged. He seemed to be gasping for air. He ducked down and came back up. A bullet caught the sailor below the ear and ripped his jaw away. He hung half in and half out of the hatch until someone from below pulled the body downward.

Ben looked away.

Moxie watched the bridge. The three-incher went off again, the round was long, over the sub.

"Three more rifles forward," Moxie shouted. "Aft men fire at the control tower and the bridge. The rest of you work over those hatches. Keep their heads down."

The *Seawitch* crept closer. Now they were two hundred meters away. There was little sign of life on the U-boat. It had no control tower designation.

"Gas," Ben said. "I think they've got carbon monoxide or gas from the batteries and had to come to surface to vent it."

"They've got other problems too," Moxie said. "Secure torpedo room, break out the rest of the small arms, including the automatic weapons. Prepare a boarding party."

Ben grinned and fired another round into the bridge of the sub.

"Are you really doing what I think you're doing?"

"Damn right!" Moxie shouted. "If we've got some hand grenades in that locker, we're going to go over there and try to capture ourselves a damned German U-boat!"

Chapter 9

Fifteen men manned the *Seawitch* decks and fired at the U-boat. A German sailor leaped from the bridge to the twin-mounted twenty-millimeter guns, but three rifle slugs cut him down and slammed him into eternity before he could even position them.

A hand lifted a weapon from the aft hatch and triggered off a dozen rounds from an automatic weapon. The German rounds all went harmlessly over the heads of the British fighters.

"All engines stop!" Ben shouted down to the control room. The submarine slid to a halt a hundred meters from the German craft. The three-incher put an armor piercing round through the side of the German conning tower. The U-boat lurched to one side as it exploded.

"Keep their heads down!" Moxie shouted to his crew. "Hold fire on the three-incher. Set up that light machine gun we have and give them a burst now and then." Moxie knew everything was under control and waved to Ben. They slid down the tower into the control room.

"Where in hell are the rest of the small arms?" Moxie shouted.

A sailor opened a wooden box. Inside were two Sten submachine guns with short barrels and big magazines. Ben grabbed one and Moxie took the other. The magazines were loaded. They charged with a simple pull of the handle.

"Grenades?" Ben yelled. "Anybody see the grenades?"

Another box appeared filled with forty hand grenades, the standard dull green, pineapple type. Ben thought they looked like the U.S. Army model. He grabbed six and clipped them to his belt by the long thin handles. Armed, the two men went back up the ladder to the bridge.

"Any change, Mr. Barry?" Moxie asked his second officer.

"No sir. We haven't seen any more Germans. She's still dead in the water."

The sea was flatter than Ben had seen it in a long time, but a squall line showed downwind of them.

"Break out two rubber rafts on the aft deck, Mr. Barry."

"Aye, aye, sir."

Moxie looked over at Ben. "Any ideas? We can't ram her without taking damage ourselves, and it would probably sink the U-boat. I wonder why she's so low in the water. We can't get close enough to drop a landing party directly on her deck."

"So we use the rubber boat, three strong swimmers and me. We board her, put grenades down both hatches and the bridge hatch if it's open, then demand they surrender."

"Sounds about right, except you don't go, I do. I'm the skipper here, and I go."

"Won't work," Ben said. "You're the skipper and responsible for this boat and your men. I'm the expendable item. If the four of us don't come back, start punching holes through the side at the water line. About six rounds from that three-incher in the same hole should put her down."

"That's it?" Moxie asked.

"Hell no. They will hear us on deck and try to grenade us off. That's my guess. So keep some covering fire on those hatches as long as you can. And let's send two boats at the same time, one to the forward hatch too." Ben thought a moment. "We'll hit them at both ends at the same time. Eight men, four in each boat, should give us a run for it. When we get inside, send over another eight men."

Moxie looked around the control room. "Pass the word that we need seven volunteers for a boarding party. Any men with combat experience are welcome. Get up here on the double."

Ben checked his British-made Sten machine gun. It had a folding stock. He locked it in a closed position so it felt like a machine pistol with a long barrel. It fired nine-millimeter slugs and could spit out five hundred of them per minute. Ben took two of the long magazines and taped them together, then stuffed one more in his pocket.

The first volunteer into the control room was the red-headed Irishman, James Leslie. Ben grinned. "Catch." He tossed the Sten gun at Leslie, and the Irishman caught it and immediately had one hand on the trigger housing ready to fire.

"Fired one of those before, Leslie?"

"Yes. I did a stretch in the Army before I joined the Navy. Infantry. I came out with the lads at Dunkirk."

"Skipper, let's put Leslie in charge of the forward boat."

Moxie nodded.

"Good. Leslie, pick three men and take them to the forward boat. We'll keep apart in case they get lucky with their weapons. The plan is to hit the forward hatch, drop in a couple of grenades, move in and mop up. I'll be hitting the aft hatch. We'll move forward and meet at the control room. Any ques-tions?"

"Any prisoners?"

"That's up to them, I'd think," Moxie said.

They armed each boarder. Moxie used the electric engines to push the *Seawitch* closer to the U-boat. The distance was now only fifty meters. The men on deck continued firing at the three main targets. No more Germans were visible.

"Keep them firing over our heads for as long as you can," Ben told Moxie. "Just don't let them hit any of us. The minute you stop firing, we'll take over so they don't know anything has changed."

Moxie pulled Ben aside. "You really know what the hell you're doing? Somebody could get hurt over there. You could get your idiot head blown off. We don't have to try to capture this hulk."

"I've got this down cold. I saw John Wayne do it once in a movie. Nothing to it. Now, you be ready to send over a prize crew who can run this pile of junk back to Portsmouth, or Land's End, or however far we can get her."

Leslie signaled he was ready with his three men in the forward boat.

Ben slid into the aft rubber boat and pushed off. He and the three men rowed across the wide expanse of ocean toward the German U-boat. He'd never seen so much water in all his life. The Sten gun swung from his neck by a stout cord. He gave his paddle to another man. He took a grenade and held it in his hand. As soon as they touched the sub, he would be the man to slither up the side to the hatch and drop two grenades.

He looked from the crest of a swell and saw the other rubber boat was ahead of them.

"Come on, lads, Leslie is out front, let's catch

him. We want this to be a lovely duet when those pineapples go off."

They paddled, fought the rising swells, and pushed forward. For a while it seemed they were making no progress. The sound of rifle fire from the *Seawitch* behind them came as a comfort.

Then, almost with no warning, the black conning tower rose up to their right. They were ten meters away. The paddlers dug in and shoveled the water; Ben leaned out in front of the tiny rubber boat.

The German pigboat seemed to loom ten feet above him. They paddled to where the craft was lower in the water. The rubber raft bumped into the U-boat, and Ben caught a vent hole, climbed upward on a bulge that must have been some kind of auxiliary tank, and pushed himself up to the slotted steel deck-plates. The sub was much too low in the water.

Ben grabbed a grenade in each hand, pulled the pins and crawled forward on the wet plates a foot at a time. He saw the aft hatch. It had a steel lip six inches off the deck to keep out free water. Suddenly, he wasn't sure the hatch was open. It could be closed from inside without exposing a man for very long. He had to get closer. He wormed his way another six feet, then heard German voices shouting from below.

Now he realized the rifle shots from behind were going over his head, not hitting the hatch. Only a few rounds thudded into the conning tower. He had to move quickly or the Germans would suspect something was up.

Ben rolled twice, saw the hatch cover was vertical, and dropped both grenades into the open hatch. He pulled one more grenade from his belt, and jerked out the pin.

The twin explosions below sounded like a block-buster. The explosions were followed by screams. Ben waited a full sixty seconds, then dropped a third grenade into the hatch and waited the four seconds. When the second blast came, he heard other grenades exploding in the forward part of the boat.

Before he could get to his feet, two men from the destroyer stormed past him, and dropped down the hatch.

Ben was the third man down. There was blood and bits of flesh everywhere. Two bodies near the bottom of the hatch had no faces. He pushed them aside. His team was in the aft engine room, the electric engine room and the single torpedo shaft. There was a steel, watertight door leading forward. It was closed and dogged down.

In front of him, a British seaman fired twice. Ben swung up the Sten gun, charged it and ran aft to where the *Seawitch* crewman had just pushed away a dead German whom he had shot at point-blank range. The seaman looked like he wanted to throw up. Ben pounded him on the shoulder and pointed to one side, past the big electric motors. They checked for more Germans and found four more dead, but none alive. There was nowhere else that they could hide. Seven men were dead in the aft section.

Ben climbed the ladder and lifted his head over the aft hatch to stare at the *Seawitch*. Two more rubber boats filled with boarders were on the way. Ben waved the fourth man in his team up to stand in the hatch for better protection. He tried to look forward, but his vision was blocked by the conning tower. Shots were audible again from somewhere forward.

Ben went down the hatch and looked at the steel door that sealed off the aft compartment. He motioned to the door. Two seamen came up and turned the wheel in the middle of the round door. The problem was that the wheel on the other side would turn too.

Anyone in there would be ready for it to open.

Ben motioned for the men to stop. He looked at the door again, and noted that it swung inward, away from them. He held a grenade, and whispered that he would drop it through as soon as the door was open far enough. Then they would have to slam it shut again. They had four seconds before the grenade would go off.

The wheel spun again and the door broke open. There was a slight hiss as excess pressured air escaped. Ben threw the grenade through and helped pull it shut. They had just relocked it when they heard the blast. There was a jolt on the deck and on the door. They hesitated a moment then reopened it.

Smoke and cordite filled the air. Ben tried to remember the diagrams of German U-boats. If this were a VII-C, the most popular model, they should be in the diesel engine, and the engine room would be just beyond and then the galley beyond that. There was a galley hatch. Ben checked to see that his man at the top of the hatch was watching behind them, serving as communications.

When the smoke cleared one of the two men with Ben peered around the doorway. A shot thundered and the sailor jolted backward. A bullet had smashed into his forehead driving him away from the door and facedown on the deck.

Ben knew he was dead. He flipped a second grenade into the confined diesel engine room, and pressed against the partition. The cracking roar was mixed with a long scream of pain. Ben darted into the room, the Sten gun in front of him, his finger on the trigger. Somebody moved ahead and he held the trigger back for a five-round burst. In a fury he hosed down the rest of the engine room and the area ahead of him with five-shot bursts. He saw pipes punctured and steam escaping. A man tumbled toward him with blood all over his face and a neat row of bullet holes down his chest.

Ben charged forward. There was equipment and gear everywhere. It was not a place to hide. He paused in the galley. The hatch overhead was dogged down and secure. Past a thin partition was the accommodation room, a ward room. One man lay on a table, blood pouring from his wounds. His right hand held a Luger aimed at Ben. Ben fired six rounds into the German submariner's chest. One of Ben's men stormed past him into the control room.

The U-boat captain hung over the periscope with a bullet in his brain. He held his own pistol in a death grip in his left hand. The control room was secure. No one else was there. Ben went cautiously up the conning tower ladder and onto the bridge. He saw the *Seawitch* hovering near and another rubber boat with four men in it approaching the aft hatch. The U-boat seemed to have slipped a little lower in the water.

Ben saw a head come out of the forward hatch. He watched and at last recognized the man as one of Leslie's team. The sailor waved, and Ben climbed down the outside of the conning tower and ran to the forward hatch. The seaman crawled out and sprawled on the deck. He had a large red stain on his upper chest.

"Troubles, sir. Mousetrapped us. Ran out of grenades." The seaman looked at Ben once more, then passed out. Ben shook him until he revived.

"Where is Leslie?"

"I don't know, sir. In the forward area somewhere. Ran into a whole batch of Germans. Leslie might be dead, I don't know."

Ben checked his belt. He had two more grenades. There was no time to get more, but just then one of his aft team checked over the conning tower. Ben asked if he had any grenades, and the man tossed two to him, then went back to the rubber boat to get more.

Ben scowled at the hatch, then hooked the grenades on his belt, pushed a new magazine into his Sten gun, and lowered himself into the forward hatch.

Chapter 10

Ben Mount climbed down the ladder of the forward hatch into the bow of the U-boat. The ugly snout of the Sten gun preceded him as he looked around after each step. He counted. Nine Germans lay dead behind him, that left thirty-five more somewhere in the craft. Where were they?

He quickly realized that he had come down beside the crew bunk in the bow section. At first glance he saw six or eight men in the bunks. They were dead, but had not been shot. The boat had been in trouble before they arrived. But where the hell were the rest? Aft of his position there should be another wardroom for the officers and then a screened-off captain's cabin.

Ben crouched at the bottom of the ladder below the hatch. He carried a grenade in one hand and looked around. A body lay against the far bulkhead, a German. Another body draped over the door-way into the crew quarters. Where were Leslie and his other two men? Ben couldn't use the grenades until he had found his men. He slid into the area beside the small bathroom and then into the wardroom. He heard someone groan. He pulled his Sten up and his finger started to tighten on the trigger, then he relaxed.

The sound had come from James Leslie. He sat against the wall of the wardroom with a tipped-over bench in front of him. He had blood on his shoulder and the side of his head. He had been pointing his Sten gun at the door, now he lowered it.

"Cleared back to the control room this way, Commander. But must be a dozen of the bastards in the bow. Some hid in the torpedo tubes and jumped out at us. My other two men are dead. Burp guns of some kind."

"You're sure they're dead, Leslie? I can't use grenades until I'm sure."

"Both of them got stitched right up the chest by that automatic in the bow. Damn good shots these Jerry sailors."

"You hit bad?"

"Just a scratch." Leslie leaned to one side and sent a deadly stream of nine-millimeter slugs past Ben. Ben spun away, pulling his Sten up as he whirled. A German sailor with a handgun gasped once and fell forward. He had emerged from a hatch going down to the battery room, which was on the deck below.

Ben surged over to the dead German and held his machine gun in the hatch and squeezed off a dozen rounds. He heard nothing from below.

"Battery room?" he asked. Leslie nodded. Ben pushed the German back into the opening and looked quickly below. A handgun blasted at him, but missed. He angled the Sten into the opening again and sent six bursts of five rounds each into the battery room. He knew he was ruining the batteries, but that didn't seem important.

He looked quickly again into the hatch but there was no fire. Once more he checked, then slid onto the ladder and checked it out. There were five dead Germans in the room. Only two dead by gunfire. That made sixteen, and with eight in their bunks, a total of twenty-four. So twenty more were somewhere.

Back in the wardroom, Ben saw Leslie send a pair of five-round bursts through the door into the crew quarters.

"Just to keep them honest. You got any grenades?"

Ben nodded.

"Might use a couple in there before they decide to charge us again. Not sure how many there are left."

Ben threw a grenade into the bow torpedo room, where the crew bunks were. He heard a scream before the bomb went off and triggered his Sten through the door as someone came running out. A German officer fell halfway through the door, his face chewed into pulp by half a dozen nine-millimeter slugs. The blast shook the U-boat, and for a moment Ben thought she was going to roll over and sink. But she steadied and trimmed out.

Before the smoke cleared, Ben threw another grenade deeper into the room. There were no torpedoes there, only corpses. Mess tables, usually set down the middle of the corridor with bunks on both sides, were stowed under the bottom bunks. Ben could see the white circular covers of the upper two torpedo tubes beyond the bunks. Six bodies lay around the tight compartment floor, but Ben was more concerned with finding the live men with guns. The silence was broken only by an occasional moan of the steel hull or the drip of water.

Ben checked into corners and under the bunks, but saw no living man. Overhead, the chains used for moving the two-thousand-pound torpedoes swung with the slight roll of the sub. Ben dove forward to the floor and rolled under the nearest bunk, the Sten gun at the ready.

He heard a gasp in the far left corner of the compartment and he turned his chopper that way. A few seconds later a man stumbled from behind the end

bunk, trying to stop the flow of blood from a massive
slash across his neck. He stared blankly at Ben, then
his eyes closed and he pitched forward to the deck.
He did not move. Ben inched ahead, stared at the
torpedo-tube covers. They were heavy metal, pressure
sealed. His nine-millimeter slugs wouldn't even dent
them. If there were Germans in there, the best thing
to do would be seal the covers from the outside. But
first he had to get in there.

Ben edged up another foot, saw a body directly
in front of him and recognized it was a British sailor.
"Sorry," he thought and pushed past. For a moment
he looked at the two upper tubes. He couldn't see
the lower ones, and they would be the most dangerous. They were at the deck level, where he crouched.

He slid forward again. He could hear nothing but
dripping water now. It probably came from some
ruptured pipes. He saw other evidences of the grenades, but they had done less damage. Much of the
shrapnel had slammed into the padded bunks of the
crew.

Ben still worried about the rest of the U-boat's
crew. At least twenty men were missing. Where were
they? He couldn't figure it out.

Without warning, automatic-weapons fire thundered
from the torpedo-tube area ahead. The slugs hit the
steel floor and ricocheted around. One rammed
through Ben's left wrist, and he slammed his right
hand over his mouth to stifle a scream. By the time
the shooting had stopped, Ben held a grenade in his
right hand. However, his left hand wouldn't obey him,
it wouldn't grab the ring to pull the pin. Hell, John
Wayne had been in the same fix. Ben caught the
ring with his teeth and pulled. He thought his jaw
would break before the metal pin wedged out of the
hole. He threw the grenade at once, aiming it for

the left side of the torpedo room. A blast on that side would have the most effect and would shield him from the flying shrapnel.

There was one shout from inside, then the bomb went off and half the lights in the compartment flickered out, then came back on.

"Charge!" Ben thought. He jumped up and swung the Sten submachine gun in front of him, his right finger on the trigger, the hurt left wrist forgotten. He stumbled over a body and crawled past the bunks, where he could see the whole space around the four torpedo tubes that extended six feet out from the front bulkhead. There were four more bodies. Both lower torpedo tubes were open. A man hung half out of one, his body a mass of shrapnel wounds. Another sat holding his stomach. He was alive, and Ben thought he was an officer. His head turned slowly toward Ben. He had no weapon. Ben aimed the Sten at him, then lowered the muzzle.

The blue eyes of the German looked up at Ben. Then he swallowed, his face working through the pain.

"Untersee-boot?"

Ben nodded. *"Ja, untersee-boot, Englisch."*

"Ja."

Ben looked around, made sure the other bodies were all dead, then checked the upper torpedo tubes. Both were closed and dogged down. Anyone inside couldn't get out now.

Ben looked back at the German. A prisoner, what would they do with a prisoner? He double-checked the route back to the bow hatch. None of the Germans on the bunks or under them was alive. There seemed no place anyone else could hide. At the hatch he called up and an English face peered over carefully.

"Get down here, the boat is secure, we've captured it. Call our medic over here pronto, and if he's here get him down the forward hatch. Leslie's hurt."

Ben went back to where the German leaned against the bulkhead. He was trying to remember his high school German. One year didn't help him much now.

"Do you speak any English?" he asked.

"Some," the German said with pain in his voice.

"You had mechanical trouble?"

"*Ja*, batteries. Poison gas. Kill twelve men. Then batteries dead. Charging no work."

The German coughed and spit up blood. He turned his head away as pain ripped through him.

"Could not dive. You came. Kapitan shot himself. It is end of everything."

"I've got a medic coming, he'll fix you up."

"No, better I go down with ship."

"Your crew, were you shorthanded?"

"*Ja*, send us out *mit* thirty men. Many short."

"Stay here, I'll be back." He ran to the officers' wardroom. Leslie sat where he had left him.

"We got it? We capture a goddamn U-boat?"

"We got it, Leslie. Thanks for blowing that Nazi away behind me before. You saved my skin."

"Hell, you trusted me for this job. Meant a hell of a lot."

"How bad are you hit?"

"Couple of slugs, probably little nine-millimeter jobs from one of their squirt guns. High up. Nothing to worry about, Commander."

A medic dropped through the hatch and called out, and Ben shouted for him to come aft. The medic looked at Leslie and had him lie down. The man checked Leslie, then put some sulfa on the two wounds in his chest with some bandages and motioned Ben to the hatch.

"He needs those bullets taken out. I can't do it.

He's probably bleeding internally. We need a ship with a doctor who can operate."

"You'll have to do it."

"No, that one slug is too close to his heart. I can dig lead out of arms and legs, but the chest makes me nervous."

"I'll tell the skipper. Now come back here and look at this German. He's in the forward torpedo room and cut up bad. See what you can do for him. I'll be right back."

Ben climbed up the ladder to the deck before he realized he still had his finger on the Sten gun trigger. He eased his finger off and let the weapon hang from the cord around his neck. The *Seawitch* had maneuvered alongside the sub, and the crew had tied the two boats together. Ben leapt on board the English boat and ran to the bridge where Moxie stood.

Two minutes later an appeal went out for the destroyer *Bulldog* to reverse course and pick up wounded from the *Seawitch*. That done, Ben and Moxie went to the U-boat and checked on the German officer. He was a first watch officer, second in command of the sub. He looked up at them and gave a feeble salute, which both Moxie and Ben returned.

"Sir, this is my kapitan, Commander Mulford."

The officer nodded. "Don't bother medicine. I am dead man. I die by my oath. We fought to death. What more can a German officer ask?"

His eyes glinted for a moment, then his head fell to one side and his eyes opened. He stared at the nothingness of eternal sleep.

"Poor bastard," Ben said. "This boat probably should never have put to sea. He said gas from the batteries killed twelve of his men before they knew it, then the batteries went dead. They couldn't dive so the boat was a sitting duck out here. Evidently they had some trouble with their diesels, too."

"Let's see what we can get off her," Moxie said. "She's too tail-heavy now. We'll check the control room, but from what I've heard she probably won't respond to the controls. I've brought two men who speak and read German. So they can try to work out the problems. At least we captured her."

Two British sailors were looking over the controls. One tried to start the diesel engines, but neither would run. There was no response to the electric drive.

"Blow all the water out of the aft tanks," Moxie ordered.

The seaman hit the levers and twisted the dials. The boat leveled off a little.

"Compressed air is all gone," one seaman said. "And we've got no power to compress any more."

"Close all watertight doors and the aft hatch," Moxie said. "Get our wounded and dead out of that area."

A sailor ran forward with the word to evacuate the English wounded and dead.

"How many men did we lose?" Ben asked.

"Three dead, four wounded. Including you. Medic!"

The medic came and coated Ben's left wrist with sulfa, then bandaged it.

"The logbook, the code books, operational manuals, let's get all the paperwork out of her we can find," Moxie said. "Let's take off everything we can of value. If we lose her at least we'll have something."

They started stripping the papers, and Moxie sent for the diesel mechanics from the *Seawitch*. They came over and dug into the engines.

As they worked, Moxie had all nonessential gear pulled off the U-boat, including the radar detection scanner, the compass, and the torpedo aimer.

"Sir, we're listing ten degrees starboard. No way to trim her without some kind of power."

The mechanic came to the bridge.

"She's blown three pistons in one engine, and the other one seems to be seized somehow. Also, there's water in the diesel fuel. No way either one is going to run again."

The English crewmen were ordered off the boat. They worked for a while stripping the snorkle and its radar-absorbing shroud. The German dead were dropped overboard.

Moxie had all hatches closed and sealed, then he put a towline on the front bollards and took off the lines that lashed the U-boat to the *Seawitch*. Two men stood on the aft deck of the British boat ready to slip the towline if the U-boat began to sink.

Back in the control room, Moxie turned to his sublieutenant.

"What's the nearest land, Mr. Barry?"

Barry studied his charts. "Scilly Islands, sir. Near Land's End."

"Distance and our approximate travel time at ten knots average speed, Mr. Barry."

He worked with his slide rule and pencil. "Estimated time of landfall, thirty-three hours and forty minutes, sir."

"Thank you, Mr. Barry. Bring her to a bearing for Scilly Islands and maintain ten knots."

"Aye, aye, sir."

Ben and Moxie went up to the bridge and kept lookouts posted.

"This would be a hell of a time to get attacked by a German fighter," Moxie said.

Ben shook his head. "No chance. They have trouble enough closer to home fighting off the bombers. Things are a lot simpler out here now than they were even a year ago. If you'd sent out a request for a doctor then like you did today, you'd have had ten U-boats zeroing in on our position."

"True, but there still are a few of the raiders around."

"Any word from the *Bulldog* on returning?"

"No, I don't expect any. But I do hope to see her masts show on the horizon before long."

As they waited, they watched the U-boat under tow. She was riding too low in the water, throwing up too much bow wave. The crew members were making bets how long she would last. Ben was taking no bets.

"Would we have a better chance at eight knots?" he asked.

Moxie stared at the low-riding boat behind them. "If she's low in the water it means her aft tanks never got completely pumped out. I hope that's what it means. If she had been taking on seawater somewhere, she might have been running with it on board and trimming to compensate. Now with no trim, we can't compensate. If she continues to take on more water the same way, she'll sink sooner or later. It's a race with the clock."

"Or with the *Bulldog*. They could put a repair crew inside that might be able to rework that diesel engine."

"Maybe," Moxie said. "Just maybe. I hope to hell that we can get her back so we'll have something to show for the loss of three good men."

"How's Leslie?"

"Fine. A couple of slugs can't stop an Irishman like him. I'm putting him in for a Victoria Cross as well as the seven others who went with him."

Moxie pounded the bridge railing. "Three good men dead; I just hope to hell that it was worth it!"

Chapter 11

Ben leaned on the cab on the *Seawitch*'s bridge until his elbows got sore, then he waved at Moxie.

"Hell, Skipper, standing up here waiting isn't going to make the *Bulldog* come any quicker. Let's go below and grab something to eat. We haven't eaten since breakfast, and I'm getting a case of quick starvation."

"Where the hell is she?" Moxie asked, taking one more look at the eastern horizon with his binoculars. "What time is it, Ben?"

"Sixteen thirty hours and counting. Now, how about some chow? If I eat with the skipper I get better food than when I go down to that restaurant of yours and try to order."

Moxie pushed his binoculars away and snorted. He checked to be sure there was a lookout on duty, then dropped down to the control room. The wireless operator told him there were no signals of any kind. He hadn't heard any traffic, not even from the *Bulldog*. Moxie sent Mr. Barry to the bridge.

Ben led Moxie through to the wardroom, and the skipper told them to whip up an early dinner. In a few minutes Ben and Moxie were eating steak, potatoes and gravy, and green peas and drinking hot black coffee.

Neither one of them talked during the meal. "Eat it while you can" was the rule they followed. When they were finished eating, Moxie went through the galley to the place where the medic had set up his sick bay. It was in the most accessible bunk in the crew quarters. Leslie and the other wounded man, Decker, who had been with Ben on his assault crew, were bedded down there.

Moxie looked at Leslie, who winced as he moved. When he saw his guests, he tried to smile. "Hi, Skipper. We still got a tow?"

"So far, Leslie. How do you feel?"

"Fine. No problem. I've been shot before."

"The medic says those bullets have to come out."

"Couple of days won't hurt much, Captain."

"Longer they stay in there, Skipper, the more damage they'll do," the medic said.

The medic's name was W. W. Hall, and he wanted to be a doctor. His grades had slipped in medical school and he was drafted into the Navy and trained as a medic. He was a skinny kid, with a lot of black hair and delicate hands. He already had a doctor's touch.

"I think I should take out the one bullet, sir," Hall said. "I think he's got a fever, sir."

Moxie looked at Leslie. The easy one shouldn't hurt. "Yes, go ahead, Hall. Get someone to help you. A mess table might work better. You decide. We hope to get some news about the *Bulldog* soon."

"Thank you, sir. I'm sure that both Leslie and I will take all of the help we can get."

"How are you doing, Decker?" Moxie asked the other man.

"Fine, sir. Glancing bullet hit me sideways. Doc pulled it out of me. I'm fit for duty now if you need me, sir."

"You just rest, Decker." The officers nodded at the medic and worked their way back to the control room.

"How's your arm," Moxie asked Ben.

"Hurts like hell."

"You take some pain pills?"

"Half a bottle."

Moxie looked up sharply with a frown but was reassured when he saw Ben's grin.

"Sorry, Ben, it's the damn waiting. Where the hell is the *Bulldog*? She should have been here hours ago."

"Moxie, that call went out only two hours ago. She could have been fifty miles ahead of us already."

"I just worry a lot. I'm going topside and relieve Barry. Want to come along?"

"No, I think I'll go to surgery. Maybe I can hold Leslie down while Hall slices into him."

"You're a primitive after all. We do use ether these days."

"Ether? What ever happened to the good old Western custom of simply biting on a forty-four caliber bullet?"

When Ben got to the crew quarters, Hall had just started operating. He had three men helping. All wore masks and had scrubbed as well as they could. The first slug he was after was just below the clavical. Ben guessed it had missed the top of the lung. Leslie was strapped down to the bunk with a second light rigged over him.

Hall had sent everyone else out of the compartment. He checked the ether, saw that Leslie was unconscious, and pulled the cloth away. When Hall made the incision through the bullet hole, the sailor holding the ether bottle sweated over his mask. A moment later, as the blood welled up on Leslie's chest, the seaman groaned, passed out, and fell.

Ben grabbed the ether bottle before it hit the steel, and Hall looked back at the incision.

"Thanks, Commander. Care to assist?"

Ben hovered over Leslie's head with the cloth and bottle of ether. Whenever Leslie started coming out of his dreams, Ben held the cloth over his nose again.

Hall probed, spread the thin flesh over the top of the ribs, and probed deeper. The second seaman mopped up the blood. Hall shook his head.

"I can't do it, Commander. The bullet went between the ribs and it's probably lodged in the top lobe of the left lung. I can't go in there that far."

He put his surgical instruments down and shook his head. He wiped the sweat off his forehead with his arm, and proceeded to stitch up the wound. He put a sprinkling of sulfa powder on it, then covered it with a compress and held it down firmly for several seconds. Hall took off the bloody compress, sprinkled on the sulfa powder again, and taped a clean compress firmly in place.

Hall pulled down his mask and slumped on a bunk.

"Damnit, it was just too deep. I don't know what I'm doing in that far. I could do more damage than good. Where the hell is the *Bulldog* and the doctor?"

Ben went back to the bridge. Moxie held his glasses up. The sun was low, it would be dusk soon.

"Where the hell is the *Bulldog*?" Moxie asked again. He didn't ask about the patient, and Ben didn't tell him. Nobody on the bridge spoke for half an hour. Ben put down his glasses.

"Skipper, those aft bollards . . ."

"Hell, I don't know, Commander," Moxie said sharply. "I've never tried to tow a German U-boat before by the aft bollards, have you? I don't know what the hell happens if the pigboat sinks. Does it rip off the bollards, or does the tow cable snap? Does the whole thing hold and she pulls us down with her? I don't have the slightest idea. I just know we can't have a man out there nursing that line all night."

"And we do have a night tow."

Moxie sighed and nodded. "Yes, damnit. So should

we maintain our speed, slow down or drift until dawn?"

"I'd go to six knots, Skipper, cut down on a lot of potential problems."

"Mr. Barry. Bring her down to six knots ahead, same bearing."

Mr. Barry called back from below. "Aye, sir. Six knots, steady as she goes."

"Lights! That would help," Moxie said suddenly. "We've got that small searchlight. We can rig it up here and have the lookout check the bollard and the towline every five minutes."

"Good idea, Captain," Ben said, stretching. "Well, I better get some sleep. I'll take the watch at twenty-two hundred hours."

Moxie looked up. "Good, thanks." He frowned. "Until when?"

"Until the tow breaks, or the *Bulldog* runs us down, or we find daylight about sixty kilometers to the east."

"Ben, thanks. How is Leslie?"

Ben told him, then went below to have Mr. Barry arrange for the searchlight to be taken to the bridge.

Ben didn't think he would sleep. His wrist burned like a white-hot poker was plunging through it. Finally, he took one more painkiller and dozed off.

The watch woke him, just before ten. He shook his head to clear it, then climbed the tower ladder to the bridge.

Moxie heard him come up and looked over.

"Not a damn thing. The light works fine. The towline is holding, the *U-133* is riding well, no problems, I've been checking the line every ten minutes now with the light."

Moxie didn't have to tell Ben about the danger of using the light for any longer than necessary. It would provide a perfect aiming point for any German submarine in the area.

"Get below and have some sleep," Ben said. "I'll call you if anything happens."

"You damn well better. This is my command. I doubt if I'll be able to sleep."

Ben waved him toward the ladder and lifted his binoculars. The *U-133* rode easily behind them. She didn't appear to have sunk any lower. The bow wake looked about the same. Ben was more optimistic about the chances of getting it to port. He swept the horizon but could find nothing.

If the *Bulldog* were coming back to help them, his guess was that it had overshot them. Without any real location they had to estimate speed and bearing and start a crisscross search pattern. Even with their radar it would be tough. They probably wouldn't see the destroyer until morning.

Ben yawned, lifted his left hand, and dropped the binoculars. His left hand was useless. He sent the lookout down for two cups of coffee, and when the hot stuff came, he took a painkiller and then once again swept the silent sea with the glasses. The heavy chop had eased in the night, but in the Atlantic calm was still far from being peaceful.

The hours passed. Clouds seemed to scurry around the moon as if playing tag. Ben watched a rain squall build to the left, pound the sea for a few minutes, and then blow away.

Every ten minutes he checked the cable. It was fine; the *U-133* stayed in a normal towing position.

When the first streaks of light penetrated the eastern sky, Ben was drinking his third cup of coffee. His stomach growled, and for the first time since he had stepped on board he realized that he hadn't even *thought* about his old claustrophobia. He was proud of himself as he watched the light creeping across the curvature of the earth's sea. When there was full daylight, he sent the lookout below to wake the captain.

Moxie came quickly to the bridge, looked expectantly around for the destroyer, then checked the tow and nodded.

"All ahead to ten knots, please, and tell the cook to roust us up one hell of a good breakfast. Your skipper is hungry!"

As they ate, the radio operator sent word that he was picking up some traffic. It was mostly shore beams to ships and convoys, and it was all in code.

"Try the VHF voice band," Moxie suggested. "The *Bulldog* might be just over the horizon looking for us."

They ate quickly. The radio man came back before they had finished.

"Sir! Just picked up the *Bulldog*! She's on VHF and has a fix on our signal. She says she can't be more than ten miles away from our position."

Moxie hurried to the radio shack and grabbed the mike, then gave it back to the operator.

"Get me the *Bulldog*'s skipper."

A moment later they were in contact.

"Good morning, Floater One, where the hell have you been?"

"Looking for you, Swimmer. It's a big ocean."

"Do you have a doctor on board?"

"No, Swimmer. But we've got a rated medic who can do almost anything but deliver babies."

"Tell him to bone up on nine-millimeter slug removal. We need a couple chopped out."

"Is the man in a bad way?"

"Yes. Put that tin can into fifth gear, will you?"

"Roger, Swimmer One, we sure as hell will!"

"Floater One, we've also got a swimmer in tow."

"Another swimmer? One of ours or theirs?"

"Theirs. It's riding low and out of power. Do you have an air compressor with a long air line?"

"We'll have it ready the minute we come alongside."

"We'll have the patient ready, he's the first order of business. He'll be strapped on a stretcher."

"Right, we'll be waiting for him. We're coming on a bearing of three-four-zero. See you soon."

Ben and Moxie ran for the tower ladder and stared at the horizon from the bridge through their binoculars.

Ten minutes later Sublieutenant Barry called out. "I have a mast, sir, and some smoke at one-six-zero."

Then they all saw it.

"Mr. Barry. Get below and talk with our mechanic and engineer to figure out how to get compressed air into the *U-133*'s air tanks."

"Aye, sir."

He turned to Moxie. "Commander, if you would check out that patient. Get him ready to move."

"Right, Captain," Ben answered. He slid down the handrails of the ladder and hurried forward through the control room into the crew's quarters.

Everyone on the ship knew the *Bulldog* was in sight. Ben told Hall what he wanted, and the medic got Leslie onto the stretcher and strapped down. He covered him with a rubber sheet and then tied that down.

"Get some half-inch line and rig a sling, Hall. Then they can pick him up any number of ways."

"Aye, Commander."

They moved Leslie into the seamen's mess. There they could hoist him out the larger forward torpedo-loading hatch. Then they waited.

"Leslie, you're first on the hit parade this time, so

get ready for a ride," Ben said before he went back to the bridge.

The *Bulldog* was well in sight now and steaming toward them at what Ben guessed was flank speed. When the destroyer was a thousand meters away, Moxie called for both engines full stop. As the submarines coasted to a halt, the heavy tow cable sank deeper into the water and the boats moved closer together. Fortunately, there was no danger of making contact.

Moxie went below and used the VHF radio to ask the destroyer captain to come in on the port side and be ready to receive a patient.

"If you people can't operate, you can get him back to a shore hospital much faster than we can," he said.

"Agreed. We'll pick him up first. I have the air line ready for your little friend. I must say that is a prize package you've hooked there."

"Right, fishing has been good. We're standing by."

Moxie had the hatches on the *Seawitch* opened. The destroyer crept alongside fifty meters away and came to a full stop. Then Moxie edged the sub toward the larger ship.

A bos'n's chair and sling was quickly rigged between the two ships, and Leslie was pulled up onto the deck of the destroyer. When he was safely on board, Leslie was rushed below. The chair was unrigged, and Moxie pulled forward until the *U-133* was directly opposite the *Bulldog*. They lowered a boat, which picked up four men including Mr. Barry. The four men went back to the *Bulldog* and picked up a pair of air hoses, which were played out as the small launch powered across the green water to the black hull of the *U-133*.

Mr. Barry boarded with the two engineers, cracked the aft hatch, and vanished below with the air hoses. Ben and Moxie watched from the bridge.

After what seemed to be ten minutes, but must not have been more than two or three, Mr. Barry came out of the hatch and waved his arms to start sending over the compressed air. He vanished and a short time later came up and held his clasped hands together over his head. He smiled and shouted.

It took a half hour to charge the air tanks fully. Then, according to Moxie's orders, Barry and his German-reading crew blew the aft tanks. Moxie cheered as the water and air foamed up around the stern and the German sub rose gracefully until she was in proper and full surface trim.

Moxie laughed and pounded one fist at the sky. "Now that son of a bitch will make it back to Portsmouth!"

Barry again showed at the hatch. He called to the destroyer that he wanted to refill the air tanks. When that was completed, the launch brought the air hoses back to the destroyer and the submariners back to the *Seawitch*.

Ben and Moxie were asked to visit the *Bulldog*. They left Barry in charge and a few moments later were on the destroyer.

Moxie asked to see Leslie. In the small sick bay, the medic had just closed up the top incision. He took off his mask and shook his head.

"That other bullet is too deep and too critically placed. We'll have to get him to a hospital as soon as possible."

The *Bulldog* captain nodded. "In that case, Commander Mulford, I suggest you continue your tow, and we'll charge back to Portsmouth as fast as we can with your crewman."

Moxie agreed, and they immediately left.

Once back on board the sub, Moxie questioned Sublieutenant Barry.

"Is the *U-133* trimmed out for surface running?"

"Right sir. She's trim and flat, ready to go."

"Did you find any other problems? Such as more water in her bilges than before, any water near the batteries?"

"No, sir. I think it was simply a matter of her running the compressed air tanks dry, and then they had no way to recharge them. That's why they couldn't completely blow the rest of the aft tanks."

"Will she make it to Portsmouth?"

"Unless she takes a bomb in her tower, or some Spitfire comes down on her."

"Very well, Mr. Barry. Let's put the *Seawitch* at full forward and see what kind of towing speed we can make."

The diesels churned, and soon they were moving easterly in the wake of the fast-vanishing destroyer. The bow wake of the *U-133* was much smaller now, and she rode steady and true.

"Making thirteen knots, sir," Barry called.

Moxie smiled for the first time in two days.

"Very well, take over the bridge, Sublieutenant. I'll be in my quarters."

Moxie dropped on the bunk. "I'll be damned, we did it! We captured a goddamned U-boat. The Royal Navy has standing orders to capture U-boats whenever possible. Not many have been taken so far. Somebody is going to be damned pleased with us, especially with you, Yank."

Moxie reached in his locker and took out a fifth of good Scotch whiskey.

"How about one small nip, to keep away the chill, and to celebrate our prize catch?"

Ben grinned. "Yes, sir, you bet!" He reached for the small glass with his left hand, his fingers closed around it, but when Moxie let go, the glass fell through his fingers to the deck, where it smashed. His left hand was limp, lifeless.

"Medic!" Moxie bellowed. Forty-five seconds later Hall was at the door.

"Take another look at this wrist, Hall. Seems his arm was hurt more than we thought. And bring him some more pain pills."

Ben could not move his left hand. The wrist was red and swollen.

"Damn, we should have sent you on that destroyer, too," Moxie said. "Why didn't you say something, man? Trying to be a bloody hero or something?"

Ben shook his head. "It didn't hurt so much before. All the action, the excitement." He winced as the medic took off the last of the red-stained bandage. "Besides, we've got to cut down that wild-eyed list for Captain White-Johnson."

"We've got more than enough time now," Moxie said. "Fix him up good, Hall. You're touching a bloody hero, you know that, don't you?"

The sub rode easily along behind them, and there was no trouble with aircraft from either side. One British fighter did sweep down low, make a second pass, then waggle its wings and proceed.

Finally, they came into the port of Portsmouth. The subs headed toward the base but were met by two motor torpedo boats and signaled to stop.

A Royal Navy full commander brought the MTB up close and called over for permission to come aboard. He climbed to the bridge, where Moxie and Ben waited for him.

"What the hell is this about?" Moxie asked.

"Commander Mulford? I'm Commander Young, Naval Intelligence. I have orders to stop your craft here. The purpose is to take your prize in tow and to remove from your submarine all material whatsoever that was taken from the U-boat. I am also instructed to tell you and your crew that absolutely no mention is to be made about the capture of this U-boat. It is an extremely important matter which I'm sure you can understand."

Moxie scowled. "Hell no, I don't understand it. Why?"

"Commander, you've been in the Navy long enough to know that is an impossible and an unwise question to ask."

"Why? What you're telling me is that as far as the Royal Navy goes, we did not capture the *U-133*. You're telling me that we did not have three men killed and four wounded in the fighting. And you're telling me that I am not going to be able to recommend for heroism eight brave men under my command."

The intelligence man stared at Moxie with anger.

"You pick up on things quickly. Are you now refusing my direct order, Commander?"

Moxie sighed. "No, because then you would simply arrest me, relieve me of command, and take what you want anyway. I might be dumb, but I'm not that stupid. I know how you desk sailors operate. I'll pass the word."

A tugboat had already pulled alongside. The intelligence man signaled, and the tug took the towline off the *U-133* and hooked her own towline on.

It took the commander and his crew of three an hour to unload the parts of the *U-133* that had been removed. Then the commander carried the logbook, code books, and other papers out of Moxie's cabin.

He gave one last order.

"Now, Captain, have your crew assemble in the seamen's mess. I want everyone on board."

"Giving us a lecture, are you?" Ben asked.

"It would take a Yank to say that. Oh, yes, Mount, we know all about you and everyone else on board, including seaman Leslie now in the hospital at Portsmouth. He's been cautioned as well. And the *Bulldog* officers and crew have been given the word. We haven't missed a trick."

Ben shook his head. "Commander, you missed two tricks, possibly three. The first one is manners, the second is humility, and the third and most obvious is good breeding," he said and headed for the galley.

The intelligence man gave a short, tough talk.

"Men, you've captured valuable war documents. Some of the best code books we've had so far were on that U-boat. This is going to be a great help to intelligence to pinpoint current squares of operation of the German sub force. It will give us up-to-date codes, U-boat procedures, methods of identification, and dozens of other vital facts, all top secret.

"The problem is if Jerry knows we have the books, they will change all of their codes and procedures, and this valuable data will become worthless. Therefore, no one must say a word about this capture. If the Germans think the *U-133* was sunk, they'll have no reason to change the code system. Are there any questions?"

There were none.

"I don't need to remind you men that any slip of the tongue by you will bring you under the most severe charges by the Royal Navy, and could result in a prison sentence of forty-nine years at hard labor. This is a serious, top secret situation. You must believe from now on that the *U-133* was not captured by your crew."

Moxie walked with the intelligence officer to the stern of the *Seawitch*.

"Just how do you suggest that I report this cruise, Commander? How do I explain the deaths of three crewmen and the wounding of four others?"

"No explanation is required, Captain. I've cleared it with your immediate superiors."

"And the parents of the dead, have you cleared it with them, too?"

"Aye, Commander. They will be notified. The sons or husbands have been killed in action at sea."

"Somebody is way off base here, Commander. I checked all of that German material. There is nothing of value we don't know and haven't known for years. The code book is the multiple date rotating number kind. It doesn't help a bit. You're going to one hell of a lot of trouble for almost nothing."

"Since when did you become an expert on naval intelligence, Commander Mulford?"

"Hell, Commander Young, I know as much about naval intelligence as you do—damned near nothing. Now get the hell off my boat before you fall overboard."

Commander Young backed up a step. "I could put you on report for that, Mulford."

"You could shit too. How are you at swimming?"

Commander Young stepped down the deck to the aft hatch and waved for the MTB. He was pulled aboard by the rest of his crew.

Moxie turned and went back to the mess.

"It's as he said it is until you hear different," Moxie told the crew. "Now let's get on into our berth."

Moxie stood on the bridge as the *Seawitch* moved slowly toward Fort Blockhouse and her greasy pilings.

"A bunch of blithering by-the-book desk sailors," Moxie said. "Those code books will be changed in two days. I had one of my German-reading seamen go through them with me. The operating procedures have been known since 1940, for God's sakes. As soon as we dock I'm going straight to see Admiral Graves. I'm not going to stand still for this kind of bullshit!"

Chapter 12

Moxie went through the routines of docking, tying up, checking in, and all the rest of the normal port operations. Then he jerked his thumb at Ben.

"Come on, let's go see Captain White-Johnson. He should be able to get us in to see the admiral today."

"What's your strategy?" Ben asked.

"Hell, I don't know. Right now it's anger. I'll think of something. I'm not going to get cheated out of that capture for my boat and a fistful of medals for my men. No way will I stand for that. Their whole reason for hushing up the capture is ludicrous. They did the same thing on the *U-110* back in April of 1941, but at least they had some damn good reasons for that. They never even got the *U-110* back to port before she foundered. Three destroyers captured her and took off tons of good strong intelligence material. But that was 1941. Four damn years ago. No sir, they aren't going to get away with this one."

"Look, Mox, he's going to want arguments, reasons for lifting the secrecy. He can't just call up intelligence and tell them to pull back the security without some damned good reasons."

"I'll think of some."

"How about what you told me: There is nothing secret they don't already know about on the VII-C-class boat. They know those subs inside out. Nothing of value to aid the allied cause is on those boats."

"Yeah, buddy. That's a start."

"And the code books. You said they were not that much good, with changing codes and numerical, dated precode progression."

"Right, keep them coming."

They arrived at the captain's office, and the WREN at the desk looked up and smiled.

"Commanders Mulford and Mount. The captain says you are to go right in. He's expecting you."

They went through the door and stood in front of the desk. The captain stood up and shook hands with both men.

"Congratulations, men! I heard all about it. This will go down on your permanent record of course. Too bad about the intelligence thing, but what the hell? That's only a small part of it."

"Captain, this whole secrecy thing is a sham of some kind," Moxie said. "Can you get the secrecy stripped off it?"

"Me? No, of course not. Not my department. They do have a point though about the code books."

Ben shook his head. "No, Captain, they have no point. There isn't a thing on that boat Naval Intelligence hasn't known about for at least two years. The code books are a waste of time at this point. The U-boat activity in the Atlantic is almost nil. Some damned intelligence officer has just cooked up a bill of goods so his people will have something to do."

Captain White-Johnson scowled, but nodded. "Of course there's a lot in what you say. But intelligence must have some good reasons."

"Bullshit!" Moxie roared. "Captain, one of our submarines has never captured a German U-boat before, let alone captured one and towed it to port. I had three good men killed in that fight, and now these patronizing, provincial, haughty, sons-of-bitching, make-work-happy desk sailors tell me to forget it? I have four more men with bad wounds. Why don't you tell them to forget it, Captain? Tell them it never happened. I'm requesting that you set up an appointment with Admiral Graves for me right now. I want to see him as quickly as possible."

The captain sat down. "Commander, you know that Admiral Graves is a busy man. You can't just go barging in on a man like that."

"Try it, Captain," Moxie said. "Give him a call. Today I think he'll make room for me. I figure that you owe me one, Captain. And I figure the admiral owes me one, too. Give him a call and see if we can't go right up to his office."

"Hell . . ." He paused. "Moxie, we do appreciate . . ." He stopped again. "Goddamnit . . ." The captain picked up the phone and asked for the admiral's aide.

Five minutes later, much to Ben's surprise, the three of them sat in Admiral Joseph Graves's outer office. The captain had been surprised too when the admiral insisted that they come right up.

"He'll want reasons, good solid reasons," Captain White-Johnson said. "The more reasons you have, the better. In fact, those four Victoria Cross recommendations might be the strongest arguments you have."

A commander came through the door and motioned to them, and they went into the admiral's large office. He met them at the door, his hand out.

"Gentlemen, I'm proud of you both. Damn fine show! A VII-C class, I understand. Good work. As you know, there won't be any official announcement."

"That's what I wanted to see you about, sir. I'm Mulford. I had three men shot to death and four men wounded making that capture. I want to put eight men in for decorations, at least four for the Victoria Cross. But I understand I won't be able to if this is kept secret."

The admiral frowned, went back to his big swivel chair, and sat down. He waved them to chairs.

"Sit down, sit down. I hadn't thought about that part. Three dead. How?"

Briefly Moxie explained the sighting, the assault on the U-boat, told of Ben's part and the casualties. "It was a hard capture, sir. The Germans fought to the last man. They were shorthanded and had lost eight or ten to gas before we got there. Our men killed twenty-four Germans on that boat, sir. None of us can just forget it happened."

"No, no, of course not. Amazing. Twenty-four dead. That's the biggest submarine hand-to-hand combat we've had in this whole war. Fantastic. Now why the hell would intelligence want to keep that all under wraps?"

"Sir, we know everything there is to know about the VII-C sub. If it had been one of the new models, I could understand it," Moxie said. "The code books aren't that much good to us with the restricted activity in the Atlantic by their subs."

"True, Commander, true. And think what the press could do with this, and with a joint forces crew! The story would be a tremendous boost to the home front right now. Not much good news coming through."

Admiral Graves looked up at his aide. "Get me that commodore who is in charge of public information. I better have a chat with him. Then find out who's handling Naval Intelligence for this area and get him on the other line. I want him to wait."

"Aye, aye, sir," the aide said and left.

"Captain, what do you think about all this?" the admiral asked.

White-Johnson flowed with the current. "Looks like to me, sir, that intelligence is up the wrong tree. The publicity value of the story and having some submariner heroes would do a hell of a lot more good than those outdated code books."

"Mmm." The admiral's phone blinked and he picked it up.

"Yes, Charlie, I've been meaning to call you. I've got something you might be interested in. But if I give it to you, you've got to blast it up big. What I have for you are some honest-to-God submarine heroes. How does that sound?" He listened for a minute. "Hell, this one won't be a hard sell. They captured a German U-boat in the Atlantic, shot it out with them and killed twenty-four Germans inside the sub. Then they blew the aft tanks to keep her from sinking and towed her home. We had only three dead and four wounded."

The admiral listened again. "Yes, that's what I figured. I'm going to be talking to a Commodore Truckingham at Naval Intelligence. Give me five minutes, then you call him. Yes, you can take it from there. Thanks, Charlie. Say hello to Ethyl for me."

Admiral Graves pushed down the lever, let up on it, and then touched a button of the desk set phone.

"Truckingham? I understand one of my S-class submarines captured a German U-boat and towed it to port and you're trying to keep a secrecy lid on it. You have about thirty seconds to tell me who authorized such a sweeping security measure and then to justify that order. And it better be damn good."

Moxie grinned. Ben slapped him on the shoulder.

The admiral listened for a minute. "What the hell is so top secret about the VII-C? We captured one back in April of 1941 as I remember. They have no new equipment we haven't seen and examined. That VII-C is as familiar to us as our own boats. We can't learn a damn thing from another one." The admiral listened again and grinned. "Just a minute, I'll ask my staff."

He put his hand over the mouthpiece. "Trucking-ham says could we claim we sank it, then the code books would still be operational."

Captain White-Johnson shook his head. "Ruin the story. A capture is more dramatic. Hell, it's ten times a better story to show how we captured the damned U-boat. And intelligence isn't going to get diddly-damn out of that code book."

Moxie grinned, surprised at the captain's reaction.

Admiral Graves went back to the phone. "Sorry, Truckingham. You didn't make a case. Your intelligence men must have something better to do. How about checking out those French coastal defenses for us? I want you to take the security wraps off that sub, the U-133 I believe she is. Turn everything back to the sub base commander and let him play with it. We might refit her and get her back to sea. Right, Commodore, that's the way it is. Good-bye."

Admiral Graves grinned. "Gentlemen, that's one of the benefits of having one more stripe than the other guy. Now, Commander, I'll look forward to seeing those recommendations for decorations. Get them to me just as soon as you can write them up. I'm sure the captain here will give you any assistance you need on form or style."

An hour later, Moxie and Ben were in the auxiliary hospital, where the navy doctor was examining Ben's left wrist.

"At least the bullet didn't hit anything important, like a bone or an artery. Your loss of use of the hand could have been the sudden shock to the muscles and tendons. It happens. I have some sulfa pills for you, and this shot is penicillin, fairly new and extremely good for infection. Keep your arm in a sling for a week, then come back and see me."

A nurse bandaged his wrist and provided Ben with

a sling, and the two men left the hospital and drove for the cottage. It seemed as though they had been gone a week.

"Tomorrow morning we write up those decorations," Moxie said. "I want your help, except for the one on you. Then we go see Leslie, or maybe just telephone him. Sometime after that we can talk to the captain about our suggestions on the sub pens."

Ben nodded. The pills were making him groggy. He leaned back in the little Austin and slept the rest of the way to the cottage.

The news story of the capture of the *U-133* came over the radio the next afternoon. For the following two days, both Ben and Moxie were targeted by half a dozen war correspondents and writers from the U.S. news services. The newspapers all carried the story, with pictures of Ben, Moxie, and Leslie and shots of the *Seawitch* with the captured *U-133* in port. There were long accounts of the sightings, the battle, and the tow job. It was a fine splurge of favorable news, and Betsy and Pru had clippings about it from eight different newspapers.

Ben and Moxie tried to get an appointment with Captain White-Johnson, but he told them to take a week's leave. "Get away and rest and relax for a few days," he had said.

Chapter 13

The two couples discussed their plans that night at dinner. Pru wanted to go up to the lake country.

"Right, and we find a little stream and rent a tent and we can camp out and have a real holiday."

"Most girls at the factory just phone in sick when their boyfriends come home on leave. We can do the same," Betsy said.

"I'd like to sleep every blessed day until noon, get up and wear me skivvies around the house, and then drink all the beer I can hold," Moxie said.

Betsy toyed with a potato. "I was hoping that we could stay right here. I mean we could go on walks in the woods, and along the stream. The men could fish if they want, and maybe we could drive into London and see a stage play in what's left of the West End theater district."

They all waited for Ben's suggestion. Finally, he flapped his left arm, which was still in a sling, and said, "I'm supposed to see the sawbones about this arm in four days. But it won't matter a couple of days either way. I'd kind of like to try some fishing. If we can rustle up some gear. Then we do some hiking in the woods. Wonder where that stream comes from, upriver? Then I'd come home to a fire, and some popcorn, and this good woman I got right here. I'd vote that we stay here and not waste a lot of time and petrol driving around."

154

"Stay here, yes," Pru said. "I'm liking that now."

"Hell, I can have another beer almost anywhere. Let's do it here," Moxie agreed. So it was decided.

The next morning Pru and Moxie went into the village for more food. Ben and Betsy took a walk along the stream and worked their way up through a patch of brush that came out on a small deserted valley. They sat beside the stream and kissed. She pulled him down and probed into his mouth with her tongue.

"That's getting to me, young lady," Ben said. "That could get me just sexed up as hell in about another minute."

"Good, because I think today is the day. Just one time I want to make love out in the open this way, with my ass in the grass, and I think this might be the time. How about over there where there's more brush?"

They jumped up and ran to the spot, worked through the small trees and brush to the center of the thicket and found a bed-sized swatch of green grass.

They undressed and made love once in the warm, springlike day, then talked about their plans for getting married. Ben had made contact with the chaplain, who had said there were no military restrictions. The chaplain would like to have a meeting with both of them first, and then they could set a date.

"It looks suspiciously like we're going to get married one of these days," he said.

"Darling, just one more time, let's pretend that we're already married."

The second time they made love was deliciously slow and gentle. Both of them were ready and keyed up by the time they coupled, and then there was furious pounding and moaning as they climaxed together. Suddenly, both got worried and pulled on their clothes, laughing as they did so. They sat side by side talking, then headed back downstream toward the cottage.

"When, darling?" he asked her.

"When do we walk down the center aisle of the chapel?"

"Yes."

"Soon." She furrowed her brow. "Now that it's almost here, it does seem a little scary, doesn't it? I mean the idea of getting married. It's always been there, the wanting to, and the settling down and not ever thinking about another man. Still it's all kind of scary now."

"I wondered if you felt that way too," Ben said. "My knees have been knocking ever since I talked with that chaplain."

"But you still want to?" she asked.

He stopped her, and kissed her lips tenderly. "Yes, I still want to marry you before I get shipped to Washington, D.C., or San Francisco, or to Manila or Guam. Hell, we can't tell what the next week is going to bring, let alone six months from now."

"Maybe we should set a date, say a month from now, and then go see the chaplain the last day of your leave. That way I won't have to take off another day of work for that. They have a fit over people being gone too much, call it absenteeism. It's a bad word."

Ben took a deep breath. "Okay, let's do it. What is today's date? The twenty-third, right? All right, how about our getting married on April twenty-third, 1945?"

"That sounds good to me." She kissed him and they walked slowly, arm in arm, back to the cottage. When they arrived, Moxie and Pru were back from the village with a newspaper and some groceries and three cases of beer.

"Guess what?" Betsy asked as soon as they went inside.

Pru looked at her. "You've set your wedding date, right?"

Ben nodded. "Right. How did you know?"

"Oh, that smugly satisfied smile on your woman's face. It meant she either had just finished a very good session of making love, or you set the wedding date."

"How about both of the above?" Betsy said and blushed.

"That calls for a celebration," Moxie said. "How about roast duck? We just bought a duck and I wanted it for some special day, and this is it! I'm the best roast duck cook in all of North London, so watch out, mates, and let me at it."

Later they ate the roast duck, and all the traditional trimmings. They also had lots of good wine figuring this was too special for the beer they had just bought. The wine was gone before the duck, so Moxie opened two more bottles. It was late into the evening before they moved the dishes away. The four of them sat around talking, singing songs, kissing, and petting.

Moxie kissed Pru and looked over at Ben and Betsy.

"Hey, mate. I thought that when a man got himself engaged to a bird, she sealed the bargain with a long romp between the old sheets. Did I miss something? You two been to bed already tonight?"

"Not yet, Mox," Ben said, feeling mellow and just a little drunk. "We've been talking, Mox."

"Hell, lots of time to talk later on. Time to be getting a little bit." He reached down and rubbed Pru's swaying bosom. A button popped off her blouse and one big, pink-tipped breast fell out.

"Yeah, that's the idea, a little action," Moxie said.

Moxie was more than a little drunk and forgot the others were there. He opened the other buttons on Pru's blouse and pulled her into a sitting position so both breasts showed.

"Let's go to the bedroom," Betsy said softly to Ben.

Ben blinked and looked at her. "Huh, why?"

"Moxie is getting serious over there."

Ben grinned. "Yeah, ain't them big ones?"

"Ben, come on." She stood, caught his hand and helped him up. Ben was still staring at Pru's large breasts as Betsy led him into the bedroom and closed the door.

The next morning no one got up until noon. Ben felt slightly hung over from all the wine and lay in bed, close to Betsy, relishing the luxury of having another little nap. Betsy poked him in the ribs.

"You were a very bad boy last night, Benjamin Mount."

"Why? Wasn't three times enough?"

She laughed and nodded. "That part was fine, Ben. You were a little drunk, remember? Out in the living room, Moxie pulled off Pru's blouse and she wasn't wearing a bra, and you kept staring at her breasts."

"Oh, yeah. I remember something about that. Damn, but she has big tits."

"Ben, shame on you, she's our friend."

"Nope, no shame. Just natural. Very few men in this world can resist a good look at a pair of female breasts, no matter how big or small or oblong or tiny-nippled. We're just kind of built that way—a built in ASDIC to locate girls. Now don't tell me you girls don't look at the bulges in men's tight pants down at the crotch."

"That's different, that's legal."

He hit her with a pillow. "Get up, woman. This is the day I teach you how to catch fish, remember?"

And he did. It was one of the best days he could remember. They caught fish, fried them for an afternoon snack, then went for a long walk and talked about how many kids they wanted, and about her parents and his mother.

When they got back to the cottage, there was a note waiting for them. Pru and Moxie had gone to the store for some more beer and wine. They would be back soon. Ben had just pulled his boots off when a knock sounded on the door.

He had expected it to be Moxie loaded down with sacks, but when he pulled back the door, he saw a memory. Lady Clifford stood in the opening, her sleek dark hair back-lighted by the afternoon sun, her striking face smiling and her devilish eyes teasing.

"Hello, Ben, darling. I've been expecting you to call me back. It's not nice to spend two nights with a girl, and then not even give her a call later on."

Ben shook his head in surprise and wonder. Then, in desperation, he turned and looked at Betsy.

Betsy was outraged. Her knuckles had turned white where she gripped the dining room table; her eyes were full of anger, disbelief, and shock, and Ben was sure that all of it was aimed directly at him.

Chapter 14

"Mrs. Clifford, that is a lie!" Ben shouted. "I haven't seen you for almost five years. You *are* the bitch your husband said you were just before he died. Now get the hell out of here and leave us alone! I mean now before I knock you off the porch!"

Cayenne Clifford smiled and Ben slammed the door in her face. He hurried over to Betsy and tried to take her in his arms but she shrugged away from him.

"Betsy, you don't believe that slut? You don't believe I've seen her lately or even thought about her? I haven't. The last time I saw her was in London almost five years ago."

Betsy held herself rigid. "She's lovely, isn't she? A beautiful woman, more money than she can ever use. So she goes around collecting men. Oh, I understand. She's beautiful and she's rich and she's so high-class British. Ben, I know you made love to her. I remember the first time you saw her at that grand estate near London. You were practically panting you wanted her so badly. She was worse, like a bitch dog in heat. And she had you, didn't she? It was the very next morning when you went walking and she went riding and you coupled in the woods somewhere like a pair of animals."

Tears streamed down Betsy's cheeks and dripped off.

She didn't try to wipe them away. She stared at Ben and shook her head sadly.

"I don't think you'll ever be able to get her out of your system, Ben. She eats away at you like acid. I've got a lot of thinking to do. Right now I'm going for a long walk, and I don't want you along."

"Betsy. You aren't going to believe what she said. It's ludicrous. Moxie was with me every minute that I wasn't with you. He can prove to you that I couldn't have been with her. Isn't my word enough? Don't you trust me that much?"

"Your ASDIC certainly is working. It found her for you again, didn't it? Moxie would cover up anything for you, we both know that. He's not exactly an impartial witness, is he, Ben?"

Betsy pulled on her little hat and sweater. She grabbed her purse and walked quickly to the door.

"Benjamin Mount, don't you dare follow me. I guess it's a good thing that we weren't married five years ago. I've learned a great deal more about you, Mr. Mount, and a lot of it I really don't like."

"Betsy, this is ridiculous. I haven't seen that person out there for five years! I haven't tried to see her. I don't want to see her. I want only you. I love you, Betsy Kirkland, don't you understand that?"

"Mr. Mount, it seems you love more than one. You couldn't really love me and keep trying to go to bed with that high-class whore. Now move, I'm going for a walk. I'll probably come back. Then we'll have a short talk and you can get your things together. I understand you men, how sex-starved you are."

She stepped past Ben, went out the door, and slammed it hard.

Ben stared at the closed door. "Go after her," he said to himself. "Go grab her and bring her back." He started once, then stopped. It would only be daylight for an hour. She would be back before it got dark, he rationalized. Then he changed his mind again and went to the door, opened it, and looked out.

Betsy was just down the lane. She turned and looked at him, then brought one hand up to her face quickly and glanced away. There was no car in the lane. Ben had no idea where Lady Clifford had gone, but he hoped that she stayed away. She was a first-class bitch, and she had proved it again.

But Betsy had been right. He had made love to the glamorous Lady Clifford the day the war began back in 1939, and later in London. But it seemed so long ago, so far away. Any attraction he had for her had ended five years ago and never could be revived. He wouldn't walk across the street to watch her pose naked, but how could he convince Betsy of that.

Moxie! Moxie had to bail him out. Moxie had been with Ben every minute he wasn't with Betsy. He hoped that when the initial shock wore off, she would realize she was being childish and was jumping to conclusions. In the end he hoped she would believe Moxie and they would be able to get settled down and back to the business of life.

Ben stormed around the cottage for a few minutes, picked up some clothes, straightened out the things on the table, then built a fire. Moxie and Pru were late getting back.

When Ben looked outside again, it was dark. Betsy had been gone for well over an hour. He slipped into a jacket, put on his navy garrison cap, and wrote a note to Moxie explaining they would be right back. Then he plunged through the front door and into the darkness.

Ben's inclination was to head up the lane the way Betsy had gone. He stepped quickly in that direction. His strides were long and sure, and he soon came to the village. He looked in the small stores. Only two were still open, but Betsy was not in either. He hoped she had gone shopping. His mother used to do that sometimes when she was angry.

The dark streets were empty. Ben walked on through to the far end of town, then down to the country road that led back to Portsmouth. Betsy was not there either. He decided he would walk another mile before he turned back. She might be any place, any place at all. He didn't think that she was in danger. Even at night this small village was the safest place he could think of, but still he shivered.

At the end of a mile, he stopped. It was totally dark, and heavy clouds had drifted in. A car came into the narrow lane, and he edged to the side. It pulled up and stopped. He saw it was a Rolls-Royce, but before he thought who it might be, he stepped forward. A gentle rain began to fall.

A light snapped on inside the car and he saw Cayenne smiling out at him.

"Darling, do come get in the car out of the rain."

He turned and walked on. Ben was so angry he was trembling. For a moment he didn't think he could control himself. The car pulled ahead and stopped beside him again.

"Ben, sweetheart. Why don't you get in now and stop acting like a silly, immature boy."

"Bitch!" he roared at her. "You slimy, fucking bitch! How could you say that in front of Betsy when it isn't true?"

"How? Darling, because I want you. I want to feel your lean, hard body against mine. I want you making love to me as you do so well."

He turned and walked away. The rain came down harder.

"Darling, don't be foolish," she said again, driving up beside him and keeping pace with him. "It's wet

out there, so get in the car. I'll just drive you back
to your cottage. No sense in your catching pneumonia.
I promise that I won't seduce you or anything."

A sudden blast of driving rain and wind hit him
in the face, and Ben staggered around and slid into
the warmth of the heated Rolls's front seat. He wiped
his wet hands on the plush upholstery.

"Why are you so bitchy? You've got money, social
position, a fine name. What do you chase people
this way for?"

"Amusement, usually," she said, holding her chin
high to accentuate her beautiful profile. Her aquamarine eyes turned toward him and she put out the
inside light. "But with you, Ben, it's something special. You're a Yank, you were my very first Yank,
and I want to try it again, to see if it was as de-
lightful as I remember."

"You're sick, Cayenne. You need to visit your psy-
chiatrist and get your head dissected."

"I'd rather play games with you."

He realized then that the car had stopped. They
were parked at the side of the road. The rain poured
down. Her hand slid over his thigh, but he caught it
and pulled it away. She held his hand and brought
it to her breasts and with a start he realized she was
bare breasted. Ben pulled his hand but she held it
tightly against her warm bosom.

"Go ahead, play with them, just like before. Remember the first time, that cabin in the woods?"

He pushed her away, his voice husky when he
spoke. "Drive the goddamn car or I'm walking."

"Oh, damn! You're no fun at all."

"I don't plan on being fun. I'm going to marry
Betsy, and if you ever come sniffing around again I'll
give that newspaper a call. *Inside,* that was the name
of it, the scandal sheet we saw at the hospital that
day. I'll spread your story all over the pages. I'll tell

everyone what a real slut you are, and how you cheated on Lord Clifford when he was dying as a war hero."

She caught his hand again and pushed it between her legs. Her skirt was bunched around her waist and she wore no panties. Suddenly his hand was pressed against her warm, wet crotch and she closed her legs, trapping him.

"Now, doesn't that feel fine, darling? I know what you want to put in down there, but that'll have to wait a minute." She jumped on him and pressed him down on the wide seat. One of her bare breasts hung over him, the extended nipple brushing against his lips. "Have a small bite, lover, all you want."

Lights showed ahead. They brightened the car until he could see her breast and the swollen nipple. Then the car swept past and they were alone again in the rainy darkness.

Ben groaned and opened his mouth, accepting her. Then he roared in anger, pushed her away from him, and sat up.

"No! Goddamn it, no! I'm not going to get caught in your beautiful, sexy baited trap again. It's not too late to settle this with Betsy, and I'm sure as hell going to try. You show up around here again, and I'll file a claim with the constable that you ran me down with your car. I can identify you from newspaper pictures, and I'll by-damn do it! And remember that *Inside* newspaper. They will always pay me well for the story of your double-timing Lord Clifford."

He jumped out and slammed the door. The rain slapped at him. He was soaked through, but it didn't matter. He walked along the roadway, blundering into the ditch now and then, but he kept moving. The lights of the big car behind him didn't come on. At last he made it to the village, and kept on going. Surely Betsy was back at the cottage by now.

It took him what seemed like an hour to walk the last few hundred yards to the cottage. When he was finally out of the rain under the small porch, he tried to wipe off the worst of the water. Then he turned the knob and pushed the cottage door open.

When Betsy had rushed out, she was crying. Tears had poured down her cheeks and she didn't try to stop them. They burned, and somehow she sensed that they were punishment for living in sin with Ben. She had never thought in those terms before. She loved Ben, that couldn't be sin. At least she *had* loved him. Betsy had looked back, but saw the door still shut. Was he going to rush out after her? Would he come and catch her and hold her tightly and say he had made a mistake and he was sorry and would never do it again?

The third time she looked back she saw Ben standing on the small front porch with his hands on his hips. He was angry. She thought his eyes showed his anger, but she was too far away to tell.

Betsy wiped a tear from her eye, then stared straight ahead. If he were coming, he would come. More tears came. A woman near another house looked at her, but she turned away quickly. She was in no mood to talk.

Betsy went through the village and beyond it to a path she had walked months ago. It circled behind the businesses to a small playground, then around to an inn. She turned that way, figuring she could still get back to the cottage before dark.

But the trail was longer than she remembered, and it was dark by the time she reached the center of the village. She was a half block from the lane when she saw Ben walk by. He was looking in the shops and stores, and along the street. At least he had come to find her. She started to call to him, then shook her head.

"No, he hasn't suffered enough," she thought. "That woman! He must have been with her, or talking to her. How else could she know where to find him?"

She walked more slowly until it was dark. The clouds gathered and a fine rain began falling. She walked quickly to the cottage and up on the porch. Moxie looked up from a newspaper as she came in, and Pru was singing in the bathroom.

"Hi, out for a walk?" Moxie asked.

Betsy burst into tears.

It took her ten minutes to explain what had happened. Moxie scowled and patted the hearth beside him. He put his arm around her.

"I've known you for five years now, right, Betsy?"

She nodded.

"Have I ever given you any bad advice?"

"No, Moxie."

"Remember that. When I went to that dance a few weeks ago with Pru, we found it was given by Lady Clifford. True. You can ask Pru. Mrs. Clifford asked me where Ben was and I said I wouldn't tell her. She must have used her connections in the Royal Navy to trace Ben and pinpoint where in this area he was assigned. She could do that, easily."

"Moxie, I don't believe you. You're covering up for Ben. I knew you would, you men stick together."

"Betsy, why are you doing this? Ben couldn't have known she was around until she stepped up on the porch tonight. God's truth, Betsy."

Betsy felt like crying again. It was plain to her now that Moxie was going to be no help at all. She was going to have to do it all herself. But what could she do? She felt so lonesome, so unwanted. What would really hurt Ben? Maybe if she could hurt him badly, he would understand how it felt to be two-timed, to have someone you loved getting sexy with someone else. Then he could feel the real pain. She turned to Moxie.

"If I asked you to do something for me, would you do it?"

"Sure, luv. Anything, you just name it."

"Make love to me, right now I want you to make love to me."

Moxie laughed. "You're joking, right? You've got to be fooling me." He put his arm around her.

"I'm not joking, Moxie."

Moxie knew what she was doing but he didn't quite believe it. In a second she had unfastened the buttons down the front of her blouse, pushed it back, and then slid her bra off her breasts.

She grabbed his hand and held it over one of her breasts.

"Please, Moxie, please make love to me! Pru will never know and I need you right now."

As she said it, the door opened and Ben Mount ran into the room. He was dripping wet. He stopped six feet from the fireplace. All he could see was his best friend, Moxie, and his fiancée sitting close together. Moxie's arm was around Betsy, and his hand fondled her bare breast.

Chapter 15

Ben stared at Moxie's hand on his fiancée's breast with an astonished, unbelieving expression. Then he exploded.

"I'll be a son of a bitch! I'm out there in the pounding rainstorm, soaking wet, worried sick that Betsy got herself lost or kidnapped or raped or something in the dark and the rain. Then I come back and find you all cozy with this guy who used to be my best friend! What the hell is going on? I'll hand it to you, Betsy. You sure don't waste any time bouncing from one man's bed to the next."

Ben spun around, and charged out the front door. He ran into the slashing rain and jumped in the Austin. He had a key. Moxie would have to worry about getting back to the base by himself. He spun the tires on the slippery footing and roared away, just as Moxie opened the door and yelled at him.

Moxie turned and shut the door. Betsy had slumped on the hearth. "Oh, God, what have I done? God, I couldn't have done something like this. He was absolutely livid. He'll never speak to me again. Why did I have to be such a pompous idiot worrying about that whore, Clifford?"

Pru came out of the bathroom, her hair in a towel and wearing a robe. She looked at Betsy crying on the hearth with her shirt open. Then she saw Moxie standing by the table.

"What the hell have you done to her, you animal?" she shouted.

Moxie moved quickly, grabbed Pru's hands, and talked softly to her, urgently.

"Now, don't you go crazy on me too. Lady Clifford was here and must have tried to take Ben away. She got Betsy wild angry and Betsy stormed out of the house. Ben went to find Betsy when it got dark, I guess. Betsy came back and she felt lonely and unloved. *She* opened her blouse. I didn't. Then Ben came in and saw her that way with me sitting beside her and he jumped to conclusions and went absolutely crazy mad and stormed out. Now I want you to calm down and help with things."

Pru understood it in a moment. She kissed Moxie's cheek.

"Sorry, luv. I've got it all." She went to Betsy, pulled her blouse closed, and buttoned it. Then she put her arms around Betsy and talked to her quietly. Pru motioned Moxie to go into the bedroom, and then she hugged Betsy again.

"Now, luv. Tell me all about it. Talk it out and let's see who you want me to shoot."

Betsy looked up and began crying again. Pru lifted her brows and tried another tack.

"Betsy, tell me about it. What happened?"

"I was here and cold and sitting by the fire. Moxie was talking to me, telling me that honestly Ben hadn't been messing around with that lady whore, and then I felt so rejected and unwanted and I opened my top and put Moxie's hand on my breasts and that's when Ben burst into the room. And then he thought . . . ohhh . . ." She cried hysterically.

Pru held her, rocked her back and forth, talking all the time. When Betsy stopped crying, she took a deep breath, sobbed a couple of times, then looked over at Pru.

"Was I a stupid, jealous woman, Pru? Did you see Lady Clifford at that dance Ben took you to?"

"Oh, gawd, but we sure did see her. She was a snippet, a real bad person. I heard her ask Mox where Ben was, but Mox refused to tell the twit."

"God's truth, Pru?"

"Damn right, or I hope to burn in hell."

"Oh, no. Then I've been a fool, a ridiculous, jealous, conceited asshole of a fool."

Pru hugged her again. "Honey, we're all fools about the men we love. How did you know Moxie was a tit man? He goes grapeshot over boobies."

Betsy shook her head. "It wasn't Moxie's doing. Not his fault at all. I just pulled his hand on my breast when . . ."

"Sweet little Yankee girl. You've got nothing to worry about from Mox and me. Hell, he probably enjoyed it, but I'll smack him if he says so. We understand all about it, and we want to help you. We love you."

She turned toward the bedroom. "Moxie Mulford you no-good boobie man. Get out here."

Betsy was surprised at the take-charge manner Pru suddenly exhibited, showing the steel beneath her jolly, calm exterior. Moxie came in, watched the women for a moment, then went over and kissed Betsy on the cheek.

Pru held Betsy's hand and Moxie's. "Now, you two, we've got a problem, a love-life problem, which is the most important kind. Mox, just how mad is Ben, and what can we do to get these two lovely people back together again?"

Chapter 16

Ben drove the Austin back to the base at Fort Blockhouse, and went to the quarters assigned to him months ago. He had kept all his spare clothes and gear there, so he showered and went to bed. He was positive that his relationship with Betsy was over, that there would be no marriage, that there was not even a chance left for friendship.

Just as he was falling asleep, he realized that he should not have bolted out, that he should not have screamed at her. But he was just coming in from an emotional scene with Cayenne Clifford, and then to walk in and see Betsy all exposed that way and Moxie's hands all over her . . .

He rolled over and blocked it out with sleep.

The next morning Ben left the hospital with word that his arm was healing well and that he no longer needed the sling. He went to his office and worked over the top five methods for reducing the German U-boat effectiveness during an Allied invasion of the continent. He still was counting on the landing taking place somewhere in the middle of France. As nearly as he could tell, the closest U-boat pens to that position were in Brest, out on the tip of Brittany. Others were scattered down the coast of France along the Bay of Biscay, but the travel time would be too much from there for a sudden strike.

Ben looked over the list he and Moxie had put together. For a moment he remembered Moxie at the cottage with his hands on Betsy's bare breasts. He shut his eyes and tried to forget. He would deal with Moxie later. He looked back at the paper.

The best methods of reducing U-boat capability to strike against an Allied invasion force:

1. A direct attack by two British submarines at the U-boat pens at Brest, France. Pens are on the broad bay of Brest. Both submarines should lay a hundred yards off the pens and systematically shoot torpedoes directly into the wide open bays, thereby destroying or disabling from ten to twenty U-boats sheltered in the pens. Return submerged out through the Goulet de Brest avoiding pursuit and detection.

2. A three-submarine attack on the pens at Brest. Submarines to approach pens submerged. Surface at pen doors, land twenty fully armed commandos from each submarine. Commandos to occupy the pens from the water side, plant high explosives on each sub in the pens, detonate all charges, infiltrate and return via the submarines and out the straits of Brest to the sea.

3. Utilize an aircraft carrier just off the coast which will launch torpedo planes. Ten to fifteen planes to attack the pens and send torpedoes directly into the pens, destroying the U-boats in the bays.

4. Send a squadron of six motor torpedo boats into the bay to launch torpedoes directly into the pens, destroying the U-boats in the facility.

5. Saturation bombing with ultraheavy bombs in the five-to-ten-ton size to break

through the twenty-six-foot-thick reinforced concrete roofs of the pens.

Ben checked the list again, dropped it off with the WREN in the captain's office, and went down to the wharf to watch the boats. He saw Moxie's *Seawitch* down the line and turned away. The men were working on her topside, but didn't seem to be in any flurry of activity. He looked for a phone.

His first call went to the commander of the U.S. Naval Forces, Atlantic. He got a lieutenant commander in the personnel section.

"Commander, I know your situation, but we've got problems here too. I know you want to be reassigned to the Pacific. Your request has been on my desk ever since you came back from there last year. My hands are banded with steel wire. Admiral Graves must approve your transfer and he says, 'Hell no,' every time we try to send through your request."

"That's what I've heard. I guess I better go over there and chew out an admiral."

"That's the place to start. But knowing Graves, I'd say you better get your teeth sharpened."

"Thanks, Commander."

He hung up and tried Captain White-Johnson. The WREN named Chappie said the captain was out for the day.

Ben adjusted his tie, pulled his hat on, and drove to the first pub he could find. He started with warm British beer, moved on to ale, then to whiskey, and by the time the pub closed, a pair of American ensigns decided they should take the old commander home. They rolled him into his bed, shaking their heads about sailors who couldn't hold their booze.

Ben didn't wake until noon the next day. He was still on leave, officially.

"Betsy, why?" he said out loud. He felt the words

slam against his sensitive head and looked for a Bromo.

Two hours later he went for a morning walk. He glanced down at the *Seawitch,* but her spot along the black pilings was empty.

Ben frowned, went up to his office, and entered slowly. Moxie wasn't there. He sighed with relief, then headed for the captain's office.

"Moxie Mulford. I noticed his boat is gone."

"Yes, Commander Mount. He was ordered on special patrol last night. He came in early this morning and cleared the harbor just an hour ago. He was looking for you and left a message."

Ben took the envelope and hurried back to his office. He tapped the thin square of paper on the desk for a number of seconds before he opened it. He didn't want to, but there was something about a message in a sealed envelope that soon made him want to read it.

It was written in a hurried Moxie scrawl.

Got orders last night to move. On patrol off the coast and I think some probing at coastal defenses. The captain said you weren't authorized for this run when I asked to take you along. Next time.

I'll be gone a couple of weeks, then we'll get this mess at the cottage all straightened out. Just take it easy and don't do anything rash like trying to get transferred. There's a simple explanation for everything. Take care. Moxie.

Ben read it over again and put it in his desk. He stared at the harbor and watched a ship coming into port. Then he sat down at his desk and looked over the other ideas they had for getting at the subs in the pens. At last he went to the officers' club and had lunch. He was not going to get drunk again. That wasn't his style. He'd had his one crock night; that would last him for a while.

Ben tried to call Admiral Graves, but he knew he had to go through Captain White-Johnson first.

"It's a personal matter, Commander."

"That won't help today, the admiral is in London."

Ben thanked him and hung up. He thought about Chappie, the captain's secretary. She was young, and pretty enough, a little heavy. He could take her out to dinner, to the show. He rejected the idea at once. That wouldn't help.

He wondered what Betsy was doing. Working, finishing her shift of putting one gizmo on top of another one to make something she had no understanding of. Then she'd ride a bus out to her cottage.

He wasn't going back there. Anyone so touchy about a former lover and who would fly off the handle that way and make wild accusations . . .

He wandered over to the ship's store, a big PX, and found two good books. "That should keep me busy for at least two or three days," he thought. He looked at the calendar—March 24, 1945. The days would drag now. He had no actual assignment. Tomorrow he would talk to Captain White-Johnson about their U-boat pen ideas, and hopefully the plans would be passed on up the line and eventually get to operations and planning or wherever they went to be approved. The invasion would be a good hit, and Ben just hoped that he would be a part of it.

In the middle of the English Channel, Moxie cruised at periscope depth for a few minutes while he used the sky periscope to check overhead for enemy planes. He had made his mandatory submerged operational check on the *Seawitch,* and now he rose to the surface and moved at ten knots on diesel power toward the coast of France. Somebody was interested in Cherbourg.

In his briefing he was told not to attach undue importance to the area. Almost every potential invasion site and supporting port along the French coast was being checked out, probed, evaluated, and considered.

His section was Cherbourg, and he had a list of orders half a page long. There was one that struck him as odd. He was to see how close he could get to the E-boat pens.

He wondered how they would differ from those of the U-boats? Smaller to hold the German torpedo boats. Cherbourg stuck out into the English Channel with Cap de la Hague on the west and Pointe de Barfleur on the east. Between these were three little towns—Equeurdreville toward the west, and Tourlaville toward the east. Cherbourg lay between them.

He didn't think there was much of a port there, but there must be something. They had a port there, a large port. Moxie had been in there once before the war, but he couldn't remember any details. He looked at the maps and charts and made note of the general layout.

His first assignment was to probe to see if he could find if any submarines were in the port area. It was thought that none were stationed there permanently because there were no huge U-boat pens. Aerial photos had showed no submarines, but camouflage could often fool the cameras.

Moxie cruised to within seven miles of the Cap de la Hague, then submerged and moved ahead at five knots, waiting for the afternoon shadows to lengthen across the water.

A half hour later he asked for the range to landfall.

"One-five-zero-zero meters to landfall, sir."

"At five hundred meters we'll parallel the coast, Mr. Barry."

"Aye, sir."

Moxie spun the periscope, found the point of land, and watched it as they moved closer. Damned routine. A torpedo boat could do this job better. Moxie relaxed. He would do it the best it could be done, that was the important point. "Who knows," he thought, "the damn invasion might even storm right in through Cherbourg."

When they came to the area off Cherbourg, Moxie brought the *Seawitch* to full stop and brought his periscope down to just over the surface of the water.

Moxie concentrated on the eyepiece. He had been to Cherbourg before the war. He remembered now. It was a major port, even though it did not have a large, naturally protected bay or a long river channel. Instead it had two massive man-made breakwaters.

The jetty was more than two miles long, and of massive construction, covering an actual land mass of three thousand, seven hundred acres. The longer arm angled to the west and the shorter one to the east. They formed an extreme obtuse angle pointing northward.

Moxie looked down at his maps and charts again. Both ends of the jetty held a fort and a lighthouse, dark now, of course. The jetty was not just a pile of rocks dumped into the sea. It was six hundred feet wide and built to withstand the pounding of the angry English Channel waves.

To the east the harbor entrance was between the end of the breakwater and the island of Pelee. This eastern entrance was only five hundred meters wide.

The western entrance between the breakwater and

old Fort Chavagnac was a thousand meters wide, and this was where the warships and heavy freighters moved in and out.

Moxie turned the *Seawitch* to run parallel with the breakwater. He could see nothing. Quickly, he checked the charts and found that there were ten fathoms along both sides of the jetty, but that much of the channel into the port was only six to eight fathoms. He guided the submarine around the end of the breakwater and viewed the entrance to the harbor. Nothing, not a ship or scow or warship, was in sight.

There was enough water to enter submerged, but Moxie wasn't sure just how far in he was supposed to go. His prime orders were to avoid contact, not to fire any torpedoes in the harbor or near it, and not to be sighted in the harbor. All in all, he was given an impossible task if he were to find out very much.

The shadows lengthened on shore. He saw little besides fortifications, coastal batteries, antiaircraft positions, and barbed wire. There did not seem to be any nets or underwater obstructions at the main port entrances. He learned that much.

Moxie pondered his orders again. He then moved the sub slowly along the entrance to the harbor, near the breakwater, but instead of turning into the harbor itself, he angled away with the jetty at the far entrance. They passed the darkened lighthouse and went back into the safety of the English Channel.

Moxie made his entries in his log. When darkness came, he surfaced and watched the blacked-out port. Few lights were visible, but across the water he could hear the hum of truck motors and the whir of machinery.

Moxie set up a three-mile patrol just outside the breakwater at Cherbourg. He rode on the surface at eight knots. There was enough light to see a ship of any size trying to slip in or out of Cherbourg. Two lookouts with binoculars scanned the landward side, and Moxie helped them.

They were on station all night. About midnight Moxie turned in for some sleep, but at two A.M. he was shaken awake.

"Target, sir, just moving out of port."

Moxie was on the bridge within thirty seconds. A merchantman, about four thousand tons, a prime target in these slim-picking times, rode low in the water. It had come out of Cherbourg, probably bound for Germany with every kind of war materiel that could be stripped out of France.

The ship was heading northwest for the Straits of Dover, or maybe just Le Havre. It was sure she would jump farther north hidden in darkness and hoped to hopscotch nightly until she got to Germany.

"Target bearing and range!" Moxie called.

The ship's crew was at battle stations.

"Bearing, zero-five-five. Range eight-zero-zero meters."

"Bring her to three-six-zero, both ahead full."

"Aye. Three-six-zero, full ahead."

From the bridge, Moxie watched as their different courses forced them slightly farther apart. That was part of his strategy. He was also slightly ahead of the other craft.

"Mr. Oliver, will you take over for the attack?" Moxie asked.

Victor Oliver, a young lieutenant, had just joined their crew during the past week. This would be his first "hot" torpedo firing.

"Right, sir. After two minutes on this course I would come to zero-five-five, sir, so we would parallel their course."

"It's your boat, Mr. Oliver."

"Come to zero-five-five," Oliver barked.

The ship swung around to the right.

"Range?"

"Range, one-three-zero-zero."

Lieutenant Oliver worked on his calculations.

"Target speed?" Oliver asked.

"Speed, twelve knots."

Lieutenant Oliver again worked with the fruit machine, plotting the relative position of the two craft, their speed, their bearings, and what heading he needed so the direction of the torpedo would intersect the path of the merchantman.

"Bearing and range?" Oliver asked.

Moxie looked at the officer. He was working at it. This would be good for him if he could score.

"Bearing one-zero-five. Range one-one-zero-zero."

"New bearing. Come to zero-seven-eight."

There was a pause. "Coming round to zero-seven-eight, sir. Coming. Mark, at bearing as ordered."

Lieutenant Oliver looked at his skipper. "Sir, the ship is ready to fire, on target. I suggest a salvo of three at five-second intervals."

"Perhaps you should ready the forward torpedo tubes first, Lieutenant Oliver."

The officer colored and turned to the voice tube.

"Prepare forward torpedo room for firing. Flood tubes one, two, and three. Then open outer torpedo tube doors on tubes one, two, and three."

The torpedo tubes were flooded with on-board seawater, then the outer doors were opened. The word came back.

"Forward tubes ready to fire, sir."

"You may fire three on five-second intervals, Mr. Oliver," Moxie said.

"Fire one!" Oliver barked.

The command passed through the ship and she shuddered slightly as a burst of compressed air shot the three-thousand-pound fish into the sea. It churned through the water at forty-five knots on a collision course with the shadow of the Nazi freighter.

"Fire two!" Oliver shouted. Five seconds passed. "Fire three!"

"All fired, all away. Closing torpedo tube doors."

They waited. Someone counted off the seconds. The officers on the bridge watched through glasses. They could not see the wakes of the fish. No bubbles showed. Someone kept up the count into the thirties.

"Too long," someone said.

"No, wait."

The flash came like a million light bulbs popping on at once in a dark room. One column of fire shot straight into the sky about three hundred feet. Fire engulfed the length of the ship in a few seconds. Secondary explosions shook the craft, and then another massive explosion blasted the ship. It burned fiercely and settled in the bow.

For a half hour the boat burned like a giant funeral pyre. Flames licked at the water, lapping up the petroleum that spread in ever-widening circles.

"Mr. Oliver, have the crew come take a look, thirty seconds per man. Move them."

"Aye, sir, in the periscope?"

"Right, Mr. Oliver."

Twenty minutes later there was another explosion, which ripped the boat in half. The bow went down first, then the stern sank, leaving a vast lake of burning fluid that floated on the heavier seawater.

"Poor bastards," Moxie said. "She was carrying petrol. Let's return to station, Mr. Oliver. I rather expect that the hunting is over for the night."

They went back to their routine three- to four-mile circle outside the jetty. Moxie had decided against a run into the harbor. The area was too restricted and too highly fortified to go in without a prize target to make the gamble worthwhile. Moxie maintained his night watch until dawn.

For the next seven days he and the crew worked the same routine, lying off the shore seven miles and watching through the mists for ships. At night they moved in and ran inside the jetty once or twice, then patrolled off shore.

The *Seawitch*'s log showed that they had one shot at a zigzagging freighter of about a thousand tons just before dawn, but missed her on March 31, 1945. A sudden flurry of enemy air action forced the *Seawitch* to dive.

Moxie stood by the forward gun mount watching the dawn. They were ready to go back to their daylight station, seven miles off Cherbourg. There the batteries would be brought up to charge, the men given special sleep time, and double lookouts would be put on all watches.

At noon Moxie put the three-incher crew through a special drill and let them fire two rounds. Then they secured the gun.

A week later Moxie was making his last entry in the log as they steamed into the bay and past Fort Blockhouse—the low, circular stone defenses that had guarded the area for hundreds of years.

As soon as the *Seawitch* had been tied up and the formalities performed, Moxie made a phone call and got permission to grant half his men a three-day leave. Then he walked up to his office, anxious to see Captain White-Johnson and ask about their attack plans on the U-boat pens.

Moxie had done a lot of thinking about Ben in the past two weeks. He hoped he was still around. He hoped that the shock of that fateful night had worn off so they could talk as friends, as adults. Moxie was still worried. He had never seen the Yank so outraged.

He went straight to their office. Moxie had his whole speech prepared and rehearsed, and it was the most convincing argument he could come up with. He was going to tell the truth. He had to win Ben over.

He pushed open the office door and walked into the room. Ben Mount looked up from his desk, his bland expression quickly changing into a frown.

"Oh, God," Moxie thought, "this is going to be a hundred times harder than I figured."

Chapter 17

"Ben, hello. Now before you knock me down or anything, let me tell you exactly what happened back at the cottage two weeks ago. Have you talked to Pru or Betsy?"

Ben shook his head. His lips were a thin tight ridge, his eyes cold, wary, yet there was a hint of softness in them.

"Ben, it was all one huge misunderstanding. Betsy came back just before it started to rain. She'd been walking in the village and back to the playground and evidently she missed seeing you on the way back. She was miserable, cold, and she felt unwanted and unloved. She needed some affection, some reassurance. So I put her in front of the fire and sat down beside her and put my arm around her. We talked a minute and the next thing I knew she had pulled open her blouse, pushed up her bra, and pulled my hand against her breast. Just then you crash into the room. That was it, the sum total of the whole misunderstood ten seconds. She was sobbing and nearly in hysterics after you ran out. It took Pru an hour to get her calmed down. The next day she was tight-lipped and cried when no one was looking."

Moxie stopped a moment. "I know that Lady Clifford was at the cottage while we were gone. Betsy told us. And I absolutely guaranteed Betsy that you hadn't seen the Clifford woman, and that you didn't even know that she was anywhere near Portsmouth. I knew she was here because I talked to her at that dance Pru and I went to. She was the sponsor. She asked me where you were and I said I wouldn't tell her. Lady Clifford got mad and poured champagne punch over my hand and my sleeve. But she must have found out where you were from the Royal Navy. She's got a lot of good connections yet."

He waited again, but Ben just looked at him.

"Ben, I don't know what Betsy is thinking now. I had to leave a day after it all happened, and as I said in my note, I tried to get you signed on my crew, but it had been filled out with some temporaries. And now here we are. Well, damnit, Ben, say something."

Ben had known that Moxie would be arriving that day. He could have been in London, or in his quarters, or out on a long walk. He didn't quite know how he felt about Moxie. He wrestled with it and at last lost. He decided that he owed his long-time friend the chance for his day in court. Ben had spent a lot of time mulling over the whole thing. Betsy had not tried to contact him in the past fortnight. There had been no messages, no telephone calls. Nor had he been out to the cottage or tried to phone the village store to leave a message.

He stood and walked to the window and looked out on the busy harbor.

"Captain White-Johnson wants to see us just as soon as you come in," he said. "It's something about the U-boat pens."

"No, Ben. This is first. Let's get this worked out now. I don't want to lose you as a friend. We've been through too much together. And it's all my fault, Ben. If Pru and I hadn't gone to that damn fancy dance, we'd never have seen that high-class bitch and she wouldn't have tracked you down."

"Moxie, it isn't your fault," Ben said. "It just happened. I've been trying to sort it out. Damn, yes, I was hurt when Betsy thought I lied about seeing Cayenne Clifford. Surprised and stunned too. Then when she got furious and stormed out of the house, it hurt some more. But I figured she'd have her mad, cry a little, and come back and listen to reason."

He walked back to the desk and flopped down in his chair. "After that the whole thing snowballed. I went to look for Betsy and it started to rain. Suddenly there was Lady Clifford driving beside me in her Rolls and offering to get me out of the rain. At first I ignored her, then rain came down in buckets and I crawled into her dry car. Lady Clifford parked and pushed a tit in my mouth just about that fast and had her panties off and tried to fuck me right there in the front seat. It took a hell of a lot of anger and some hatred and then more willpower than I thought I had, but I pushed that luscious body away and charged out into the rain again.

"Then after walking two miles home in that slashing, wind-whipped rain, I come in and find your hand around Betsy's bare breast. It was the capper that blew my stack."

"Lady Clifford hung around?" Moxie asked in surprise. "She even followed you. That bitch! Ben, you've got to believe me that nothing happened between Betsy and me. I'd never start anything like that. And she was angry, mixed up, confused, and suddenly had an urge to be petted, that's all. Then ten seconds after she pulled her blouse open, you came through the door. Don't let one little ridiculous incident like this ruin two people's lives, and end our friendship."

Moxie walked up to Ben and held out his hand. "Hey, am I forgiven? Let's get this all behind us, what do you say? I need you as a friend."

Ben stood and stared hard at Moxie. Then he reached out and grabbed the hand and shook it.

"I believe you, Moxie. Damnit if I don't believe you! I don't know why really, but I want to."

There were tears in Moxie's eyes as he pumped Ben's hand, then slapped him on the shoulder. "Now, this is more like it! I've been scared as hell these past two weeks that something might go wrong, that you'd already be on your way to Hawaii or Guam or somewhere. Christ, but I'm glad I got back in time."

They sat down in their chairs. "That day after you left, Betsy was all broken up. She kept wailing about how stupid she'd been. She said she believed you, that you hadn't been with Cayenne, that you hadn't even known she was in town. She cried more than I've ever seen her. I hope you two will get back together."

Ben's face clouded. "I think that will have to be up to Betsy. She knows where I am. She can get to a phone."

Moxie sighed. "Well, one out of two ain't bad. You said the captain wanted to jaw at us?"

"Right. He's been stalling me for three days now until you got back. Let's go see what he has on his mind."

A few minutes later they sat in Captain White-Johnson's office, and the officer was smiling.

"You two seem to lead charmed lives somehow. I've seen a dozen ideas shot down at this level on those sub pens, but somehow you found a niche. Your first two ideas have been cleared by Admiral Graves, and are now up for consideration by the high command. You know things are gearing up for the big swim across the channel, whenever it comes. Something like this obviously would be an advance raid, to try to cut down on the available subs the Germans could throw at our forces.

"I've seen some figures on the mass of ships, troops,

planes, and even gliders that are going to be used when
we make the big leapfrog across the water. It just can't
be believed. They say if this comes off it will be the
largest amphibious invasion in history. And that's
been a damned long time."

"So we've still got a chance," Ben interrupted.
"What's your guess at the odds for our getting one of
the two raids approved?"

Captain White-Johnson fidgeted in the chair. "Off
the record. You didn't hear this from me. Don't tell
anybody else. Now that Admiral Graves has given it
his approval, I'd say it's a ninety percent chance we'll
get a go-ahead."

"The invasion must be coming up soon," Moxie
said. "What's the date today, April sixth?"

"Right, Moxie. Hell, I don't know when the crossing is coming off. Probably not more than six or eight
people in Ike's Supreme Allied Headquarters know
that. But it's got to be soon. The channel is calmest
these next three months. But almost everything we do
now is pointing toward that big day. It's a chess game
now, isn't it? We move and countermove, and they try
to figure out if it's a fake into the king's row or if
we're really going to bring a queen and bishop in for
a checkmate."

"Captain, I just hope you build me into any plans
for a raid. I'm feeling like an outsider lately. I need
something to do. How about assigning me as exec
officer on Moxie's boat for a while? He's been running
one and two officers short all the time."

"If this plan goes through, Ben, you'll be having a
boat of your own to run. That's true for either plan.
So just relax for a week or so. The Royal Navy and the
Supreme Allied Headquarters do not move fast on
this kind of decision."

Moxie handed in his written report on the patrol,
and the captain nodded. He skimmed it.

"A freighter with petrol?" he asked.

"I thought it was petrol at first. Now I think it was a freighter converted to run as a tanker, and loaded with that new synthetic fuel they've been making. It was lighter than the water and burned hot as Hades."

"Good, good. The brass wanted another check on that breakwater. I don't know why they asked us to do it, but we're not in the new weapons development stage now. Gentlemen, I'll let you know the second I hear anything about that raid."

They saluted, flirted with Chappie at the outer desk, and went back to their office.

"Let me buy you dinner tonight, Ben."

"All right, I could use a good meal."

"I'll serve it up at the cottage," Moxie said.

Ben hesitated, then shook his head. "No. It won't work that way, Moxie. You can't slam us back together. Betsy is an independent woman with a strong mind of her own. If she wants us to get back together, it's up to her to call or send word or something."

Ben shuffled some papers, then brightened. "Now we have that problem out of the way, you're just in time for my workout."

"Workout?"

"Right. If we're going in with the commandos, which is my pick of the two now, I want to be in good condition. Those guys are so hard they have muscles on their muscles. They are like steel. I feel more like clay. So I've been working out every day. You want to try it?"

Moxie shrugged. "Sure, I used to play a damn good game of rugby."

"Good. Get on your shorts and sneakers and we'll go over to that little park the other side of the stream and have at it for a while."

They started with a fifteen-minute regimen of exercises. Moxie soon found that he wasn't in as good shape as he'd thought. Ben slowed the pace of the exercises. After a short rest he jumped up.

"Now, mate, comes the interesting part. A five-mile jog around the park."

"Jog, like running? Are you blowing your tubes, man? I've used up twice the energy I've got already."

"Drop out anytime you want. We'll take it slow for you beginners."

Moxie made it almost two miles before he gave out and sagged onto the grass.

"I'll meet you back at the car," Ben said as he kept running. He picked up the pace a little and grinned back at Moxie. He could do it. He was ready. Running let him think things through. And now he needed to think.

By the time he saw the car with Moxie sitting on the fender, Ben had it all worked out. Betsy did a foolish and cruel thing. He had let her storm off and then gone back to her. Later on he did a stupid thing too by getting so angry. Now it was her turn to come back to him. If she did, it would be a lot like it had been before. Not the same, but much the same. He wasn't sure about marriage now.

He ran up panting and fell against the Austin. When he could talk normally again, he looked up at Moxie.

"Dinner is on me tonight at the officers' club. You get the best dinner and all the wine you can slosh down."

"You're on," Moxie agreed.

The next day they both worked hard. They got the latest marine charts on Brest, the straits getting into the harbor, and the surrounding area.

It was close quarters, but not impossible. They could go in submerged at periscope level and slow enough so there would be little feather. They probably would be in there at night for the attack either way.

Together they spent the day working out every problem they could think of. They devised ways to carry extra torpedoes in the crew quarters of Moxie's sub, and so that it would work in other boats assigned to such a mission. They hoped to have four extra fish below decks.

They would get a new sub that had two external torpedo tubes aft. These could be used by the sub against anyone trying to chase them into the straits.

By the end of the day they had moved a torpedo out of the usual storage area in Moxie's boat and lashed it down in the crew space immediately behind the mess area. The arrangement would work, but they could only safely stow two additional torpedoes there.

The sailors moved the three-thousand-pound fish back into its usual reload area and kept asking questions about what they were doing.

"Research," Moxie told them. "We're simply trying to decide if this boat could take two more torpedoes if it had to, a special emergency load."

It was too late to order Moxie's boat to be refitted with external torpedo tubes on the deck. Some British subs had two external tubes on the bow and two on the stern. Other subs had four external tubes amidships with two facing forward and two facing aft. Ben wasn't exactly sure how they were fired. They would be flooded anytime they were underwater. He suspected that it would be a matter of aiming the submarine and firing the torpedoes with compressed air, the same way the internal bow tubes were fired.

The next morning Ben and Moxie tackled the other problem. What if they had twenty, fully armed, combat-ready commandos to put on board Moxie's ship. Where would they stuff them? How many in each compartment.

"They would have to be able to disembark both at

the bow and stern hatches," Moxie said. "So they should be positioned in those areas."

"We could leave the six reload torpedoes home," Ben suggested. "That would save weight and help give us more maneuvering room."

Again they took a tour of the *Seawitch* and looked over the space. They had already figured their time to Brest, planning it so they would be at the entrance to the straits at the first dark. The discomfort factor wouldn't be severe, and each boat would carry a fully qualified Royal Navy doctor, they hoped.

Later in the day, as they came out of the forward loading hatch, they saw Chappie, the WREN who worked for the captain. She rushed down the dock. Moxie waved and she motioned. The men looked at each other, then ran up the boarding plank to where she stood.

"He wants to see you right away," she said. "From the look on his face I think it's some good news."

Both Ben and Moxie kissed her on the cheek, and they hurried back to the captain's office.

"We must have got a plan approved!" Ben yelped.

"How about both of them approved?" Moxie asked.

"Whichever one, I vote that we take Chappie along on the mission as our engineer," Ben said.

"Not me," she said. "I'm afraid of a half-full bathtub. I don't see how anyone can stand being under the water."

Ben laughed and tapped his head. "You just have to be a little bit crazy."

Captain White-Johnson was ready to pop when they ran into his office.

"Damn, it took you long enough to get here," he said, trying to frown. "We've got it. The head of the Joint Naval Forces has approved the hit on the sub pens!"

"Great!" Ben shouted.

"Which plan?" Moxie asked.

"The commando raid. You'll be bus drivers with a lethal load of expert sappers as your special cargo."

Chapter 18

It was April 8 when they met Major Dustin Varner of the British Commandos. He was six-four, two hundred and twenty pounds, twenty-six years old, and so hard his muscles squeaked when he moved. He looked them over in the captain's office. His eyes glittered, and Ben decided Major Varner was one of those men who did not consider the possibility of his own death. He shook hands all around then looked back at the captain.

"We have two weeks. The raid is set for April twenty-second. Before that we must learn about each other, plan the raid in detail, figure the best way to get in and out of the area. I'll want all my men to be familiar with your boats before we go. Sixty men will not be enough. For a raid like this we're authorized seventy-five men. It's a large area we have to secure. I suggest we get busy. I'll have Captain Engle come to help us set up the raid and work out the details. He'll be my second in command. Is there an office we can use? I'd also like quarters for two of us."

Captain White-Johnson assured him that all of that had been taken care of. Major Varner looked at the two submariners.

"I understand that this raid was the brainchild of you two men. Are you excited about it?"

"Damn right," Ben said.

"Should be effective," Moxie said.

"Good. I also have a rule of never going into an area with a force of this size in the blind. We have intelligence reports and French underground information. However we have decided on an in-person reconnaissance of the pens six days before the raid. I'll want one of the sub commanders to go, taking our sub as close as we can get it, and another of the sub commanders to land and assist in the recon. I'll need him to give me advice about the subs, approaches, et cetera." He took out a detailed chart of the Brest area.

"As you know, this *goulet* is well protected on both sides. But it's over a kilometer wide, and you should have no trouble working up the middle of it at periscope depth. It will be a trial run for the sub commander on our recon. We need a reconnaissance of the facility, and a double-check with our French friends in the underground so we can finalize our French diversion. That's set to take place in front of the pens at the same time we hit them from the bay side. Any questions?"

"What are our chances for success?" Ben asked.

"Commander, we don't take chances. Rather we guarantee success. If we can blow up one, five, ten, or twenty German U-boats in those concrete boxes, it will be one hell of a lot more efficient than trying to chase them down at sea."

Ben grinned. "Major, I've never met a commando before, but I think I'm going to like working with you."

The major stared hard at Ben for a minute, then his face cracked and he smiled. "Hell, Commander, that's good, and I hope it'll be a long friendship, not one shortened by the failure of this mission."

The major, Ben, and Moxie went back to their office and discussed details.

They decided first of all to tour the *Seawitch*.

"Little, isn't she?" the major said. "Can we stuff twenty-five fully armed commandos in here?"

"Easy," Moxie said. "Remember we'll have only a skeleton crew, short trip rations and fuel, and we'll not carry the six forward reload torpedoes. Those six fish alone weigh nine tons. Major, have you ever been in a sub before?"

"Several times. What's your estimation of our running time to Brest?"

"About twelve hours, running on the surface at fourteen knots."

Major Varner led the way back to the office, sat down, and pulled off his tie. "I'm beginning to think you men have done your homework on this one."

"We have, Major. Could you use a beer?" Ben asked.

Major Varner laughed, some of his ultratoughness dissolved. "I think I'm going to like it here. Damn right, bring up a case if you can. It's going to be a long night."

They worked until almost two A.M. putting together the various elements of the plan. Now and then they came to a dead end and had to scratch out the arrangements and start over. But gradually it came into focus and meshed. Ben showed the major the photos and material they had on the U-boat pens at Brest, as well as on some of the others.

"Can we run your boat right up to the entrance of the pens themselves? There must be some concrete platforms where my men can debark."

"We hope so, Major, but we just can't be sure," Moxie said. "We know their subs go in and out of there, so it has to be open and deep enough, but about the footing, the landing areas, we just don't know."

"That's one of the points we'll answer when we take our hike in there," Major Varner said. He popped the cap on a warm beer and tipped it, still looking at the picture of the U-boat pens.

"What are they like inside, do we know?" Varner asked.

"Not much. We don't have any eye-witness reports. We guess that some of the pens are wide enough for U-boats to go in side by side, at least for the VII-C class. But most of the openings at Brest appear to be single width. However, we're sure they are deep enough to allow two subs to be lengthways in each of the slots."

Ben interrupted. "We expect that inside there are concrete platforms along the side of each of the long berths. This would provide working space, areas for retrofit and repair as well as for resupply. Some berths probably are for repair, some for fueling, and so on. We know some of the pens can be drained and used as dry docks, but we don't think the ones in Brest have that capability."

Varner looked at the photo with a magnifying glass. "So each of these doorlike openings could have two to four U-boats behind it?"

"Right. We've counted what we think are twenty separate slots at Brest. Some are double width, but most single. We guess the most U-boats that could be in Brest is forty-eight."

Varner shook his head. "Doubt if they have that many there now. Intelligence says the Nazis have a total of only two hundred subs they can put into action. We understand that they also have a shortage of crews as well as U-boat crew training. But I doubt if they would put twenty-five percent of their whole sub fleet in one location." He scratched his ear. "But if that is the potential, we have to go in with charges for forty subs at least and forty teams to take care of them." He opened another beer and put his feet up on the desk.

"I don't know if you gentlemen understand how we function, but the commandos are special troops in many ways. We all have parachute training, the toughest hand-to-hand training, as well as dozens of specialty areas. Our one biggest asset is speed. We hit a target quickly, do the job, and get out before the Germans wake up to the fact that they have been put out of business. On this mission speed is going to be mandatory. Brest is one of the most heavily fortified ports along the French coast. That means they have a lot of manpower there as well as equipment. There is no possibility that we could hold the inside of the pens for more than five, perhaps six minutes. In that time we must capture the pens, plant our charges, and get the hell out before the Germans break in and before the charges go off.

"Even if we get inside without firing a shot, which is unlikely, that would mean a total engagement time of seven to eight minutes. The Jerries can bring up a thousand troops in ten minutes, and every one of them will be spitting lead of some kind."

He took a long pull on the beer.

"The key is surprise, then fast action and a fast getaway."

"Then you'll want a day or two to run your men in and out of the subs, right?" Moxie asked.

"Yes, and with full packs and their demo loads. Let's say two days. We can work with one sub, or all three. Your other two boats should be assigned today and be on site tomorrow. I spoke with the admiral earlier today." He nodded, then looked at the fuzzy photos of the Brest pens. "The key is to get off and get back on the subs. We can blow up the subs with a waterproof, specially formed charge slapped on the hull at water level. It's magnetic and the fuse can be set easily for ten minutes, or five minutes. But getting to the subs, getting off the trolley, and then getting back on without getting the shit shot out of us is going to be the critical period. Those machine guns on the bow of your boats will be essential."

Ben wanted to ask what machine guns, but he let the major roll.

"Damnit, I wish I knew how much space we have to disembark, two feet or twenty? Can we get from one of the slots to the other on the bay side, or do we have to go to the far end? It's got to be the far end and that involves more time, and more risk. Three subs, twenty doors, so each sub's commandos will take care of three or four slots of subs."

Major Varner sipped his beer. His eyes closed, and Ben decided he was trying to visualize the attack inside the pens. He took out a pencil then and sketched it out, all twenty slots, where the subs would come in and how the men would work.

"Hell, I don't know. My guess is that we'll have to nose our subs right inside the damn sub pen doors, and get the men over the side on the platforms between the berths."

"We better plan on taking along a plank of some kind to use as a gangplank down from the forward hatch," Ben said. "It probably will be too far to jump."

It was just after one A.M. Ben yawned.

"Not yet, Commander. We've got to lay out our straw man schedule. Tomorrow is the ninth of April. We get boats assigned and start making any retrofit we need. You mentioned pulling out the reload torpedoes. I think it might be good to weld or bolt a heavy machine gun tripod on the front of each of the boats. Then one of my men on each boat can rush out a heavy machine gun, mount it, and use it as cover for our landing. Might even have to surface out a ways and get the machine guns going as

we move in, if we get any enemy fire. Looks like
we're going to have to nose right into those pens
themselves."

"Two days for training your men in loading and
unloading?" Moxie asked. "Want that in the last
week?"

"No, sooner. Tomorrow or the next day. We have
our recon set for what, the sixteenth? That's a week
from tomorrow. I'll pick the sub crew to go in and
I'll want one submariner to go along on the recon
hike to give me input on what the subs can and
can't do. I'll make my choices soon."

"Casualties?" Ben asked.

"We'll request a junior medical officer doctor to go
on one of the subs," Varner answered. "Chances are
we'll get three rated medics instead. Doctors are hard
to get on dangerous missions like this. We lose too
many. There should be few if any casualties by the
submariners, unless we run into a big force in the
bay, or if we lose a boat, of course."

"We'll have skeleton crews," Moxie said. "So if
we do lose a boat, the crew and the commando passengers can transfer to either of the other boats with
plenty of room. I figure on taking eighteen men.
Usually I'd have about forty-five, so a second sub
could take on my eighteen crewmen and twenty-five
commandos with no problem for the run home."

"Are those straits going into Brest mined?" Ben
asked.

Major Varner grinned. "That's one of the interesting little factors we'll have to find out on the night
of the sixteenth."

An hour later they quit. The major had been assigned quarters near Ben and Moxie. They agreed to
get back to work at eight thirty the following morning.

Moxie dragged in the next day at nine with a cup

of coffee and glassy eyes. Major Varner and Ben had been working since seven thirty. They had completed a lot more of the planning work. The three men went down to the docks to look over the two new submarines.

One was the *Topflight*, a T-class boat, and the other the *Underworld*, another S-class. The T was larger, two hundred and seventy-three feet long as opposed to the two hundred and seventeen feet for the S-class. The T also carried more torpedoes, with eight twenty-one-inch tubes in the bow and three in the stern. For a moment they considered using only two of the T-class boats, but they changed their minds. They liked the idea of three boats. They liked the backup potential.

The sub commanders were experienced men. Both were lieutenant commanders and each had spent several years as a sub skipper. Lieutenant Commander Roland Rogers, who captained the *Topflight*, was a slight man with a high forehead and light brown hair. He had the looks and style of a professor of ancient literature, but he handled the T-class submarine with easy confidence. Ben liked him at once.

"Hi, Yank. You the bloody hero we've been hearing about? Good to see that you've got only two legs like the rest of us."

They then took a brief tour of the improved T-class boat, which had been launched in 1941. Ben and Moxie were surprised by the amount of space it had inside.

"You're our designated hospital ship if we need one," Major Varner said. "If we have any casualties, we'll meet and transfer them to your craft if it seems reasonable. Oh, we'll all have VHF voice radios, just like the flyboys do, so we'll be able to talk to each other on the surface or whenever our antennas are up. That will help. We'll hope the Jerries aren't monitoring the one band we'll be using."

They moved from the T-class to the smaller S-class boat behind it and began the next tour. The captain of the *Underworld* was Lieutenant Commander Hal Iverson, a short and stocky man who looked like he could be a prize fighter. He also had a perpetual smile. Ben had heard of him before. He was said to be one of the best submarine tacticians in the fleet.

"Hi, Yank. Good to be on board this project. Understand we're going to have a go at some sub pens."

"Right, Commander Iverson, but no heroics. We're just the bus drivers on this job, taking the real fighting troops down to the corner field and back."

"True, true. But then again, Yank, you never know what might happen once we get out there into the thick of it."

After the tour of the *Underworld,* all five of the officers went back to the office. They were given use of a conference room with a long table. Major Varner quickly briefed the sub commanders.

"So, that's about it. Nothing too complicated. We expect some resistance, but just how strong and exactly when, we're not sure. We'll go in on a recon on the sixteenth. If everything checks out, we'll shove off from here on the twenty-second so we can hit the straits out from Brest at first darkness. Are there any questions?"

"Are we to be combat ready all the way?" Rogers asked.

Major Varner pointed to Moxie for an answer. "Almost. We'll be combat ready but only with our loaded torpedoes. At least our S-boats won't have any reload fish. This will cut our weight and give us some additional space for the commandos. We'll also travel with a skeleton crew. Now if the T-class boat doesn't need these precautions, we'll talk about it. The *Top-flight* looks like she has room and speed to spare. But both the S-boats should have this setup for the raid."

Major Varner stood up. "Gentlemen, I suggest you see to your boats. I'd like them stripped and ready for practice loading of your human cargo in four hours. Pick the crew you will use, get rid of extra torpedoes, whatever needs to be done. Commander Mulford said something about stocking only short-cruise stores. I'll let you gentlemen get to work now."

The submarine skippers stood and talked together in low voices as they left. Varner looked over at Ben. "What do you think of the two new men?"

"Both look like good ones. I think we had a lucky draw."

The major snorted. "No such thing as luck, Yank. I put in my order with the admiral for the two best damn sub men he had within five hundred miles. No luck to it. I have a hard job, I demand good men," he said and paused. "You must have figured out by now that I'll be using you on the hike into the pens on our recon. We'll let them run their boats and you can play soldier with me. You know the subs, and besides, I want a man who can take care of himself. I read the report on that sub you captured. You did such a damn good job I thought there for a few minutes that it was me."

They both laughed. Varner sobered.

"So, I want you with me when we check out Brest. I also hear that you're a runner. Good, let's go for a jog."

They ran ten miles. Ben couldn't believe it. He couldn't believe that he had run ten miles, but he was astonished that Major Varner had enough breath to talk almost continuously while they ran. He had continued to plan as though they were sitting around the table. He also had said he liked to run because it seemed to stimulate his mind and he could think more clearly.

After a shower and lunch, Ben still felt as though he had a hole in the pit of his stomach. He mentioned it to the major.

"Trace elements. Your system used up a lot of trace mineral elements in the run that you haven't replaced yet. Water can't do it. Orange juice is the best I've found, but even that isn't right. After twenty miles you really notice that hole. It'll go away in a couple of hours."

"I'll never make twenty," Ben said.

Major Varner brushed aside Ben's remark. "Hell, if you can run ten, you can go twenty. It's mostly mental. Now, about the pens. We'll go in with Moxie's sub, surface, and use a rubber boat to get to a spot where the French underground says it will be safe to land. They will either keep the Nazis away from that place or pull an attack to draw them away from it, so we can get in without being seen. From there on, we move by land to the closest possible area to the pens without being seen. We've got a twenty-power scope we'll use, which should give us some answers about the pens. I'm sure we won't get into the immediate area. That whole land mass must be highly fortified, and it will be crawling with guards. Three of us will go in so we shouldn't have much trouble slipping past them."

"We leave the raft on shore or signal for a pickup?" Ben asked.

"Leave the raft with two Frenchies, then we'll signal when we start moving out."

"I hope it goes as easily as you make it sound."

"It won't. Not one mission I've been on in this war has gone the way it was supposed to. There are a hundred factors that can go wrong. That's why we take care of every goddamned eventuality that we can think of *before* it happens. That's how we cut down the odds. That's how we live to enjoy our retirement."

"So what else can I check now?"

"I just told you."

"I don't have a submarine."

"Then make damn sure nothing can go wrong with the others. Get your ass down there and double-check all three, especially that big one. It looks soft. You've got to stay hard to stay alive, Commander."

Ben went down to the *Underworld* and talked to Captain Iverson.

"Commander Iverson . . ."

"Yank, call me Hal. I'm not that stuffy."

Ben nodded, smiling. "Good. Hal, call me Ben or Yank. The major is running this operation, as you can see. What I'm doing now is looking for any problems. How's it going?"

"Come take a look," Hal said. "Any suggestions that you have, just speak up."

They looked. The reload torpedoes were being pulled out the forward hatch. A pile of food stores lay on the dock awaiting transport.

"Small arms?" Ben asked.

"Sure, a few, issue stuff."

"Has it ever been out of the locker?" Ben asked, then added, "I'd suggest ten Sten guns, machine guns, with plenty of ammo, and a case of hand grenades. Never know when they might come in handy. Also set up some range practice for your men who are designated to handle the Stens. They tend to climb a little, so get in some range time."

"We going in as infantry?" Hal asked.

Ben lifted his brows. "I was damn happy to have both the Sten and the grenades when we needed them. On this raid, who knows what's going to happen. It's better to be ready, and now is the time we try to shortstop all the problems."

They went on through the ship. Ben suggested more medical and first-aid supplies and a stretcher. They figured how they could hang bunks where the reload fish had been.

"Anything we can do to make these commandos happy, comfortable, and eager, we'll do it," Ben said. "This whole mission depends on them."

Hal Iverson agreed. "Just damn glad that I'm not the one to charge into those sub pens," he said. "Anything those commandos want, they'll get it from us."

When Ben looked at the T-class *Topflight* he was again impressed. He'd seen the T-class boats but had never spent much time in one. This sub seemed like a palace compared to the cramped S boats. Ben and the skipper, Lieutenant Commander Roland Rogers, decided they could leave the reload torpedoes in place.

"We've got a complement of five officers and fifty-eight ratings. We can run the boat easily with eighteen men and officers. We'll leave twenty-five men off our crew and let the commandos have their bunks," Rogers said, smiling. "I want to get those boys into the sub pens fat and happy, so the Jerries don't blow us out of the water."

Ben suggested they requisition ten Sten guns, get hand grenades, and then put in some range time. Rogers agreed. Ben also made suggestions for more medical supplies and then continued on to Moxie's ship.

Moxie had done everything Ben had asked the other skippers to do. He had already brought two cases of hand grenades on board and had a Sten gun for every man in his crew. Ben suggested range practice for the men, and Moxie agreed.

"What do you think of our leader, the major?" Ben asked.

Moxie rubbed his chin and looked out across the harbor.

"Damned good man as far as I can see. Anyone who has led the raids and missions he has into France and even one into Germany has to be made of steel. He seems to know his job. I guess we're in the best hands we could ask for."

"I'll tell you what I think after the seventeenth," Ben said.

"So you're the one going on the hike with him."

"True."

"No sub command?"

"Not with you three blokes on board."

"Unhappy?"

"Hell no, I get to play soldier. As I have it figured, I'll be the link from the major to the boats."

"In the attack, will you go in with him?"

"I don't know. We'll just have to wait and see."

Ben walked up the gangplank to the dock and looked back at Moxie. "Hear anything from Pru?"

Moxie nodded. "I phone her every day. She says they both are fine. Betsy is working, eating, living, but not smiling much these days."

Ben sighed. "After this is all over, this raid, we'll see what happens."

Chapter 19

The next day the commandos arrived at the dock precisely at 1000 hours, as ordered. They came in two buses and turned out to be quiet, alert, orderly, and serious young men. Most wore red berets. Ben asked the major why.

"Those men have been blooded, with at least two missions against the enemy. It's a kind of badge of courage. The green berets are for less than two missions. There'll be only ten greens in this group. Six of the men have the Scottish Cunningham plaid beret. Those signify ten missions and still around to brag about it. Those men are team leaders."

"I don't see any rank on the uniforms," Ben said.

Ben looked over at the major. He wore stiff, new green fatigues like the rest of the commandos. They had been camouflaged with irregular blotches of black, brown, and gray. There were no oak leaves on his collar.

"We don't use any insignia of rank in the field, Ben. We don't need it, and the enemy can use that against us. Usually we work in extremely close contact with the enemy."

"I understand," Ben said.

They went down to the dock and watched the commandos fall out. Each had a light backpack, and each carried a forty-five caliber on his web belt. Every man had a first-aid packet, a bayonet, and a Sten gun over his shoulder with the stock folded down. About half the men carried chest packs as well.

"No supplies?" Ben asked. "Is this all they need?"

"Those forty men with chest packs are carrying enough high explosives to blow up half of this base," Major Varner answered. " 'Have you heard of plastique?"

"Heard of it, that's about all."

"It's a new kind of explosive, more powerful than anything we've had before, and it's malleable. You can mold it like soft clay. A quarter pound of it is more powerful than you can imagine. We use it with small timer-detonators. We could give you a demonstration, but we probably won't have time."

The submarines were ready for the drill. Both front and rear hatches were open. However, there was only one gangplank, which was a single two-by-twelve plank twenty feet long. It was the same plank they would land and get back on board with at the sub pens. The three boats had one plank apiece.

A man with a plaid beret stood in front of each group of twenty-five commandos. Ben heard nothing; everyone was at attention. Then he saw a hand signal from the major, and the men ran to the three planks and stepped quickly across them onto the subs. Men moved alternately, forward and aft.

With their heavy packs the commandos seemed to run effortlessly, drop down the hatches like Navy men, and vanish below. When the last man entered, he pulled the hatch down after him and dogged it from inside. When the sixth hatch slammed shut, Major Varner thumbed his stopwatch. He scowled at the time, then made two quick gestures toward the middle sub. A commando came from near the conning tower and rapped on the rear hatch. It opened. He said two words, and the commandos emerged. The men in the other two undersea craft followed suit.

There was no rush. The men came up the hatch, trotted up the plank, and fell into formation. All of this was done in a remarkably short time.

Major Varner walked in front of the three double rows of commandos.

"Not bad for the first time. But we need to cut at least twenty seconds off the boarding time. Remember, this will be no tea-time picnic. Germans will be shooting at your asses, so get them moving on my signal. This time, inside the sub, go directly to your assigned station, area or bunk."

He moved to the side. A dozen seamen had paused along the dock to watch. Major Varner looked at a man who obviously was another officer.

"Captain Engle, would you see that those seamen move on about their duties. If we wanted an audience we would have sold tickets."

A moment later Major Varner gave a motion with his hand and punched the stopwatch. The commandos sprinted forward in close order, went down the planks to the submarines, and vanished down the hatches again.

"How many times will they run this?" Ben asked.

"Ten, maybe twelve. Let's get back to the office and work out the last of the plans for our hike. I've had a signal from France this morning. The partisans will send two people to meet us. They will be a great help."

A few minutes later in the conference room, Major Varner stabbed a finger down on the map.

"Right about here we will meet our French cousins. First we have to sail around Pointe de Portzic. Usually there is a light there, but it's not working now. We'll bear left and stay along the shore as close in as Moxie wants to go. We have charts on the bay along there. We'll come past the White House, and keep moving toward the pens. This is the uncertain part. Along this half-kilometer stretch will be our Frenchie friends. They'll give us a signal with a flashlight. We'll have to be alert. If there's any trouble, or a heavy concentration of guards, they will use a small diversion, such as a fire, to draw off some of them and open up a stretch of beach for us. I'd rather they wouldn't do that, it simply draws too much attention to the general area, and we don't want that."

"How far are we from the pens at that point?"

The finger stabbed again. "We think the facility is here, just a little to the west of the French Naval College. We have several objectives on this recon— to check the straits for mines and hope we get through any that are there, to tie down the exact location of the pens, and to check on fortifications and disembarking areas for our men. If we can complete those tasks, we'll be a leg up on our mission."

"Who else is going in the rubber boat with us?" Ben asked.

"Sergeant Andrews. He's six-six, two hundred forty-five pounds, and he can run thirty-five miles without breathing hard. Best backup man I've ever had. Weapons, hand to hand, tops in all fields. And he can carry out either one of us if we pick up too much lead to walk."

"You're making this hike sound like a barrel of laughs, Major."

"It will be. Had your run yet today?"

"I thought I'd rest up today."

"No way, Commander. Not if you're going in with me. We'll pick up Andrews and go for a few."

"How far? I'm still stiff as hell from yesterday."

"You'll run that out the first mile."

Sergeant Andrews looked about twenty-two. He had short, soft blond hair and a stiff blond mustache that was hard to see from a few feet away. He took Ben's hand firmly and smiled.

"Commander Mount, I've heard a lot about you," he said.

"And I've been hearing about you."

Major Varner snorted. "Enough of this damn back-slapping contest. Get your shorts on, Andrews. We'll meet you here in twenty minutes for a run."

They had run for five miles before Ben had any idea of where they were going. They ran farther and farther away from the base. Suddenly, he remembered the range. It was used by several branches of service, and was thirteen miles out of town in the rolling hills. No way! They couldn't be running out thirteen miles and then turning around and running back thirteen more!

Ben felt as if his lungs were pushing out of his throat with each breath, but they made it to the gates of the range. Ben had no ID, but Major Varner produced a celluloid-encased card, and the guard snapped to attention.

"Yes, sir, Major Varner. Everything is set up. That's your jeep right over there, sir."

Varner returned the salute, walked over to the jeep, and sat in the passenger's side.

"Come on, you goldbricks. We've only got so long on the range. Let's not waste it."

Ben jumped in the back, and Andrews sat in the driver's position. He gunned down the road in the direction the major pointed. When they stopped a mile from the gate, Ben saw that indeed everything was set up. A three-quarter-ton truck had backed up to a folding table. On the table were a variety of hand weapons. Targets stood fifty and a hundred yards downrange, poking up from behind solid earth mounds.

"Some familiarization for you, Commander. First the Sten. I understand you can use one. This type is a little different, it's fully silenced. We'll each be carrying one of these on our hike into France."

For the next hour Andrews demonstrated. Ben then fired two dozen different weapons, both Allied and Nazi types as well as a few Russian automatic burp guns. They had a contest to see who could throw a live grenade the farthest. Surprising himself, Ben won.

With the sniper rifle, Andrews, standing offhand, placed twelve shots in a row in the hundred-yard target. Ben tried the same position and got one bull's-eye. The last weapon was a thirty caliber heavy machine gun that sat on a tripod.

"Ever shot one of these, sir?" Andrews asked.

Ben said he hadn't, and was given instructions on how to load and charge a belt of ammunition and how to set the small green box so that the rounds would feed in automatically without an assistant gunner.

"I might leave you on the deck with a thirty heavy to cover us going in and coming out," the major said. "But I'd also like to have you on a radio. We would have a radio operator with us but the signals won't penetrate those damned cement and steel bunkers, so that's out."

Ben squeezed off three- and five-round bursts on the machine gun. He learned how to traverse the weapon and fire again. Then he tried it for a moment in free movement.

"Try that fifty-yard target with it on freewheeling, sir," Andrews said.

Ben squeezed off five five-round bursts and missed the big target with all twenty-five shots. He could see the tracers going all over the place.

"The machine gun is best utilized in the locked and traversing position," Andrews said.

Major Varner checked his watch. "That's it. Let's move out."

They drove back to the gate, the major waved at the guard, and they passed straight through.

Ben shouted with delight. "I was afraid we were going to run all the way back to the Blockhouse."

Major Varner shook his head. "I push my men, but I never work them to death. You aren't ready for twenty-six miles yet, Mount, but you will be before we go in on the twenty-second."

Ben ran every day for the next four days. He slept in on the morning of the sixteenth until eight A.M., had a big breakfast, then went for the final briefing at nine. Captain White-Johnson was there, as well as Ben, Moxie, Major Varner, and Sergeant Andrews.

"We don't have much more to do," Major Varner said. "Moxie, your boat is ready. We'll leave here at ten A.M. That gives us twelve hours to get to the straits, and then two more hours to position ourselves along the Brest bayfront. Any questions?"

There were none.

"Gentlemen, I invite you to board the *Seawitch* at any time," Moxie said. "We'll cast off all lines in about fifteen minutes."

Ben wore a set of commando camouflaged fatigues, as well as high lace jump boots with a knife scabbard on the right side. The blade was six inches long, thin, and could kill a man at any number of points on the body.

Ben, Varner, and Andrews had a short meeting and discussed exactly what they would do in the rubber boat. They carried no packs, only Sten guns with full silencers, forty-five-caliber pistol on the belt, four grenades each in the high pockets, and other assorted goods including penlights.

"Might be hard, Mount, but I suggest that you have a nap. Makes the time go faster and it will keep up your strength. We'll have a good meal at five this afternoon."

Ben nodded and left. He found the bunk assigned to him. It was Moxie's, in the skipper's cabin.

Before he went to sleep, he lay on the bunk listening to the undersea craft and making note the life-sounds of the cocoon of steel while it charged along on the surface of the Atlantic. He knew they were making fourteen knots. He could tell by the hum of the contented diesels aft. He heard a murmur of voices as the men went about their normal routine of surface running. He heard boots going up the rungs of the ladder into the conning tower to the bridge. He felt at peace, at home on the sea. Then he closed his eyes and went to sleep.

The five P.M. meal was just finished. The *Seawitch* had dropped to periscope level and begun a cautious approach around the point of French soil called Minou. The mouth of the straits of Brest was almost two kilometers wide, and Moxie was in the middle of it aiming his boat up the Goulet de Brest at four knots. He sweated at the scope. He felt blind. The night was too damn dark. He checked the skyscope and could find no moon, no stars. Clouds?

"All stop!" Moxie barked.

"All stop, sir."

He looked around the control room, found Ben leaning against the rungs to the tower ladder, and motioned. "Take a look at this."

Ben stared into the night lens.

"Look at what?" he asked.

"That's the trouble. I can't see anything, not even a shadow of the shore. We're going to go up with the control tower out of water, the decks awash. Be a larger target that way, but at least I can see from the bridge where the hell we're going."

Ben nodded. Moxie gave the orders. The *Seawitch* lifted gradually until they could hear the bridge and the control tower break the surface. Ben moved to the tower ladder and unlocked the first hatch.

"Decks awash sir," a sailor reported.

Moxie climbed through and onto the bridge. He checked to his right and then left. Now at least he could see the faint, dark shapes of the shore on both sides but he was still in the middle of the straits. There was nothing ahead but a lighter shade of blackness. Moxie checked the flow of water around the *Seawitch*. She was too high.

"Drop us down two feet," he whispered into the voice tube. "We're showing too much for decency up here."

Ben climbed up beside him.

"Now, if we just don't run into half the U-boat flotilla heading outbound from the sub pens, we should be all right."

Moxie looked over at him and lifted his brows. "Thanks for the encouragement, buddy." He was sweating. He increased his speed to six knots and crept along, trying to stay in the center of the straits. Although the straits had narrowed to less than a kilometer, there was still plenty of room.

By eleven thirty Moxie saw what he thought was the blacked-out lighthouse he was looking for. "It has to be Pointe de Portzic," he said. "Send Major Varner to the bridge," he called into the voice tube.

The major used his twenty-power scope, which was sixteen inches long and looked like a junior telescope. Varner studied the area for several seconds.

"Yes, that's the point. Now work in closer to that

side and come around the point and close in toward the shore. Our French contacts can be anywhere along here, so let's keep a sharp lookout."

Moxie slowed the *Seawitch* to four knots, still running it on the electric motors, and edged along as close to shore as he could. It was six to eight fathoms to within fifty meters of the shore. They crept ahead.

Ben could see little even with his binoculars. They moved closer.

"A hundred yards to landfall," Moxie said. "I'm not going any closer than that until I have to."

They inched along. Suddenly, Moxie felt a new force.

"The tide is changing," he said. "It's going out, we're just past flood tide. I don't know if that helps us or not."

"It will be going out when we leave," Ben said.

They all watched the shadowy shore. The White House landmark slid by. The shore swept inward, and Moxie turned the boat in with it.

"It's eleven fifty," Ben said, reading the glowing hands on his wristwatch. "Anytime now."

Nothing happened.

"We've been stood up," Ben said at ten minutes past twelve.

"We'll give them another twenty minutes," Varner said. "Then we make a return sweep along this half kilometer."

At twelve thirty Ben thought he saw something on the dark shore. Then he saw it again.

"I've got it," Ben said. "Bearing almost ninety degrees. Three flashes, pause, two flashes, pause, three flashes. That's it."

"I saw it too," Varner said. "That's the correct recognition signal. We're okay to land. Stop this thing, Moxie, or put us in closer, your choice."

Moxie stopped the boat. "Let's surface and trim

out," he quietly ordered through the tube. Below the order was passed and the *Seawitch* gently rose to the surface and trimmed.

Ben and Major Varner had left the bridge as soon as they saw the light signal. They hurried aft to the hatch, pulled on jackets and waited with two folded rubber boats. Sergeant Andrews joined them.

"Open aft hatch."

A seaman on the ladder spun the handle, lifted the hatch, and leaped onto deck. He took the first rubber boat passed up and opened it, then popped the inflating valve and watched it billow out to full size. He stowed a reserve boat inside the first one. A second seaman with a Sten gun came topside and faced the shore. Then Varner, Ben, and Andrews climbed up on deck.

Word filtered up from below. The *Seawitch* would move in closer, to a point about seventy-five meters off the shore. Moxie checked for a sighting point he could use to return the boat to the same spot. The plans were fluid. If the raiding party had no pursuit, they would try to get back to the same position. The French would leave a man and give a signal every five minutes.

"Put the boat into the water," Moxie ordered.

The seamen pushed the boat off the stern into the water, and the three men climbed into it and stayed low—just as they had practiced in Portsmouth.

"Good luck!" Moxie whispered, and the three men headed for the shore.

The paddles dipped and pulled the water noiselessly. There was a slight swell, but nothing they couldn't manage.

Ben thought the fifty meters he had rowed to the German U-boat were miles, but this seventy-five meters seemed like a trip around the world. No one spoke.

They dipped and pulled the oars. Ben looked up from the crest of a swell and saw the blinking lights from the shore. He rowed harder.

They came to land fifty meters down-tide from the lights. The French had seen them. Ben jumped into a foot of water and pulled the boat forward. Then they all jumped out and ran, pulling the black rubber up the shore toward a ten-foot-high pile of rocks. Someone ran toward them, and Ben raised his silenced Sten gun.

"Here, we are over here," someone called softly in English with a heavy French accent.

Ben and Major Varner dove into the dry sand and waited. Andrews was in the sand as well, but facing the other direction.

"We are friends," Major Varner called softly with the recognition phrase.

"And we will help our friends," replied the man. It was the correct countersign in the same French-accented English.

Major Varner started to move. Ben touched his shoulder.

"It isn't right. I don't know why, but it isn't right. I don't like it."

"They don't want us to shoot them thinking they are Germans," Major Varner said. He started to get up, but Ben pulled him down.

"Second password," Ben said less softly. "Who sleeps with Maggie?"

There was a stunned silence. A fluttering of soft French came back. Then the same voice in fractured English replied. "Who sleeps Maggie? Who is Maggie? Husband sleeps her. We only one password. Come, we have far to go."

Varner grabbed Ben's shoulder. "They have no idea where we are going. Standard procedure with the underground."

Ben motioned and all three men moved to the protection of the rocks. Everything was quiet.

"My friends. Do not fear. Everything is right. Just because I do not know this Maggie, and who beds her . . ."

As the voice came to the last word, three hand grenades exploded with a shattering roar on the spot where Ben, Varner, and Andrews had been lying.

Chapter 20

Ben and his two companions raised their guns and stitched silent deadly patterns in the sand on either side of the place the French voice came from. Someone screamed, and Ben threw two grenades. Andrews did the same thing, and the four blasts shattered the night air again.

"We have infrared night scopes on our silenced weapons. We can see every move you make. Don't anyone lift a finger or you'll be riddled. First, lay down your weapons, stand, and walk toward my voice," Ben yelled.

For a moment there was no sound.

"You have ten seconds before we start firing again."

The three allies had split so that there were ten yards between them as they faced the sandy beach and the unseen enemy.

"No shoot!" someone called. They saw a shadow emerge from the mists. The figure held a submachine gun and quickly brought it up to fire. Ben sent five slugs into the German's uniformed chest, slamming him backward into hell.

They waited two minutes. Nothing else happened. Varner waved his hand forward, and they moved cautiously, fingers ready on triggers. They found two dead Germans in Army uniforms. To the side they found a third man. He had been tortured, seemingly for some time. He was dead. The civilian was elderly, perhaps sixty, with a Van Dyke beard.

Ben searched the Frenchman but found no papers. They held a conference.

"Three-man patrol of Nazis probably caught the man on the beach, found his flashlight, and tortured him until he talked," Varner said. "Then when they knew we were coming in, they set a trap for us. It probably happened so late that they couldn't send word back or get any more men. At least we have to assume that, otherwise we bug out for Moxie's boat right now."

"Would the French underground send out one man on a mission like this?" Ben asked.

Varner shook his head. "No, at least two." He gave a call, some kind of lonely bird whistle, into the slight breeze. He gave it again. "It's the sea tern," Varner said. "A second recognition signal." He made the call again, waited, and then made it once more.

From inland they heard the call repeated once, faintly.

"Underground," Varner said. "We set it up for this mission only. They have to be friendly Frenchmen. But they might have some deadly Germans with them. And after our small war out here, they will be ready."

They moved cautiously, ten yards apart. Varner in the middle made the call again, one time. The answer came from behind a small sand dune fifty meters inland. They went around it in a rush from both sides, their Sten guns at the ready, fingers on triggers.

At the back of the dune a girl sat leaning against the mound. She was tied, both hands and feet.

Varner dropped down beside her and cut her bindings loose. He talked with her in fluent French for a moment.

"Pierre?" she asked.

Ben and Andrews stood on either side of her, each facing away, with the Sten guns pointing outward.

Varner switched to English. "I'm sorry, the Frenchman on the beach is dead. Tortured."

The girl brushed back silent tears, and blinked.

"Your party, any wounded? Any dead?"

"No, no casualties. I'm Major Varner, commandos. This is Ben and Andrews."

She nodded to them. "I'm Lilette. I'm glad you're all safe."

"About Pierre, we can't leave him on the beach. Where can we take him for you?"

She rubbed tears away again. "Up this way, about three hundred meters. We can leave him hidden."

Varner pointed at Andrews. Andrews jumped up and ran back the way they had come. As they waited, Varner talked with the girl.

"How far are the submarine pens?" he asked.

"Yes, the pens," she said. "I thought it would be about them. They are over a kilometer away. Many guards, a big facility."

"Have any of your people been inside them?"

"Yes, before to build them, Henri was there, but now he is dead, we think. He was the only one left. They have excellent security."

"How close can we get to them, on the bay side?" Ben asked.

The girl looked up at him, and in a sudden splash of moonlight he saw that she was tiny and thin, but with a fierce look of determination on her pretty face.

"Close? Barbed wire, fences, a hundred meters."

"Good," Varner said. "That will be fine. Can you take us there now?"

"Yes. This was Pierre's section, he knew it best, but I can do it."

"How did the Germans catch you?" Ben asked.

"Pierre had one of his bad spells. Sometimes his heart is weak and for a few minutes he can't walk. We were crossing the road in the forbidden zone and it hit him. I couldn't carry him and the patrol came. I couldn't leave Pierre alone, so I told them he was ill and I was taking him home the shortest way. They could see he was sick, but they didn't believe me. So they started to slice him with a razor, and then . . ."

Major Varner made a sound low in his throat. "And when he broke and told them why you were here, they took him with them to the beach for more questioning and to lay out the trap. They were saving you for later."

"Yes. After it was over they would have raped me and then taken me to the Gestapo. They are all dead, *non?*"

"Yes, and we almost were. Ben tripped them up." Varner turned to Ben. "By the way, who does sleep with Maggie?"

The French girl laughed. "*Oui,* I know that. It is Jiggs. The Maggie and Jiggs funny papers in America, *non?*"

"Comics? Funny papers? Ben, how would a Frenchman know that?" Varner asked.

"I didn't expect him to, I just wanted to hear him talk a little more. There was something wrong about the voice. Then I caught it. We had a neighbor who had come from Germany. He had a lilt, a rhythm to his words, and I thought I heard it in the way the guy spoke. I had to hear him talk some more."

"We have American newspapers in underground," Lilette said. "I like to read about Maggie and Jiggs."

"I'll damn well remember Maggie and Jiggs from now on," Varner said.

A noise came from behind them, and Ben spun around, his Sten gun ready.

"*Seawitch*," Andrews said softly. Ben lowered his weapon as the Englishman came into sight with the small Frenchman draped over his shoulders in a fireman's carry.

"Poor Pierre," Lilette said, touching his hand, then kissing it. "He was almost seventy, and he hated the Germans." She wiped her silent tears again. "*Bon, we should go.* This *Seawitch* will be our password. But we must stay together."

Andrews handed a German submachine gun and two spare magazines of ammunition to Lilette. She took them, made sure the weapon was charged and ready to fire, then slung it over her shoulder and led the line of march. She went northwest toward Brest, following the edge of the bay and staying between the soft sand and the hard-surfaced roadway to their left.

After a few hundred meters the girl dropped into the sand in foot-high dune grass. The others followed her example. A minute later a vehicle with its lights masked to small slits ground down the road. The occasional beam of a searchlight swept the grass and sand between the road and the bay. The light passed over them. They waited until the rig was well down the road.

"*Vite! Vite!* We must hurry now," Lilette said.

A short way ahead they came to a ditch that emptied into a culvert under the road.

"We will leave Pierre here," she said. "I will send someone soon to take him for burial. No questions will be asked. He was an old man and of no use to the Germans. All of Brest will soon know of his heroism."

When Pierre's body had been put on the dry culvert, they talked quietly for a moment.

"The patrol will be missed," Lilette said. "They will send out another patrol to find it."

Andrews smiled in the dimness. "I launched the three Germans into the water. With the tide going out, they could be halfway to the Atlantic before they touch ground again."

Lilette smiled at him. "Andrews, you are smarter than all the rest of us. Good. The sub base is perhaps a kilometer ahead. Not far. But there is a roadblock and a fence this side of it."

"We do not wish to make contact with any more Germans if possible," Varner said. "We don't want them to know we've been here."

"Yes, I understand," she said and thought a moment. "Let's move up closer to the road and the fence, then I will decide. The fence is maybe half a kilometer from this end of the submarine base."

Lilette led the way, and Andrews covered the rear. The moon came out from behind a cloud and Lilette sank to the ground, motioning the others to do the same. They waited five minutes for the clouds to darken the light of the nearly full moon.

As they came closer to the roadblock, Lilette took them closer to the bay. They walked along the edge of the wet sand. She cautioned them, then climbed a thirty-foot-high sand dune and knelt down.

"From here we can see," she said. The men climbed up and stared through the tough sand grass.

At first Ben saw little. Then, as he concentrated, he made out the dim outline of a small building beside the tarmac road fifty meters ahead. There was an entryway through the gate, with a wooden barricade that was lifted by hand with a counterbalance. On a six-foot platform at the near side he saw a heavy-duty machine gun mounted and ready to use.

Major Varner had opened his leather tube and extracted his twenty-power scope. He studied the fence. "Some kind of heavy wire mesh. No chance to cut through it. Barbed wire on top. Little chance of going over it without making too much noise."

Lilette stared at Ben, who lay beside her. "How important is it that you get closer to the submarines?"

Ben looked at Varner.

"Tell her."

"Yes, it's vital. We have to know as much about them as we possibly can. We especially want to see the entrances, and if there are any dividers, landing platforms, any structures of that sort."

She nodded, her eyes closed for a moment. "All right, you don't have to say more. We have a hole in the fence the Germans don't know about. We use it only for escapes, for saving lives. But this is important enough. We shall go through in fifteen minutes. That's when the Germans change the guard at the roadblock. They are not as watchful then."

The time showed 0130 on Ben's watch. They had been in France for a little over an hour.

As they waited, Varner continued to study the fence and the German roadblock at the gate.

Lilette turned toward Ben. "You are the American, *non*? We hope that soon many Americans will come with the English and you will land on France and drive the Germans back to Berlin."

Ben nodded. "Everyone knows that there is going to be an invasion. My guess is that it will be in France somewhere. Not out here, closer to England. But I don't know where or when. Just wish I did." He smiled. "Can you really use that submachine gun you're carrying? You look so young."

"I am not young, Ben. I have been fighting the Germans for five years. I am nearly eighteen. Yes, I am a woman. Yes, the Germans have raped me. You English and Americans always wonder. I am French, it does not embarrass me. But I say quickly that I killed four of the seven Germans who raped me. I killed them with their own pistols or knives. When a man is at the peak of sexual fulfillment he is weak, do you not agree?"

"I suppose you're right. I've never thought about it that way, or had to defend myself then."

She smiled. "You are very nice. I will kiss you before you leave, but there will be no time for making love. It is a shame. You are a fine and gentle man. I have learned to decide quickly. Life must be lived moment by moment in my land." She touched his cheek and smiled.

"Someone is coming," Varner said.

She looked. "The guards come to change. They're early tonight."

A vehicle pulled up to the gate. The gate was fifty meters to their left. The fence extended in front of them twenty meters away, and continued to the right well into the water. The wire was higher at the water's edge.

"Come," Lilette said. She led them toward the water and out of sight of the gate. At one small dune she stopped.

"The hole is a slice of the wire along one of the steel posts. A small bush is growing beside it. I will bend the wire inward. Be careful not to harm the shrub. The last person through should push the flap of wire back in place by the post, *oui*?"

They nodded and she moved ahead, crouching low for ten meters, then dropping to her hands and knees and crawling forward. It took her a moment to open the wire. No alarms went off, nothing happened.

Major Varner hurried after her and went through the fence. Ben was next. Behind him came Andrews, who pushed the wire back in place.

Lilette motioned them forward, crawling again. They had just slid behind the first small sand dune when a roving vehicle splashed the fence line with a shaft of bright yellow light. It snapped off a few seconds later.

"*Mon Dieu!*" Lilette said. "Never has it been so close. A few seconds earlier and they would have seen us."

She led them out again. They moved inland, and she pointed out a silent craft in the bay that moved without running lights—a ghost patrol craft of some sort. Varner frowned when he saw it. That one could be trouble.

They moved faster through the center of the dune area. The sand seemed to get firmer, and soon they came to the last remnant of the dunes. There was a small knoll not a hundred meters from a high wire-mesh fence with barbed-wire coils on the top. Just beyond it loomed a huge structure. In the moonlight it had a ghostly gray color—concrete.

A searchlight swept the fence every few seconds. The hummock they were on was just out of reach of the finger of light.

"Best I can do," Lilette said.

Varner looked at the end of the submarine pens. They were almost even with the front of it.

"Could we get farther out, more toward the water?" Varner asked.

She said yes and moved toward the bay, but in doing so they lost the height of the hill. Varner was satisfied. He lay flat in the soft sand and aimed his twenty power scope at the dark doorways of the Brest submarine pens.

"The one on this end says twenty-two. It's painted on the wall," Varner said. "That must mean there are twenty-two of them. Come on, moon, break through again."

He checked the fronts of the pens. "Looks like some kind of mechanical bumpers, maybe hydraulically activated. Instead of pilings that give way when you bump against them. This looks like it does the same thing. It's a divider between the openings of the pens."

"Yes, a safety bumper. How big is it?"

"Not big enough. I don't see any kind of platform out front. None at all. It's like a wall, those damn doors, all in a line, and the little bumpers. Not a damned place where we could put ashore our seventy-five, without nosing into the pens themselves."

"Maybe at the other end," Ben suggested.

"But we can't see the other end, and we have no way to get down there. We have to go with what we've got."

"So we come straight in, clear the way with the heavy thirty, and maybe a few rounds from the three-inchers," Ben said.

"Might have an idea there."

The light swung around again, and they ducked behind the three feet of sand that hid them.

"Damn, I'd like to get closer," Varner muttered.

"And I'd like to be in London," Lilette said. "But you can't get any closer without getting killed, and I have to stay in France."

"Come back with us," Ben said. "We have plenty of room. Ever taken a ride in a submarine?"

"No." She leaned over and kissed Ben's cheek. "But thank you for asking. When the invasion comes, all the French underground members have definite jobs to do, even if the landing is up in Calais, or Le Havre, or somewhere else. We have jobs to do. I must stay here and fight for France."

Varner handed the scope to Ben. "See if you can find anything out there I missed."

Ben studied the closest opening. It looked like a mass of gray on another of black, but gradually he was able to make out the bumpers Varner had spoken of. He thought they might be spring loaded, but they were not big enough to be of any use in landing. If it were daylight, he would have been able to see right into the end of the slot. But if it were daylight, his ass would be shot full of holes. He looked to the far end but could see nothing. The pens had to be at least a quarter of a kilometer long.

"Nothing new," Ben said.

Varner thumped the sand with his fist. "All right. Lilette, we go on the principle that if a person does not know something that person can't have the answer tortured out of him. We want you to know something of what we're doing, but not all of it. That's not because we don't trust you, it's because we know how brutal the Germans can be during interrogation.

"What we want is some kind of a diversion from you. We'll want it at the French Naval College, or as close as you can get to the sub pens. What we need you to do is tie up a lot of Germans so they won't have time to come see what we're up to at the sub pens. If you can even divide some of their forces, that will help. A large fire would be good. Most of this area is going to be devastated anyway during the coming fighting. If you could burn down a warehouse, or the German officers' quarters, or a big supply dump, it would be most helpful."

"When?" Lilette asked.

"That's one of those things you can't know yet. We'll get word to you twenty-four hours before we need it done. Time enough?"

She nodded.

"That's it. I'm ready to go home, anybody with me?"

They went back the way they had come, got through the fence with no trouble, and fixed it so it looked normal. Then they went back to the spot where they had come ashore. They sent Lilette home. She kissed each of them good-bye, wished them a safe trip, and vanished into the French night.

Ben led the trio as they neared the high dune where Lilette had been tied. They were spread out in the best combat fashion, ten meters apart, so no one grenade could kill them all.

For five minutes they flashed their lights at the bay —two shorts, two longs, one short. There was no response.

The three moved up another fifty meters. They hid in the sand dunes just in back of the pile of rocks where they had left the rubber boat. They listened— wind, the slosh and pounding of the small waves on the shore, a cry of a night bird, a cough. Ben frowned. Had it been a cough? He moved like a shadow to where Varner lay.

"Did you hear a cough?" he asked in a whisper.

Varner nodded. He pointed below them to the left. There through the twenty-power scope Ben saw a German lying behind a smaller dune, his rifle pointing at the rock pile. Quickly Ben searched and found a second man, almost directly in front of them. A third one was hunkered down to the right. They had set an ambush around the rockpile where they must have found the rubber raft.

Varner pointed to Ben, drew his boot knife, and motioned to the man on the left. Varner indicated he would take the one in front. Ben could see Andrews moving up on the German on the right.

"We can't risk using the silencers this time," Varner said. "We don't want any stray patrols coming to investigate. Use your knife. Let's move out now. After you take care of him, come to the rocks."

Varner pushed away and started around the dune. Ben stared at his knife, then moved ahead. It had to be done, and done this way. He lost sight of Varner, then concentrated on his own route. He would come up just to the left of the man, surge over the top of the small rise, and dive on him. It was the safest way. He moved quietly, got his bearings, and moved again. He worked up silently to the top of the eight-foot pile of sand. The German was on the other side.

Ben drew his knife and held it in one hand. He laid his Sten gun down, careful to keep the muzzle out of the sand. He didn't like to use a knife, never had. He held it tightly and looked over the dune. The German was just below. He had clasped his hands behind his head and lay on his back. He was sleeping!

Ben sucked in a deep breath, then went over the top of the dune. He took two long running steps downward and lunged at the German. The knife blade went in just below the ribs and Ben tried to pull it upward. Suddenly the man below surged against him, struggling with powerful, strong arms. Ben thrust the knife upward again, then ripped it sideways. The arms around him relaxed and fell away. Blood surged from the German's mouth and Ben smelled a potent stench as the dead man's bowels emptied.

Ben rolled to one side, the bloody knife still in his hand. He knew he was going to throw up. His stomach ground and the bile pumped into it. Before he could turn his head the fluid flew from his mouth and his back arched. He couldn't stop. He gagged and vomited until there was nothing left in his stomach, then he rolled over in the sand and tried to stand. Something was in his hand.

He looked down, saw the knife with blood still dripping from it, and threw it toward the bay.

He gasped for clean air, then shook his head and staggered toward the pile of rocks. By the time he got there he could walk normally. The other two were there.

"Is he dead?" Varner asked.

Ben nodded.

"Good, now go back and get your Sten gun, we don't want the Germans to know about this silenced model. Rush it."

Ben turned and ran back to the top of the dune. He avoided looking at the dead German, picked up the Sten, and ran back to the rocks.

At last he could breathe normally. At the rocks he saw that the raft had been slashed to black strips of rubber. Varner checked the pile and found the second folded-up life raft they had brought. He pulled it out and opened it.

Andrews was steadily sending out his dots and dashes of light to attract the submarine.

Varner popped the package open and hit the valve, and a moment later the rubber life raft billowed into shape. They ran with the boat to the edge of the water and waited. Andrews kept up his flashes. Still, they waited. The water sloshed over the tops of Ben's jump boots. He bent and washed his face with the salt water. It felt good, but he didn't feel clean. The stench of vomit clung to him. He was sure the others noticed it, but they didn't say anything.

Five minutes they stood, taking turns signaling.

Then Varner saw the three flashes of light.

"To the left a little, yes, there she is!" Varner said. "What a beautiful little *Seawitch* she is."

Twenty minutes later all three were back on board the submarine, and heading out toward the open sea. The men changed into dry clothes and sat in the officers' wardroom, sipping at a ration of the captain's grog.

Moxie joined them.

"How did it go? Did you find out what we need to know?" he asked.

Andrews motioned to the major. The major looked at Ben.

"Yes, we found out what we wanted to know. There are no landing platforms at Brest, we violate those pens with the bows of our submarines if we want to rape her. And there will be French Resistance and underground help."

"So it was a successful trip, a good recon, right?"

Ben looked at Moxie but couldn't speak. Finally, he sighed. "Yeah, it was just lovely." He got up and went topside to the bridge and the fresh air.

Moxie looked at Major Varner.

"What happened to Ben out there tonight?"

"He earned his red beret—one for going in and one coming out. He'll tell you about it when he's ready. It's never pleasant the first time you kill a man with a knife, and you're so close you watch his eyes turn cold, see him sag away from your blade, hear his death rattle. He'll tell you about it when he's ready."

Chapter 21

The last two days before the raid were hectic. There seemed to be so many things to do. The commandos had to go through their drills of embarking and debarking from the submarines under a stopwatch again. Stores had to be carefully inspected and reduced. Even the T-class boat had to cut stores to lighten the ship so she was ready in case she were needed for hospital work.

Ben did not go to the cottage. He wanted the raid on the pens to be over first, then if he were still around, there would be time enough. He stayed in the quarters on the base. Once he took out the red beret and the official commendation he had won for the recon. He tried on the beret. He couldn't wear it with his uniform. It did look a little rakish.

Soon it was the twenty-first of April, 1944. They were to sail in the morning at 1000 hours. They had one last briefing the night before, at which Major Varner was the spokesman.

"Gentlemen, I have just had word that the emplacements around the sub pens at Brest have been hit tonight with a bombing raid. Six flying fortresses made the attack, scattering high explosives directly around the perimeter of the U-boat pens. The aim is to reduce any fortifications and emplacements that might bring fire directly on our boats going in or out of the area.

"To prevent suspicion, similar raids were made at Cherbourg and Le Havre on their port fortifications. I hope the flyboys did some good."

There was some general talk about the effectiveness of the bombings. Then Varner took command again.

"Submarine commanders, are there any questions?"

Ben hoped there wouldn't be. The plan of attack had been worked out, adapted, reworked, and discussed until they had it down to perfection. Rogers of the T-class boat shook his head. Moxie remained quiet, and Hal Iverson of the *Underworld* frowned, but said nothing.

"The voice radios will be a great help. If there's any changes in plans, or if we have to pull back without landing troops, we go to the second attack plan of launching all our torpedoes into the slots of the pens." Varner looked around. "Gentlemen, that's it, then. We'll cast off tomorrow at 1000 hours. Have a good night's sleep."

Varner signaled Ben to stay and caught Moxie as he was leaving. When the two other sub commanders had left, Varner closed the door. Captain White-Johnson had also remained.

"Ben, I know you wanted a sub command for this mission, but the captain and I felt this would be a needless complication, a disruption of a submarine crew with a new skipper, and a waste of manpower. I want you with me inside the pens." He paused and looked at Ben. "If you don't want to play commando with us again, I'll use you as radio control from the bridge of the first boat in line. The choice is up to you, but I'd appreciate it if you would come fight with us."

Ben hadn't slept well since he had returned from the recon mission a week ago. In his dreams he could still see the blood pouring from the German's mouth just before he died. They were waiting for his answer.

He stood and nodded. "I'll go wherever Major Varner wants me to go, however I can help. But I want a silenced Sten gun and about a dozen fraggers."

Major Varner grinned. "Ben, you've got them! By the way, the men voted this afternoon to ask you to wear your red beret on the mission. They say you've earned the right."

"Thanks."

"That's all," Varner said. "See all of you in the morning."

Moxie didn't go back to the cottage that night. He made an hour-long telephone call instead. Ben went to bed and tried to get to sleep. It took him a long time.

Moxie led the trio of killer submarines into the straits of Brest. He'd been there before. All three were riding low, half submerged with only their conning towers and bridges out of the water, the decks awash. They sailed a hundred meters apart so they could maintain visual contact. Long wires on the microphones and small speakers had been extended to the bridges for the skippers to use. The radio communication was excellent, but they transmitted only when needed, and then briefly.

Moxie's sub was moving along at six knots. They had timed it so the tide would be coming out when they did. They would attack at two A.M.

"Once we get inside, we've got to work fast as hell and blow up those subs, then get our asses out of there," Major Varner said. "The Jerries have over three thousand men at Brest from what I've been able to find out. I mean three thousand attack troops with guns."

Ben and Varner sat in the wardroom on the *Underworld*, the second ship in the line. She would be the first boat to slip into slot number four at the pens.

Varner assumed that all of the pen openings would be numbered. They depended on it.

The second sub, Moxie's, would move into the number eleven slot and discharge its work force. The *Topflight* was to go into slot eighteen. The commandos would spread out from there, fighting their way to the far end of the pens, and then disperse to the walkway fingers on each side extending between the moored U-boats. There they would set thirty-second fuses on the specially prepared magnetic charges and blast as many of the subs as they could before the time limit of five minutes was up. Then they would haul ass or swim.

Major Varner spoke again. "As soon as the subs hit their assigned positions, we discharge our men. Each team of commandos has seven to eight slots to cover, three or four on each side of the embarkation point. The biggest problem is that we have to work all the way to the back of the pens on those three positions before we can get our men up the other walkways beside the other U-boats. Then the men have to fight back to the far end of the pens, blowing up U-boats before they can run back out the key walkways they came in on to get back to the subs for escape."

"We may have to fight through the same spot two times," Ben said. "I hope there aren't many Germans inside when we hit it. Then we can move to the U-boats, blast them, and get out without having to battle for every inch of concrete."

"That probably is a dream, Ben, but we will hope."

Ben looked at the tall commando. He seemed so right for the job, as if he had been born for the position.

"What will you be doing after this is all over, Major?"

"Do? Haven't thought about it much. Probably the same thing I'm doing right now. I'll stay in the Army, no doubt about that. If I'm lucky I'll get busted back only to a first lieutenant. I can't see myself in a business suit going to work from eight to five every day of the week. I'd be bored to death the first month."

"Not much of a market for commandos between wars," Ben said.

"Hell, I'll fight for anybody. There's always a place for a really good mercenary. Maybe I'll jack up my price, get two or three of my best men, and form a team. We could charge twenty thousand pounds a month. We would have more work than we could handle."

"God, I hope not. After this war is over, I'd hope the world can settle down and lick some wounds."

"Just my luck it will do that," Varner said.

Ben waved and climbed to the bridge. Iverson nodded at Ben and looked back into his binoculars. It was a clear, cool night. No clouds, and only a sliver of last week's full moon.

Iverson looked over at Ben. "Scared?"

"Hell yes, scared shitless."

"Me too," Iverson said, "and I'm not even going into the pens. Just nosing my damned bow into the fucker."

The small speaker hooked onto Iverson's jacket sounded.

"Passing point A, let's line it up."

"*Ja*," Iverson said into his mike. A moment later they heard a "*Si*" over the speaker, and Iverson asked for more power ahead as his boat pulled forward and to the right. It was now the first boat in a three-ship line.

Ben saw the outline of the cape and the lighthouse slide by on the left. He shivered. So far, so good. He should get to the forward hatch with the others. He adjusted his red beret. If he were going ashore he had decided on a steel helmet. He'd use one the 3-inch gunners usually wore. Might as well go in with the best protection. If the GIs could wear the steel piss pots in combat, so could he. To hell with the beret, he'd wear that on parade . . . if he lived. It was the first time Ben had considered the point. He felt death staring at him, mocking him. He had killed, now was it his turn to be killed?

"He who lives by the sword, shall die by the sword." "An eye for an eye, and a tooth for a tooth . . ." And a life for a life. He was too far ahead on that score now for the fates to try to get even. He could always refuse to go with the commandos into the pens. He snorted. Like hell he could. He dropped through the hatch and walked forward. The twenty-five commandos stood lined up, waiting. It would be five minutes yet.

Ben felt the boat turn to port almost ninety degrees. Then it came up to surface trim. The commandos felt it too.

"Not long now, men," Ben said. He checked his gear. He had everything—the Sten submachine gun, a new boot knife, four special long magazines, the fraggers. A small chest pack held two more filled magazines. It was going to be one hell of a war out there.

Captain Iverson stood on the bridge with Major Varner. They looked ahead at the ghost shadows of the pens, a thousand meters off.

"Basic team out," Varner said.

Iverson repeated the words into the radio mike and into the voice tube at the same time. He saw the front hatch crack open and two commandos climb out. They slapped the heavy thirty-caliber machine gun on the mount near the bow and brought up two boxes of ammunition. In a moment they were ready to fire.

Varner could see no lights on the pens. Darkness. Nothing showed inside. Perhaps they had installed doors of some kind, black doors, shrouds? He did not know. He closed his eyes and said a small prayer, a prayer for his safe return. No one ever knew about these attacks of self doubt.

He looked again, this time through the twenty-power scope. No doors, no shrouds, a lighter shade of gray inside, even one winking light now. Not much activity. Good. The three boats had spread to their assigned distances. Now if the numbers were printed on each slot they would be set.

He held his breath, just as if he were waiting for the red jump light to turn to green in an aircraft as a paratroop mission started.

Closer now, closer, within five hundred meters. No sign of any patrol craft. Were they going to be lucky? Were they going to slip in with no challenges? This was the part he feared. On land with a team behind him, he could take on anyone, anywhere. Out here he felt trapped, limited, caged.

Closer.

Three hundred meters.

He could see inside the pen doors now. Through the scope he spotted the numbers. Yes, they were lined up on number four. Iverson had been giving orders quietly down the tube. It looked good.

Another hundred meters slipped by. Iverson kept the troops at the forward hatch informed of the progress. No need for the MGs yet. Varner hoped they didn't need them. Ben would be the first man out of the hatch. Varner would go down to the deck over the gun mount.

Closer.

A hundred meters away. He could see inside, dim lights, shielded. He saw two men deep in the number four slot.

Closer.

Fifty meters.

"Start the men coming on deck," he told Iverson, who passed the word down the voice tube. Ben moved forward to the machine-gun crew. More men came; twenty were supposed to be on the deck when they nosed into the opening.

The big door of number four slot gaped open at the bow!

No attack yet, no challenge, they were going to get inside!

A thin voice came from a loudspeaker deep in the bowels of the pens.

The two words boomed out again. They were German. They sounded like "identify yourself," but Varner wasn't sure.

The *Underworld* nudged the bumper, and the bow pierced the magic curtain of the German U-boat pens at Brest. The submarine edged forward twenty feet and stopped. The plank went down. It was almost level with the concrete walkway work space. Ben ran across and ducked behind the first huge pillar holding up the massive roof. A dozen commandos charged along the pier, then raced forward. Still no shots. They were well into the pens before Varner got across the gangplank to the concrete. He was with a dozen sappers. They ran ahead. He had paused long enough on the bridge to see both the other submarines nosing into the pens.

Ben had been the first off the boat. He held the Sten gun in front of him, ducked behind the concrete pillar to the side of the number three slot, and ran forward. He saw a man far ahead who simply stood and stared at him. He kept running until the man turned and yelled. A three-round burst from Ben's silenced Sten cut him down. He ran past him. He heard boots on the other side of the concrete pillars moving with him. He passed the first U-boat and saw another one ahead. A man showed on the bridge in back of the antiaircraft guns. Ben sent a six-round silent burst at him, and the German vanished.

There was shooting now on the other side of the concrete barrier, then farther down. He heard the muted explosion of a grenade and pulled out one of his own. Two Germans jumped up from a wall near the end of the sub and fired. Ben poured two five-second bursts at them, dodged behind a concrete roof pillar, and pulled the grenade pin. He threw it too far, but it bounced downward off the wall and landed behind the barrier. The explosion blew one German halfway over the small wall. Ben charged, saw a red beret come around the other side of the concrete, and waved him to the right. He wanted three men down the walkway between slots one and two.

A German officer came from an office on a high platform just in front of them. Both Ben and a commando beside him threw grenades. One bomb went into the office and blew the officer off his perch. He died on the concrete floor below. Ben and two more commandos rushed past him, cleared another small room with a grenade, then saw half a dozen French civilians with their hands up, standing next to a wall. Ben motioned for them to get into the safety of the small room. Then he rushed with the commandos down the slot one-two walkway, hosing it down with deadly lead messengers as they ran.

Ten seconds behind them came the sappers. They raced to the far end, swung charges down on two subs, set the fuses, and attached the magnetic explosive charges below the waterline. They turned and raced back toward Ben and the second sub.

There was only one more U-boat in the two rows. One man took care of it and was back before the first explosion shook the underground structure. Ben's ears throbbed from the sharp explosion, then a second blast came almost on top of the first and he saw the two U-boats in front of him start to settle into the water.

Ben and the three commandos ran to the juncture of the walkway between three and four. They saw no more Germans. The U-boats on that walkway would be blasted as they ran back to the *Underworld*.

"Where are the others?" Ben asked.

"I don't know," a commando answered. "The major took six men down toward number seven."

Ben and five commandos ran that way. A grenade blasted in front of them and all dove to the concrete. Someone threw an answering grenade toward the Germans. Two of the commandos were hit and didn't get up from the floor.

"Don't shoot!" Ben ordered. "We've got men down there." They edged around the concrete partitions. Ben took a quick look and saw a German run from one pillar to the next. Ben rolled a grenade to one side of the pillar and listened for the blast. As soon as the bomb went off, he jolted around the post with two commandos, moved up to the blast site, and slid next to the safety of the rough concrete. Hedgehopping, they moved ahead, grenading as they went. A German submachine gun chattered ahead of them. The bullets didn't come their way. Where was Major Varner?

Ben motioned two of his men to check one side of the next slot. He looked down the other side. Nothing. He waited, looked again, and spotted a German moving out cautiously. Ben aimed a burst at him, saw him hit and go down. Still the German raised his weapon. A commando from the other side put ten slugs into him.

Quiet. Even the echoes of the machine-gun fire had faded away. A man cried out in pain and frustration. Ben checked the end of the pens again, then slammed a new magazine into his Sten. There were no doors here, only the rough concrete where the forms hadn't met.

"Cover me!" Ben shouted to the two commandos with him. He ran out and around the next pillar, then the next, and the next. He slid behind the concrete support post. Ahead he heard a burp gun chatter. Seven, slot seven. This was where the major had come. Ben sent a burst of gunfire down the work space, and three commandos with red berets roared into the danger zone and dove in beside him.

Far ahead of them a U-boat blew up. The charge must have been placed near the bow and caught a German torpedo warhead. The explosion set off the other three or four fish in the reload racks on the U-boat. That whole end of the pens was filled with smoke and fumes, and was raining pieces of metal. Ben pointed at the commandos.

"You. Check out this number seven pier. I'll take six. You two cover us. Find the major."

Ben rushed from pillar to pillar. He saw that the U-boat on the far end was sunk but the near one was intact. A red stain flowed from behind the next pillar. Ben rushed around it, his Sten gun ready. A commando sat there, blood still pouring from his chest. He looked up at Ben and his voice came high and unnatural.

"Father, forgive me for I have sinned." The commando's eyes drifted closed, popped open again, and he fell facedown in his own blood.

Next to him sat Major Varner. The side of his head was red with new blood. His eyes had closed. Ben shook his shoulder.

The major opened his eyes.

"Ben! Damnit to hell! God damn it, Ben! Get the troops out of here," he said and collapsed.

Ben yelled for the men he had been with. They

came, dodging and throwing lead to the side. The slots beyond seven evidently were back in German hands.

"Move it or we buy it right here!" Ben yelled. He put the major over his shoulders and lifted him. Ben dropped his Sten gun and struggled forward with the two hundred pounds. The men behind him were firing as he smashed into a pillar and bounced off.

The boat seemed a million miles away. A grenade went off behind them, then another. They were U.S. fraggers. Ben knew the sound. His troops were keeping the avenue open. They had almost missed the three-four slot walkway. A commando with a green beret pulled Ben into the slot and tried to help with the major but couldn't. Ben nodded at the U-boats they passed, a VII-C and a newer one.

"Find a sapper and kill those boats," he shouted and stumbled on. More grenades went off behind him and on the far side. The whole world was one big bang. He heard a charge go off behind him and he guessed it was the VII-C. He knew another U-boat was going down. He tripped over a dead German, went down to one knee. Two commandos helped him up, and they carried the major between them.

"Another twenty meters, sir. We can make it!" one of the men shouted. Rifle fire raked the *Underworld* just ahead.

Ben was near the last post between them and the boat. "Put some concentrated fire down there on those German rifles," he yelled. "They've got slots five and six. Hit them hard."

Six commandos poured fire into the offending area, and the attack against the sub slackened. Ben and another commando picked up Major Varner and rushed across the no-man's-land of concrete. Ben shouldered Varner and tried to walk across the plank to the aft deck. He slipped and fell. The deck was bloody. He dragged Varner to the hatch.

"Man coming down, wounded. Major Varner. Catch him." Ben bellowed it down the hatch, then handed the major down to reaching hands.

"Move out," Ben shouted toward the men still on the dock. "Come on, let's get out of here!" he roared. He saw one man after another break off fire and run for the sub. Then he noticed that the machine gun was unmanned at the bow. He ran to it and pulled the trigger. The gun fired.

He swung it toward the pier and chattered off five rounds. Ahead of him someone rose to throw a grenade, but a blast from a Sten gun cut him down. The German fell beside the grenade and it exploded. Ben aimed down the next pier, swung back to the other side of slot four, and saw a dozen men rushing forward. Ben held back on the trigger and felt the gun getting hot. The lead sprayed into the bodies. The Germans fell like toy soldiers, one on top of the other. Then the gun sputtered and seized and wouldn't fire. Somebody called behind him.

"Come on, we've got everybody on board who's alive from our sector. Come on, Commander, let's go!"

They had to smash his hands with their boots to make him let go of the machine-gun handles. They carried him aft and pushed him down the hatch. One of the men who helped bring him down reached up to pull down the hatch. Shots boomed and he pulled his hand back—a shattered, splintered mass of bloody flesh. He screamed. Another man jumped up and closed the hatch.

From a distance, Ben heard the command to dive. They started down while still at the dock, and moved backwards all at once. Now they would turn around and dive.

Ben looked at his hands and couldn't figure out why they were mashed and bleeding. They hurt like hell. He wanted to sit up, but he couldn't. Someone was lying on top of him. It was the unconscious commando with the shattered hand.

Ben could feel new explosions in the water. He thought he felt one hit the ship, the stern area.

"Medic! Medic!" someone screamed nearby.

"How long were we in there?" Ben asked.

Nobody seemed to hear him or pay any attention.

"Damnit, how long were we in there?"

"Eleven minutes," someone said.

"Too fucking long. Shore batteries. Sure as hell it's the shore batteries now. Why so long?" Then he remembered the major. The men wouldn't leave without the major. Hell, *he* wouldn't leave without Major Varner. His team must have been stopped cold and cut to pieces.

Ben wiped a bloody sleeve across his face. His eyes wouldn't focus. Why was it so dark? Where was the major?

At last his vision cleared and he rubbed his fingers over his face. It was covered with blood. His eyes were blinded by the blood. Somebody handed him a towel and he wiped his face, then his hands. It was red—British blood? American blood? German blood? He didn't know. It didn't matter.

"The major. Where is Major Varner?"

As he asked, Ben realized he lay where he had fallen. A young commando with a small purplish hole in his forehead lay beside him. Ben knew the boy was dead. He shivered.

Ben sat up. "Major Varner, where is he?"

A medic in bloodstained clothes looked up. "The major is over there in the lower bunk."

"How is he?"

"Take a look. I'm no doctor."

Ben tried to take a deep breath. He heard the sound of the water surging around the deck. It seemed like the right sounds for a diving submarine, but somehow now it was different. Ben prayed that they were going down. Down away from the explosions, from the chattering machine guns, from the flaming blasts and the slashing bullets, down from the redness of bloody death. Down to safety and quiet and peace. He got up and struggled toward the bunk. The deck was slippery. He looked down. It was red with British blood.

He paused. Twenty-seven of them had left the boat. How many returned? He looked around but could count only twelve men, twelve commandos. Everyone seemed to be wounded. Where the hell were all the others?

Ben heard voices aft. "That must be the other commandos," he thought. He went to look at the major. The bullet crease on his forehead looked worse now, deeper. But it wasn't bleeding anymore.

He touched the major's face and jerked his hand away.

"No. Oh, sweet God in heaven, no!"

Ben put his fingers to Major Varner's temple. There was no pulse. The skin was cooling. He lifted the major's eyelid. It stayed open.

"Oh, God, no!" Ben moaned, then collapsed in a wailing scream of anger, frustration, and loss.

Chapter 22

Searchlights crisscrossed the bay beyond the sub pens. Machine guns hammered away from shore. On the bridge of the *Underworld* Captain Hal Iverson zig-zagged his boat in a determined effort to avoid the patterns of light that brought death.

He had seen the other two submarines load their men and leave promptly on schedule. His commandos had run into more trouble than they could handle. He had seen some of them cut to pieces on slot seven. The survivors had come staggering back to the boat, wounded and dying. Of the twenty-seven who went out, he had seen only a dozen, perhaps fifteen, make it back. The delay meant he had been four minutes late casting off from the pens. One of his seamen had been killed manning the machine gun to cover the commando's retreat.

Now he zigged again, ran through the edge of the giant beam coming at him, and crouched lower on the bridge. Machine-gun fire came too late, but tracking where the sub might be.

Hal swore roundly. He was trapped on the surface. He had taken two rounds of artillery early in the run from the sub pens, and while both were super-ficial, one had sprung the aft hatch so badly that it had popped open before they could submerge. Now it would not close watertight. He had two men on lifelines working on it with sledges, so far without any hope of success.

Hal zigged again, slamming along through the darkness of the huge bay at fourteen knots. He had lost contact with the other two subs when they had left. He only hoped that they would surface out of the combat zone and listen for him. He had his radioman making a call every two minutes.

"*Underworld* hit, can't dive. Aid requested."

He heard the radioman making the plea again. He was heading in the right direction but all along the narrow stretch to the channel, the searchlights were snapped on. They tracked him like a pack of hounds with a fresh scent. The lights shone from both shores, so he plowed along in the middle and hoped. The ship passed the lighthouse and a shore battery opened up with three rounds. It was a guess, but still the rounds came too close.

Hal couldn't worry about the score, but he knew that well over fifteen U-boats had gone to the bottom by the piers. He kept hoping it had been worth it.

He quietly ordered two fresh men to the aft hatch to work on pounding it back into shape. He suddenly heard a new sound sneaking into the programmed background noise.

"E boat," he thought. "Gun crew, report. Prepare for action," Hal Iverson said into the tube. He had to make one lucky shot with the three-incher. It was possible, but not likely. If he didn't blow it out of the water, they were all dead. There was not a chance in hell he could tangle with a German torpedo boat on even terms and win. It had all the advantages. On a sudden impulse he made sure the E boat was coming from the rear, and he turned the *Underworld* around to face it. It was a chance, not a good chance, but a fighting, clawing, scratching, last blood try. He bent to the speaking tube. "Ready all forward tubes to fire."

"All six tubes, sir?"

"Right, ready all six tubes, quickly."

He listened to the E boat coming closer. Iverson looked at the speaking tube with impatience.

"All tubes ready to fire, sir."

"Stand by for firing."

He thought about two methods. He could fire a salvo of six and hope, but what if there were more than one E boat? He decided to use the "down-the-throat" method. He had heard about this one from the Yank skippers in the Pacific. Yes, it might work. Better potential. The E boat probably had picked him up on radar; he hoped so, and he prayed there was only one E boat coming. They had almost seven of the eight kilometers of the straits to negotiate before they could call for some help from a friendly destroyer, or hope to raise the other two submarines. Surely they hadn't abandoned him.

Iverson looked up and heard the high-pitched sound of the E-boat motors. Then he saw a trace of it far off.

"Range and bearing," he barked into the tube. He hoped the ASDIC man had picked up the craft.

"Forward, sir, I have a single craft. Range, four-zero-zero-zero. Bearing zero-nine-six."

"Ahead slow, come to zero-nine-six bearing."

"Aye, sir."

Now he was closing with the raider. He was attacking the attacker.

"Range?"

"Three-five-zero-zero. Closing fast."

The fish were set for shallow running. He just hoped that the skipper or a lookout on the E boat could see the wakes of the torpedoes in the moonlight. His whole attack plan counted on it.

"Sound off range each five hundred meters," Iverson ordered.

"Range three-zero-zero-zero."

It was coming faster than he expected. "One boat?"

"Yes, sir, one signal."

Iverson stared ahead into the gloom. Just when should he fire? The E boat could turn so fast, it wasn't like a tanker or even a destroyer. Decisions had to be made quickly on a submarine, and he decided. He would fire two torpedoes at two thousand meters, then if they missed, fire two more at one thousand meters, if there were no change in course.

"Gun crew ready," the gun captain said.

"Load and be ready to fire. Don't fire until we are at five hundred meters, and then only on my command."

"Aye sir."

"Bearing zero-nine-six, no change. Range two thousand meters."

"Fire one and two," Iverson barked. He heard the command go down, felt the double surge as the two fish jolted out of their forward tubes. He knew they would quickly reach a speed of forty-five knots slanting at the E boat dead ahead.

Iverson had never tried this before. He'd heard that in the Pacific the submarines with stern torpedoes would fire two parallel fish at a destroyer or other ship chasing it. The plan was to hope the lookouts spotted one of the fish, and turned the boat away at a forty-five- or ninety-degree angle to avoid that torpedo. By doing that they would present a broadside target for the second torpedo.

It worked best in daylight, and it would work only if everything went right. Now Iverson counted the seconds, wondering how far the fish had moved. There might not be time. The E boat and the torpedo were closing on each other at ninety knots.

"Bearing, range?"

"Same bearing. Range one-five-zero-zero meters."

They were about a thousand meters apart, and closing rapidly. How long? How long? He stared ahead with his binoculars.

"Let me know if there is any change in bearing," Iverson said into the speaking tube.

Another few seconds. Then ten more seconds slid past.

"Bearing changing sir. She's swinging away, making a port turn of about ninety degrees, sir."

Almost at the same time the words came there was a splash of brilliant orange and red flame a thousand meters ahead of them. The E boat dissolved in a crackling, flaming mass of steel, wood, fabric, and exploding petrol tanks.

"We have a hit, control room. Scratch one raiding E boat that didn't want us to go home. Inform the crew. Then bring her around to a bearing of two-six-zero and let's get the hell out of here."

Hal Iverson checked his position. He still had seven miles to go before clearing the straits. Another search-light snapped on, combing the water. He thought of putting a gunner on the bow machine gun to put out the light. But one of his crew said the gun had burned up.

"Gun crew, secure," he shouted at them over the railing. They went about their work, and a few min-utes later the word came that they had secured the gun and closed the exterior ammo hatches and the crew was below.

Two more searchlights came on, and with them the boom of a shore battery. Target practice, Hal decided. Then, just for a moment, his boat was caught in the crisscrossing of two beams of light. He surged ahead, but the light trailed and caught him, and no matter how he turned or slowed, or speeded up, the lights stayed with him.

The roar of three or four guns came from the north shore, and Hal knew his boat was in trouble. Just one lucky shot was all it would take. He couldn't submerge and he was running as fast as he could on diesels. He was trapped in the unrelenting arms of the battery of searchlights.

The first round went over them, the second went over, the third was short. Hal changed course and charged straight away from the guns toward the southern shore, then wound to the west again. The searchlights stayed on him. A new light from the dark southern shore picked him up and pinpointed him. He slowed to two knots, then ordered full ahead and hard left rudder.

Rounds came again, two at a time now, with the guns taking turns, the gunners guessing which way he would turn. One round came dangerously close, but a call showed no damage.

"Radio room, sir. Should I continue sending the message? We're getting no response."

"Change to 'Under attack shore batteries. Assistance required.'"

"Aye, aye, sir."

Six rounds came in, then six more, and before Hal could get to the tube he knew they were in trouble. The guns had the range. Now it was a matter of pure chance.

"Full left rudder," he shouted.

Ben Mount climbed the ladder into the bridge and held on as the *Underworld* turned sharply. He saw the searchlights and heard the rounds striking the water. He wore the same bloody fatigues he had at the pens.

"Good God, Hal, you've got your own war going on up here."

"Right, any good ideas?"

"We're still afloat, you're doing fine. Depends how many guns they have and how lucky they get."

His words were drowned out by twelve rounds. Some fell short, but they saw them moving toward the *Underworld*. Ben and Hal ducked.

One struck just beside the conning tower forward but didn't penetrate. The second slammed into the stern and exploded behind the aft hatch. The *Underworld* shuddered, rolled ten degrees to port, then steadied. A gaping hole three feet wide had been ripped into the stern. Already she was taking on water.

Hal grabbed the radio mike. "Moxie, we're hit aft, taking on water. Estimate buoyancy for ten to fifteen minutes. Making ready the life rafts. Shelling continues. *Topflight,* hope you can hear this and find us. We're just off Point Minou somewhere. This is Hal."

"Damage report," he shouted into the tube.

"Stern is hit, taking on water. Have evacuated all personnel in stern section, watertight door is sealed."

"Trim the ship."

"Trying, sir. We've taken on a great deal of water."

"Blow some tanks if you need to."

"Aye sir."

Another volley of rounds came from the north shore. Four of them were wide. The next two came closer and one gave the forward deck a glancing blow, failed to detonate, and splashed into the sea.

"Come to bearing two-six-five and give her all ahead. Let's get away from those guns."

Another pair of rounds came in, one hit the bow, peppering the bridge with shrapnel. Neither Hal nor Ben had time to duck. Ben felt something hit him in the back, but decided it was nothing major. He turned to where Hal had been and saw the commander lying on the bridge deck. The boat pitched to one side and Hal's head came off his shoulders and rolled to the far side of the bridge. Ben grabbed the side of the bridge and closed his eyes. He shook his head and looked again. Hal's eyes stared at him. A large piece of shrapnel must have barely missed Ben and decapitated Hal. Ben grabbed the mike to the radio, sat down behind the bridge shroud, and wiped his face then spoke.

"*Topflight,* Moxie. We're hit again, we're on a two-sixty-five course outbound. Hal is out of it. Not sure how long we can keep it above water. The shelling is slacking off. Hal blew an E boat out of the water, so nobody is following us. Hope you can get over here quick. We've got wounded."

Ben felt the wetness on his back now, and knew it wasn't water. He might have been hit worse than he thought. He looked at Iverson's body, then over at his head. Ben shuddered and went down the ladder toward the control room. His back felt like a hot poker was gouging him. In the control room the short-manned crew looked at him.

"The skipper caught half of that last round forward. He's dead." Ben waited a minute. "What is the latest damage report?"

"Aft compartment flooded. Bow is leaking and we're taking on water slowly. Repair crews are working there. Engines are in good shape, no danger of water getting to the batteries. Fuel adequate for return trip."

The engineering officer looked up. "If it goes sour we have four hours of buoyancy, sir. We're on an outgoing tide, and it should be getting light around five A.M. It's now 0245. With light we could rendezvous and unload wounded, personnel, and vital records."

"Torpedoes left?" Ben asked.

"Four, sir."

"Make ready to fire the last four torpedoes," he said.

No one questioned his orders, his right to command.

"Numbers three through six ready to fire, sir."

"Fire three through six," Ben said.

The command was repeated. Soon they felt the jolt of the firings, one after the other.

"Torpedoes all fired, sir."

"We just bought ourselves another half hour of buoyancy."

Ben looked around the control room.

"The captain. How?" someone asked.

"That last round on the bow, a head wound, massive. Instantly." Ben paused and watched them. "Now, I want a complete list of dead and wounded, and a roster of all personnel. The first officer to the bridge."

Ben went back topside, and when the first officer came up, Ben held out his hand. "Finster, isn't it? This is your command if you want it."

Finster was at the ladder, staring at Hal Iverson's head, lying on the deck.

"Oh, my God!" he whispered as he turned away. Tears sprang to his eyes. He shook his head. "My God, just like that? In a half a second he's dead?"

"I'm sorry, I should have told you."

Finster turned, braced his shoulders, and came up the rest of the way. He wiped his eyes then shouted below.

"Bring a blanket up here, and two men, on the double!"

The blanket came up. They rolled Iverson's body into it. Ben put the head on the torso, and they wrapped it up, then tied and handed it down the hatch.

Finster stood and looked at the shore batteries. He shook his fist at them. The rounds had stopped now. The next set of guns had not come in range.

"Finster, I should have taken care of this before I brought you up here. I forgot. I'm sorry. Do you want command?"

"You're doing fine, sir. I'd rather you continued."

"Very well. Keep the radio operator sending out our request to *Seawitch* and *Topflight*. Send it every two minutes. They may be out of range, or our receiver may be malfunctioning."

Ben stared at the shoreline. "We should be through the worst of the shelling. No more good points for shore batteries. But with first light the Jerries will send some land-based planes and E boats out to finish us. There is no way we can row this thing back to Portsmouth, agreed?"

"Agreed, Commander. The patch job in the bow is holding, but it won't last forever. We continue to take on water and the pumps can't keep up. In effect we're slowly sinking. That flooded aft compartment is dragging us down."

"How many rubber boats?"

"Six-man boats, there should be eight, sir."

"Aren't some of them in that flooded aft compartment?"

"Yes, sir. I'd forgotten. Four."

"Get those four available next to the hatches and make them ready."

"Aye, sir."

"Stand steady." Ben knew the map by heart. Once they passed Point Minou they were still deep in French waters, and German patrol craft could be on them at any time. They had thirty more kilometers before they could even start to breathe easy.

"How many knots are we making?" Ben asked through the tube to the control room.

"Six, sir. Engineering has recommended no more than that due to our damage."

"Aye. Is that roster complete?"

"Almost sir."

"Bring it up when it's done. I want totals first."

"Finster, how many crewmen did you sail with?"

"Seventeen, sir. There were twenty-seven commandos counting you. That's forty-one all together."

"Give me a verbal on that roster," Ben snapped at the voice tube.

"Yes, sir. Royal Navy crew: four dead, two injured, eleven fit for duty. We lost two in the aft compartment. Commandos: four dead, eight wounded, and two with minor injuries. That doesn't include you, sir."

"Then there are only fifteen of the commandos accounted for? We have twelve commandos missing in action in Brest?"

"Yes, sir, that's my count."

"Carry on."

Ben looked at Finster. "Sixteen dead out of twenty-seven. Major Varner thought he might lose seven or eight from the troop." Ben sighed. "Take the helm, Mr. Finster. Steady as she goes, I want to check below."

Two hours later, Ben was back on the bridge. He estimated they were somewhere below Pointe de St. Mathieu. If his calculations were right, they were some seven or eight kilometers south of it and nearing the area where they could expect friendly forces.

The first streaks of light daggered in from the east.

An urgent voice came over the tube.

"Sir! Radio contact with the *Topflight*. Your extension mike is dead up there. They want to talk to you."

Ben dropped down the ladder and grabbed the mike.

"*Topflight,* this is Ben. Where the hell are you?"

"We're out here in the soup with you. Is this Ben? What happened to Hal?"

"He's busy. We've got trouble. Another hour on top at the most."

"Just keep on talking, we're taking a reading on you. We've got a direction finder. Keep talking and we'll home in on your signal. Remember we can't be more than eight or ten miles away. These things don't carry much farther than that. We got you because our antenna is higher. Moxie is in the area."

"So we keep talking. We've lost some men, have some shot up. Your medical people will be busy. Our aft compartment is flooded and the bow is leaking. The pumps can't really keep up, so bust your ass and get over here."

"Right, we're moving at almost sixteen knots and on the way. Yes, we have a bearing. Just stay on that heading and we've got an intercept. You're at six knots forward?"

"Right, hurry home, Mother. We need you."

Ben sat down heavily. He wasn't sure for a moment where he was. Then his eyes cleared. "Mr. Finster, requesting that you take command."

A seaman grabbed Ben before he toppled. "Requesting permission, Captain, to leave the control room," Ben said.

"Permission granted, Commander Mount," Finster said. He motioned to two men to help Ben, and they walked him through to the wardroom and helped him into a bunk.

Ben's mind swirled and swept away like morning surf foam, then it came back a jumble. The T-class was coming. Their hospital people were standing by. The *Underworld* had another hour afloat, engineering estimated. Plenty of time. Why the hell was he almost passing out? What the hell was going on? The fog and sea dust closed around him and then he realized someone was talking to him and he got on his hands and knees and tried to creep out of the dense fog bank.

"Sir, we're going to turn you over on your stomach. Someone said you have a wound in your back, and I want to take a look at it." It was a medic. Ben nodded. He didn't remember seeing him come in. The medic turned him over, slit his shirt down the back. There was a silence then. The medic sprinkled something on his back, then must have put on a bandage.

"Just lay on your stomach and take it easy, sir. We'll get you fixed up soon."

Ben swore silently. Why did he collapse? Psychosomatic end of mission wipeout? That must be it. His damned back began to hurt. When did he get hit? He couldn't remember. In the pens or on the bridge? He couldn't figure it out. Everything was fuzzy again.

Later Ben remembered the transfer to the *Topflight*. It hurt like hell climbing up the ladder. He wouldn't let them strap him to a stretcher. The men took everything they could out of the *Underworld*—all instruments, the logs, code books, radios, small arms, all the stores, everything that would come loose in a reasonable time. The *Underworld* edged lower in the water. At last Finster ordered his men out and refused to let anyone else inside. They dogged down the hatches and attached a light tow cable. She might stay afloat, who knew?

Ben demanded to be left on the *Topflight* bridge to watch the tow. Moxie had been alongside but now he moved off and they steamed for Portsmouth.

An hour after they started the tow at eight knots, the *Underworld* began to sink. A sailor slipped the towline, and the *Underworld* slid under the waves at 0842, April 22, 1944. All her dead had been removed to the *Topflight*.

In the wardroom Ben asked for a combined casualty report. He knew the one from his boat. The *Topflight* had lost two dead, two wounded commandos, no Royal Navy loss. Radio contact with Moxie brought in his report. The *Seawitch* had one commando killed and one wounded, one Royal Navy sailor killed. A total of twenty-four dead on the mission.

They made an estimated tally on the number of U-boats sunk. Ben's men remembered eight going down in their section. The *Topflight* reported twelve blasted, and Moxie's boat commandos put seven down.

Twenty-seven U-boats were either sunk in the pens or were badly damaged. Ben wanted to stay in the wardroom, but the medics came. One of them gave him a shot, and he was placed on a stretcher. They had worked on the most seriously wounded first.

After a ride the lights were brighter and Ben tried to look around, but someone held his head and then they put a strange-smelling cloth over his nose. Slowly everything faded into a soft fuzzy fog, a real London fog, and he relaxed. Betsy would be there. Betsy would come find him in the fog. He relaxed, and then he remembered nothing more.

Chapter 23

U-boat Kapitan Wilhelm Fricke stood on the bridge of the *U-2321*, the first of the new breed of German submarines that were going to sweep the seas clean of the English and Americans. He felt it. He watched the boat making way at two knots along the Elbe river between Hamburg and Kiel. It was the first test run. She hadn't even been underwater yet. The *U-2321* was a Twenty-one-class U-boat. She was huge compared to the VII-C boats he had been used to. So large, so spacious, and with such deadly potential. Six torpedo tubes in the bow, but none aft. How he would have loved to have had those six bow tubes in 1939 and 1940!

Now his first shakedown cruise was underway. He would work down to sea and back today, watching, looking, testing. He would not even think about submerging today. There were dozens of problems to work out. Changes in minor designs that would make the next boats better, more perfect. He had two weeks to find out where the problems were, and to make his report in Berlin, to Admiral Doenitz himself. Fricke had no idea why the routine changes should go all the way to the top, but he was following orders.

It would give him another chance for a direct appeal to Doenitz. Twice he had asked for a U-boat, an operational fighting ship to take back to sea and sink some more enemy ships. The rumored invasion of France could not be far off. He could tear into a dozen enemy troop transports if and when they left England.

He deserved a chance. Doenitz might give him that chance with a personal appeal. His immediate superior said such an assignment was impossible, that they had more important work for him. The Twenty-one-class boats were needed, and his touch would get them into operation more quickly. They needed his genius for getting to the heart of a problem and learning how to correct it, to move from experimental to operational in the shortest possible time.

Problems. Yes, the Twenty-one U-boats had their share of difficulties, but they were so beautiful, fast, and powerful that he had swallowed his disappointment and flung himself into the task of working out the bugs and getting them into the underwater fleet.

Usually workers from the shipyards went along on shakedown cruises, but the workers had all been drafted into the army, and the women, old men, and children did most of the work in the shipyards. Gone was the pride in worksmanship. Gone were the skilled workers who knew how to form a good weld, how to fabricate a steel hull. Gone, too, was the reliability of the VII-C class boats.

There were not even any experts among the workers to send down the river on the ship. Fricke didn't even know if the hatches were watertight.

Schedule? There was no schedule. It had been postponed so many times it finally had been forgotten. How could you build U-boats when the shipyards had three, four, even five air raids a day? The damage was tremendous. This was the first and so far the only Twenty-one-class boat in the water. He would make it into a reliable fighting machine. If he had time.

Fricke had never been partial to hydraulics. The

reliable electric motors had functioned so well and so long without problems in the U-boats that he had grown to appreciate them. But now in the Third Reich there was a shortage of electric motors. They simply were not available even for top-priority jobs. So hydraulic components had been built and the systems were engineered for them. The Twenty-one had many, many hydraulic units on it, handling jobs that should be done by electric motors.

The hydraulic systems had been the cause of ninety percent of the problems on the Twenty-one. They were working on them, but it was becoming clear that redesign and retrofit would be mandatory. No one would be pleased. It might be months, even a year, before Fricke had the first Twenty-one truly operational and ready to go to sea as a fighting ship.

Fricke walked the decks, amazed again at the space. The boat was three compartments high in some sections, and, as an added feature, it had an electric deep freeze for food. There also was a full-time ventilation plant to purify the air.

Wilhelm Fricke pounded the bulkhead with his hand, and wished that he had been provided with an efficient, working war machine like this back in 1939. The record in the Atlantic would have been far, far different.

Fricke remembered how the British aircraft carrier *Courage* had steamed out into the Atlantic with its entourage of protection, and how he had sliced through that protection with his VII-C-class boat, surprised them, and put the massive carrier at the bottom of the English Channel with four torpedoes. It had been a glorious day for him, for the Fatherland. It had won for him the Iron Cross and the favor of Adolph Hitler, and his status as a continuing favorite with the chief of the submarine service, Admiral Doenitz.

Fricke lifted his brows as he thought of the attack. Four torpedoes, fired in quick succession. The danger, the risk, the prize, the triumph!

He looked at the Twenty-one's hydraulic loading mechanisms, which brought a second torpedo to a tube after the first had been fired. All six of these tubes could be reloaded in ten minutes by hydraulics.

He marveled at the time. In the VII-C-class U-boat it took ten to twenty minutes and four men to load one torpedo! And that was done with back-breaking work with hoists and chains hung from the overhead.

The maker of the double-hulled Twenty-one assured Admiral Doenitz that his craft could dive to a depth of five hundred meters! They could go lower than any depth charges the English had!

Fricke went to the bow of the big submarine and checked the internal action of the torpedo doors. The six torpedoes in the tubes were useless if the exterior torpedo doors on the bow would not open. This was the latest hydraulic problem. He would have to go in between the hulls when they got back to the submarine pens at Hamburg.

Oh, he would solve this one, and the others, but could he do it in time?

Fricke remembered the date, April 23, 1944. He wondered how much time he had before the English invaded France. He was sure the invasion would be in France. The German High Command had told him the invasion would come at Calais. Every bit of intelligence information the Germans had pointed that way.

Fricke would put in another request to take command of a VII-C U-boat out of Hamburg, and go at once to Calais and simply sit off the coast until the invasion came. It must be soon. It must! But the last three such requests had been refused, and by Admiral Doenitz himself.

Fricke slammed the palm of his hand against the sleekly painted bulkhead and checked the hydraulic lines again. Why in hell wouldn't the pressure in the lines open those exterior torpedo doors?

Chapter 24

Commander Ben Mount remembered nothing more about April 22, 1944, or the long ride back on the submarine *Topflight*. The medics took one look at the shell fragment nestling next to his spine and immobilized him on a hard stretcher. They kept him heavily sedated until they arrived in Portsmouth. He was moved by ambulance with the other casualties to the closest hospital, and there he was quickly taken into surgery.

Ben regained consciousness in the postoperation recovery room. A nurse and a doctor stood next to him.

"He's starting to come around, Doctor," he heard a woman's voice say.

It was the first thing he had heard, but also the last coherent thought he had for several minutes. Drugs played with his mind, and the room swirled and plunged, came back upright and then dived again like a submarine crashing with three German destroyers on its periscope. No, that was ridiculous. He wasn't sure if the Germans had three destroyers left on the water. His eyes were open but he couldn't see. Blind? No, they had been jabbering about his back, not his eyes.

"Damnit!" he said, fighting the blindness. When he heard his own voice, things seemed more natural.

"I think you're feeling better," the woman said.

The wild colors and shapes gradually faded, and

he turned and saw the woman sitting by his bed. She wore one of the volunteer corps uniforms he'd seen in hospitals. She had soft brown eyes, matching short hair, and a puckish grin.

"Hey, am I alive or is this dead?" Ben asked.

"Quite alive, and swearing a blue streak. My, my, but you do know a huge variety of bad words."

"Learned them in the Navy."

"That's what I keep telling my father." She stood. "There's someone who is waiting to see you. Shall I have her come in?"

He looked at the woman. "Her?"

"Yes, a Miss Betsy Kirkland, a Yank like you. She's been here ever since you got off the boat. You should see her. She's used up a dozen handkerchiefs already."

"Yes. I'd like to see her."

Ben watched the slender girl go out, and a moment later Betsy pushed the door open quickly, then slowed as she came inside. She smiled, her eyes anxious, wary.

"Ben?"

"Yes, Betsy."

She let the door close and looked at him. She wore the red and white polka-dot blouse and the short reddish skirt he liked. Her hair was mussed and so was her makeup. When he smiled, she ran over to his bed.

"Darling, you gave us a few anxious moments. Moxie has been here, but he's back at the base now. I said I'd call him when I talked to you." She bent and kissed his forehead.

"Ben, I'm sorry. I'm so very sorry I made a big scene at the cottage about Lady Clifford. I was jealous, and wrong, and I apologize. In the cottage I was acting like a spoiled child. I was so miserable and angry and stupid. I pulled my bra up and grabbed Moxie's hand. He wanted nothing to do with me. So it was just another, stupid, spoiled, juvenile trick I pulled. Can you forgive me?"

He smiled. "Lean down here."

"Oh, I had to promise not to jump on your bed. Your back is badly hurt and you're not supposed to move. You can't see it but you are strapped to a wide board."

"All from that little chunk of lead in my back?"

"Darling, it was a large piece of shrapnel and it was dangerously close to your spine. That's what frightened everyone. If it moved it could have paralyzed you for life. They were amazed at all the running around you did after you were hit. I told them you always had been an amazing person."

"Can I kiss you?" he asked.

She laughed. "I think that would be perfectly all right, medically. Emotionally I hope it's fine, too."

"Yeah, great. You tell Moxie he owes me one for bugging out and leaving our boat all alone. He pops for a pint."

"I'll tell him. They say I have to leave now. But I'll be back tonight after my shift. Can I come in my work clothes?"

He nodded. His eyes closed, and before she left the room he had slipped into a natural sleep.

Betsy was sitting beside his bed when he woke up that evening. He felt better. The pains were muted with sedation and he could move a little. There was no paralysis, and the doctors told him he'd be good as new in two months.

"I have to lay here for two months?" he'd yelped.

At last they consented a gradual increase in activity after a month. He would then start getting his body working again.

Betsy was bubbling and happy as a teenager but Ben sensed the false gaiety. He didn't question it. He knew she was trying to cheer him up. They talked about her parents, her mother's war projects, and where her father was stationed.

"How is Pru?"

Betsy told him a long, involved story about Pru getting mixed up in a problem at work.

"Moxie and Pru are waiting outside. Can they come in?"

"Damn right!"

Moxie was in uniform and Pru had on a dress and a hat that looked cute, sexy, and stylish. Pru cried as she rushed into the room. She bent over and kissed Ben's cheek and wiped her tears away.

"Ben Mount, we've all missed you so much. I'm glad you're safe and getting well and that we're one big family again. You hurry up and get well and come home."

Ben grinned and said he would, then Moxie took his hand. He stared down at him soberly.

"Jesus, what some blokes won't do to get out of straight sea duty." They all laughed.

"How the hell did you get your boat away from that slot so fast, little buddy?" Ben asked.

"Easy, we didn't have forty Germans to wade through. From what the other men said in the de-briefing, there was a nest of thirty to forty German guards who swarmed in from some central door. When Major Varner took his four men into slot seven, they got cut to pieces. When you came with your grenaders, it forced them back into the other slots that had been vacated already by sapper teams from the *Top-flight*."

Ben sighed. "Twenty-four good men we lost, Moxie. Is that still the total?"

"No, we lost one more commando."

"Twenty-five men dead. I just hope to God it was worth that much blood, that many lives."

"We've put in an official estimate of twenty-seven German U-boats sunk in the pens. I hear there's going to be some medals tossed around."

"Just so Major Varner gets one. He's the guy who died making the mission work."

They were all quiet for a moment. The girls stayed in the background letting the men have their reunion, their memories.

"You lose any of your crew?" Ben asked.

"One. McPherson. He volunteered to go on the cruise. Then he volunteered to fire the machine gun. He was up there when he caught the rifle rounds. McPherson wouldn't leave the gun until all of our commandos were back on board. He was a fine, brave man."

"I'm sorry, Moxie."

Moxie nodded, then deliberately tried to brighten up the conversation.

"So, what are they telling you? Two months in here loafing around, eating good?"

Ben laughed. "Loafing and pinching bottoms on pretty nurses. But they say I'm too sick for the special midnight nurse therapy sessions that are wilder than hell."

Betsy bristled.

"Commander, stow that talk. When you are ready for that kind of special therapy, whether it's midnight or midday, I'm the one who takes care of it. I'll see to that."

The other three chuckled, and Ben reached out and took her hand.

"I thought you'd dropped off to sleep over there," he said. "So what's the brass got you doing, Moxie? Any missions coming up? What about Hamburg, Kiel, Trondheim? We've got lots more sub pens. Now we know how to do the job."

Moxie shook his head. "I've heard they aren't going to go after any more pens. Too high a risk factor, and they say the German subs are not now considered as a major threat. Everyone is concentrating on the damned invasion. I wish it would start. The pressure is building and building. I don't see how it can be more than a week or two away. This is the best time of the year, weather-wise, coming up."

"At least twenty-seven U-boats won't be on hand to put any of our troop transports to the bottom of the channel," Ben said. He looked around at all of them. "You're getting fuzzy out there." He squeezed Betsy's hand. "Damn, but I think I'm going to have to cut out on you folks. Sorry. Just not much left in the old batteries. Come back real soon."

He felt Betsy kiss his cheek, then before they started for the door he dropped off to sleep.

A month after he'd entered the hospital, Ben was up and walking. He underwent therapy to re-establish his former motor control and was progressing well. There would be no permanent damage. Betsy came every other evening and talked and walked the aisles with him. It was almost as it had been between them before that rainy night at the cottage when everything blew up.

Two weeks later, Ben was listening to a radio in a recreation room when Betsy rushed in. She grabbed his hand and sat beside him. They listened to the news together.

"We repeat, the historic landings made on Normandy beaches this morning, June 6, 1944, by the joint forces of the Allied armies under the Supreme Commander of the Allied Expeditionary Forces, General Dwight Eisenhower, have been a success. The Germans expected the landings to come at Calais, well north of where they actually took place, and had massed men and tanks in that area.

"Total surprise was achieved, and beachhead commanders say the beaches are secure and forces are driving inland. It is the historic start of the attack on the continent and against Germany that we have waited for for so long. French Resistance groups carried out specific missions against the Germans just before and during the invasion, and the sky was filled with paratroopers and glider aircraft depositing large numbers of fighting men inland to block access roads to the beachheads, preventing German reinforcements from moving up.

"We have had few indications of casualties. The Royal Navy has reported that there were 'far fewer attacks by German U-boats than anticipated,' and that the landing force consisted of some seven hundred ships, four thousand landing craft, four hundred minesweepers, and a total of thirty-seven army divisions. There were thousands of aircraft in the fight, and the Allied warplanes have almost total control of the skies over the invasion area.

"The BBC repeats this bulletin. The Allies have landed on the French coast between Cherbourg and Le Havre. The beaches of Normandy were attacked at dawn this morning by the largest amphibious invasion force in the history of the world. The beachheads at 'Utah' and 'Omaha' have been established. Further reports will come as information is released by the War Department."

"Goddamnit!" Ben said in anger and frustration. "I should be over there helping. I should be out in a boat protecting the ships or chasing U-boats, or some damned thing, not just sitting here on my ass letting those other guys get killed."

"Ben, you've done more than your share already," Betsy said. "And didn't you tell me that the submarines wouldn't have much of a part in the invasion? You said it was all the surface guys' show."

"Yeah, right. But I'm still mad. Is it all right if I get mad?"

She kissed his lips and held him close. "Ben Mount, every time I think about that submarine, and Hal Iverson, and how close you came to not coming back to me at all, that's when I'm overjoyed that you can get mad, that you can shout and rage, and laugh and swear. I'm delighted that you're still alive. Yes, please get furious." She smiled, then kissed him. "Damnit, Mount, let's go see if we can find a cold Coke somewhere and talk about Michigan and New York City and Groton, Connecticut. Right now I'm so damn homesick that I could scream."

"Yeah, right, let's find a Coke. Christ, but I should have been there!" Ben said once more. Then he grinned and kissed Betsy. "Thanks for letting me get mad. I can see it now. In about fifteen years one of our kids will say, 'Daddy, what did you do in the big invasion of France?' And I'll say, 'Hell, kid, I did it almost single-handed. I was sitting on my fat ass in a hospital in London without my pants on, and wishing like crazy that I could make love to your mother.'"

She kissed his lips. "Oh, Lordy, me too! Let's find a dark corner somewhere so I can get you all bare."

"In here there isn't a dark corner that doesn't already have a waiting line."

"Then let's go back to your room and get sexy."

"Okay, my three roommates will enjoy it."

"Damn!"

"Another week, and I get sprung. One more week."

"A whole week?" She pressed against him as they walked. "Darling, I'm going to have something very special at the cottage. It will be a day and a night of lovemaking you'll never forget."

Chapter 25

Ben stood and stared out his window at the U.S. Naval Headquarters, Atlantic Theater of Operations. It was hard for him to believe that ten months had slid by since he had been released from the hospital in Portsmouth. He had worked with the British submarine service for another three months, and then one day he was transferred without request or explanation to the U.S. Navy headquarters in London. There he pushed paper, served in a minor advisory capacity on submarines, and asked for a transfer to the Pacific. He desperately wanted to get back into action.

The sea war in the Atlantic was over. When the invasion began, the Allies had so many supply, support craft, and warships in the English Channel that the German U-boats seldom ventured out of their French ports. They were restricted to those friendly waters and stymied. Many boats returned to French ports, and the men were ordered to leave their U-boats there and take land transportation back to Germany. Other submariners were taken from their boats, given rifles, and told to defend the ports.

British submarines had virtually nothing to do. Now and then a supply mission to some still-occupied point would be undertaken, but it was generally slack time for the underseas service.

Moxie phoned whenever he was in London, but

gradually Ben lost track of him. Moxie had been on a few supply missions, took a saboteur into Norway, but he too had little to do. He had also requested a transfer to the British force in the Pacific, but he was refused.

The best part of the whole assignment was that Betsy had moved to London, found work, and they had taken a small flat. Ben looked forward to going home each day. He had a nine-to-five job, and almost nothing to do during the day at the office. Each time he put through a request for transfer to the South Pacific, it was turned down.

Betsy had worked for the Royal Navy in one of its many offices, then landed a job in the same office building where Ben was, with the U.S. Navy. She was a secretary-office manager for a Captain Archibald. She was vague about what the captain did, and Ben wasn't that interested. He and Betsy saw every play that struggled to the boards in the West End. They went to the headquarters' movies, and checked out the best of the museums and galleries in London.

Ben found some real popping corn at the headquarters PX and had talked the manager out of a full case of six-ounce Cokes. At a greengrocer he found some apples, and he walked home a happy man.

Betsy had said she had an errand. By the time she got home, Ben had a spaghetti and meatballs dinner almost ready. She dropped down on the sofa and sighed. She patted the spot beside her.

"Come on over here, sweetheart," she said.

He saw a strange glint in her eye as he sat down next to her and took her in his arms.

"Now, tell me what the problem is. You've been edgy and worried, and a little bit snippity for the past week."

"You noticed. I had a doctor's appointment today."

"Oh?"

"I went to see a gynecologist. My period is three weeks late."

Ben held her away and looked at her.

"That's what I thought," she said. "I was sure as hell that I was . . . that *we* were, pregnant." She watched Ben a moment, then she grinned. "*We* aren't pregnant, so *you* can relax. Nothing serious is the matter with me. There's no real problem the doctor could find. He said it was probably that virus flu I had three weeks ago."

Ben kissed her, then pulled her across his lap and kissed her seriously, his tongue touching hers. He made the kiss last a long time. When she stirred he pulled away from her.

"Did you hope that you were pregnant?" he asked.

"I'm not sure. I must admit that I did think that now we would have to get married. Did you listen to me? I didn't say that now Ben would have to marry me. I am highly *we* centered these days. But I'm not sure if I wanted to be pregnant or not. This doctor told me the same thing my young doctor had told me at the college infirmary. He was young and sexy and I think I got him all excited when he gave me a pelvic exam. It took him long enough. He told me I have a tipped cervix and it might be hard for me to get pregnant."

"That's what a lawyer would call an evasive answer."

"I don't want to get pregnant before I get married. I am definitely old-fashioned about that."

"But you don't mind sleeping with me in your unmarried state?"

She stared at him. "I said I wouldn't on the *Queen Mary*, remember, back in 1939, and we didn't on the trip over. It was just when we got to England, and war was so close. . . . I guess I do mind it, a little. I'd rather be married. But it's all so complicated, and we've been sleeping together for so long. That piece of paper and a few words seem so unimportant. But I really don't want to get pregnant before I get married. I can't even guess what my parents would say. Daddy would want to shoot you, Mother would cry."

"But you're not pregnant, and the war is still on . . ."

"Are you trying to seduce me?"

"Yep."

"Try harder, will you? I'm feeling so sexy I could scream. A pelvic always does that to me."

"Those lucky gynecologists, they must get laid all they can stand." His hand rubbed her breast. Her hand rubbed at his crotch.

"My, my, what have we here?"

"That's called the staff of life. Since you have that tipped cervix and all . . ."

"Hey, why don't we eat your old spaghetti dinner a little later . . ."

He unbuttoned the top of her dress and pulled her bra up over her breasts, then bent and nibbled on one mound, making her nipple blush and flood with hot blood, standing up to twice its normal size.

"Right here?" she asked.

"Why not? A first. Let me lock the door and put on the chain."

She undressed him first, and marveled at his smooth, strong male body.

"Such a beautiful sexy creature, this man animal of mine. I'm glad that I've got you."

He undressed her and teased her.

"You play your cards right, sailor, and I might get friendly with you," she said.

"You probably say that to all the sailors you undress, just to lead them on for a free drink."

"Think it would work?"

He lay on his back and pulled her on top of him and let her play until she became serious. Then she made the connection, and slowly, gently, they completed their lovemaking.

Later that night they listened to the BBC. The war news was good. The Allies were driving toward Berlin. Stiff resistance still came as the Germans fought for every foot of the Fatherland.

"It's just a matter of time, now," Ben said. "They can't hold out long. Only a year ago we invaded France, remember? June 7, 1944, I remember that day. Now here it is April 15, 1945, and Germany is reeling. I don't see how she can hold out another month."

"And then?"

"I'm U.S. Navy. I go where they send me. I'll have to take a cutback in rank to stay in after Japan is whipped, but I want to stay in. There must be fantastic new ways to improve the submarine. I've been hearing about some of the things the Nazis tried. Their new Twenty-one-class boat could be terrific, if they could get it into action. Intelligence says they only have a few of them at sea now, two or three, and there isn't much left they can do that would make any difference. After it's over in Germany, I'd like to go to Hamburg and Kiel and the other big sub bases and see what I can learn from the German U-boat people."

"How long will you be here in London, after Germany gives up?"

"Who knows? The Navy is strange sometimes. I'd still like to go to the Pacific. I put in a new application for combat duty every month. Every month it gets turned down."

"I don't want you getting shot at anymore, Ben."

"I know."

He popped some corn and they ate it with the apples. They drank a few Cokes.

Betsy watched him. "Darling, sexy Ben. Do you think we'll ever really get married?"

"I don't know. I guess I'm waiting for you to say the word. It's up to you. I don't want to be without a family forever. I'd kind of like a couple of kids. Rounds out a person, completes some experiences in life you can't know anything about any other way. But we're not exactly senior citizens yet."

"I'll remember that. Heard from Moxie lately? I thought once that he and Pru were going to take the big step, but it never happened."

They talked on and on, about home, about the States, jazz and the tragic loss of Glen Miller, about ration stamps, clothing allotments, nylons and painting seams on girl's legs. Then they made love again.

Before he went to sleep, Ben knew he would be late getting to work in the morning. It really didn't matter; the work he had to do could be finished in an hour, any hour of the day. The talk they had that night was more important, much more important.

Ben finally fell asleep just before dawn.

Chapter 26

Ben arrived at his office the next morning at 1015 hours. He had been vaguely aware that Betsy had got up, punched him, and left. When he sat down at his desk there was a note written in heavy black ink asking him to report to the Chief of Naval Operations at once.

"That would be a two-star admiral," Ben thought as he tried to remember his name. Then he remembered. It was Rear Admiral Zilke, a stickler for regulations. Ben sighed, carried his hat under his arm, and marched to the elevator. He had no idea what Zilke wanted. It might prove to be the highlight of an otherwise dull and dank London day.

A few moments later, Admiral Zilke stared at Ben, then at his permanent service record file on the desk.

"Mmmmm. Ben Mount. I just wanted to meet you and have a little chat, if you're not too busy. You're the one who sends through a request for a transfer to Sub Pacific all the time, right?"

"Yes, sir. Once a month, sir."

"Good. I like to see that kind of drive. Just keep trying. We're overstaffed here, and we should be shipping lots of people to the Pacific soon. Especially to the submarines." He glanced back at the file. "You were assigned to the Royal Navy way back in 1939. Before we got into the war."

"Yes, sir. We were working on submarine nets to

protect British ports and on adapting radar to the English ships."

"Yes. Well, looks like you've picked up half of the medals the Royal Navy gives out. This latest one the DSC, Distinguished Service Cross. Damn good record, Mount. Trouble is you'll never get a promotion around here. You need a billet that calls for a captain's rating."

"Sir, I'm not that anxious about rank. What I've been doing lately is a lot of thinking and investigating about new designs for submarines. Have you seen anything about the new German Twenty-one-class boat?"

"No, I haven't."

"It's much better than what we have now, from what I hear. I'd like to get into the design and development of a new generation of submarines."

"You want that even more than getting to the Pacific?"

"No, sir. The fighting comes first. But I'm not doing much fighting in here. I think I could be of more use to the Navy in the Pacific. Can you help me get there?"

"Probably." Admiral Zilke watched Ben. "You've had more than your share of combat, Mount, and I won't order you to take on any mission, but there is something coming up that we think would be right for you."

Ben sat up straight. "For me, sir? Almost anything is better than sailing a desk."

"Yes, I agree with you there. Your file shows you've been wounded twice under enemy fire. That you were trapped inside the Brest U-boat pens while on a mission with the commandos and fought your way out leading the survivors." He tapped Ben's file. "I'm curious, Mount. Did you actually have claustrophobia, yet you stayed in the submarine service?"

"Yes, sir. I whipped it. Meanness and youthful stubbornness, I imagine. Now I could go to sleep in a Japanese torture box."

Admiral Zilke lit a cigar.

"All right, Mount. It's yours if you want it." He moved to a map stand at the side of his desk and flipped back a covering sheet. A map of the north coast of Germany centering on Hamburg was revealed.

"This is Hamburg. Our troops have bypassed it and we own part of the forty miles of the Elbe River going into the port of Hamburg from the North Sea. There are submarine pens in there, as you know. Big ones. We're not sure what is taking place at those pens now, but Ike and his people charging for Berlin don't like it. We know there are U-boats there. In fact, the report we have says this is where two of the new Twenty-one-class U-boats you mentioned have been commissioned and are stationed there for final sea trials.

"We've sent individuals in there to find out what is going on that is so top secret. We lost two good men. We've tried to get German partisans to infiltrate—they have been killed. A commando raid is suggested, but how to do it has been up in the air.

"We don't have to know what Jerry is doing in there if we can destroy the project. Bombs won't work. Sapper teams will, as evidenced by your work at Brest. There were to be no more Brest-type raids, but this seems to be an exception. Any questions?"

Ben nodded. "Yes, sir. This strange activity, what is it? It can't be a new weapon, it's far too late for that. Do we have any idea what the activity is?"

Zilke stood and walked around his desk. He puffed on his cigar, straightened the picture of his wife on the desk, then looked out the window.

"I wasn't supposed to tell you, but I don't see

what it can hurt. You are not to tell anyone else." He went back to his desk and sat down in the swivel rocker chair and leaned back.

"Ben, the war is almost over in Europe. From one to two months more at the outside. The Allies are in Berlin waiting for the Russians to move in to where they are supposed to be. When a war winds down, almost always the top political and military people on the losing side start looking for a way out, an escape hatch, a new identity, a hole to crawl into.

"The *Luftwaffe* is not the answer. With our radar and our air power we can prevent any large-scale or long-range flights by top Nazis."

"Yes, sir. I see the connection. Hitler and Goering and Doenitz and any number of the Hitler gang could get on a long-range U-boat like the Twenty-one and be in Africa or South America before the Allies knew they were missing."

Ben moved forward on his chair. "But would they try to leave from Hamburg when they know they could get caught in the forty-mile run to the sea?"

Admiral Zilke lifted both hands. "That's one of the points we don't understand. It doesn't seem logical or good planning, and our German friends are out-landishly good planners, and logical to a fault. So why? Where else can they leave from? Wilhelmshaven is cut off; Brest and the other French sub bases are all captured or out of commission. That's why we need to go into Hamburg, torpedo everything we see that can move on top or underwater, and if possible put a detachment of commandos in the pens to in-vestigate."

"That last part is going to get messy," Ben said.

"We know. And we realize that you have been there and have the scars and medals to prove it. However, in this case you will be instructed to remain on your ship if commandos do go ashore."

"How many of the commandos are experts on German subs?"

Admiral Zilke laughed. "Yes. I told them you would say something like that. I didn't think you would settle for half the apple. Well, what do you think of the plan? Is it a mission that has a sixty percent chance of success?"

"Yes, I think so."

"Do you want to be involved in it?"

"Damn right!"

"Good. For this raid you'll have the temporary rank of captain. We don't have an American submarine, but we do have a British T-class boat. The skipper has just been promoted and the ship is now ready for you to take it over for a familiarization run. You can report to her at 0800 hours in the morning at the Thames and take her out. She's called the *Thor* and she has a complete complement of men and officers, except for the skipper. You have the next two days for trials, then report back here for your briefing and the final plans for the mission. And *Captain* Mount, good luck!"

Ben saluted, did a snappy about-face, and almost ran out of the office. He found out where the *Thor* was moored and went down to the Thames to look at her. He couldn't help but go on board. He was met at once by a British sublieutenant.

"Captain Mount?" the man asked.

"Yes."

"I'm Sublieutenant Quincy. The first sends his compliments and invites you to the control room."

Ben accepted and they went through the forward hatch. The *Thor* was much larger than the S boats Ben was used to. He had been on the *Topflight,* but it was different now. This was his command. The boat was clean, looked fairly new, and the crew members he saw were smiling and seemed contented.

In the control room he met Lieutenant Commander Bernard Bacon. Bacon was a tall man, broad, heavily muscled, with keen blue eyes and a tousled head of brown hair. The first officer saluted and Ben returned it sharply, then held out his hand.

"I'm Lieutenant Commander Bacon, Captain Mount. We heard you might be coming on board."

"Thank you, Commander. I like the looks of our ship. Are you aware of the upcoming mission?"

"No, sir. They said you would tell us when we need to know. But the sooner the better."

"Let's go into the wardroom and talk. I could use some coffee or tea, whichever you might have."

Coffee was quickly brought. Ben guessed they had made a special purchase of coffee for him and had made it fresh every hour until he arrived.

"Now, gentlemen," he addressed the two officers, "we do have a mission. Tomorrow I'll tell you something about it. In the morning I want to cast off for a two-day cruise. During that time we have to learn to work closely together as a team, to understand each other, and to show that we are ready for any combat situation. We are going on what could turn out to be one of the most important submarine missions of the entire war. Any questions?"

"We have some men on pass, sir," Bacon said.

"Misfortunes of war, Commander. Try to get back those you can. We'll sail with what we have here at 0800 hours. We can run shorthanded for these two days. This training cruise is for my benefit. I take it for granted that the crew is highly trained and everyone can do his job efficiently. How long have you been with the boat, Mr. Bacon?"

"Almost two years, sir."

"You will have your own command soon, Mr. Bacon. Now, I'd appreciate a tour from bow to stern. It's been some time since I've been on a T-class, and I want to be reminded about every nut and bolt. Shall we, Commander?"

Three hours later Ben had a much better idea of what the *Thor* could do and what she couldn't. He was especially pleased to find eight forward torpedo tubes. This was an improved T with more sting than the *Topflight*. She also had three tubes in the stern. If he got in a trap he could play "down-the-throat" with a German river patrol boat the way Hal Iverson had.

The captain's cabin in the corner of the control room was small, but private. It contained a bunk, tiny closet, a chair, and a small table. Ben smiled as he looked at it. It would work nicely.

Back on the dock, he tried to call Betsy, but she had already left for the day. It took him an hour to get to their apartment.

Ben thought about the importance of this mission. The end of the war might not prove to be the end of Adolph Hitler. The madman could very well try to escape to Brazil, or Spain, or some other nation where he would not be considered a war criminal. Hundreds of top Nazis might try to escape. Twenty-one-class boats could take a hundred passengers each! They also might try to take jewels, art treasures, and gold worth literally billions of dollars. The thought made him even more determined to make sure that the monkey business in Hamburg would be dug out and stopped.

Speculation. It all was speculation, and it would remain that way until somebody blasted his way into the pens for the express purpose of finding out what was going on.

Ben tried not to tell Betsy about it that night, but

in the end he told her. They talked for hours about it. Then Betsy cried and begged him to be careful.

The two-day shakedown cruise for the new captain worked out well. Ben learned to rely on his first, Mr. Bacon, and to appreciate the smooth way the crew handled the big craft. He would let the first officer bring the ship into firing positions and launch the torpedoes. Ben's job would be to get them in and out of the river.

Ben hated to leave the *Thor* in the evening. She was what he had always wanted, but he knew it would be a short stay. He went back to the flat and told Betsy about his new craft.

The next morning he was in Admiral Zilke's office at 0930 as ordered. They began to make detailed plans. Then on April 20, 1945, Ben and five other men met in the admiral's office. Ben knew the commander of the other T-class boat involved, Commander Hoyt, and he had met the commando officer, Captain Lester. Suddenly, he did not want to become good friends with either of them. Losing good friends hurt too much.

They worked out final problems, details, plans. They would take two boats in. Each boat would have fifty commandos ready for combat. They would sink surface and underseas craft at the pens and in the port, and then fire remaining torpedoes at the boats in the pens. If the action seemed warranted, they would land troops on the pens and clear them of all personnel, and blow up all U-boats there.

"Gentlemen," Admiral Zilke said, "we have had increased reports of unusual activity at Hamburg, and this puzzles us somewhat, since almost half of the Elbe River is now in our control. Granted, the situation is in flux, and we might be pushed back tomorrow, but when Hamburg was bypassed in the race for Berlin, huge stocks of stores, arms, equipment, submarines, and groups of fighting forces were left behind.

"Most of that is useless now, and with Berlin ready to fall, we're positive that the war is almost over. But that also is the trigger of what we think is a well-thought-out plan for dozens, perhaps hundreds, of top Nazis to escape. We hope to block off that escape, but the Elbe is a wide river, and submarines can sneak in and out. So we have to go in and settle the matter at the Hamburg pens, before they can load and sneak out with their criminal cargo.

"Our new target date is April twenty-ninth, which gives us another week for training and preparation. Right now I'd like reports from both submarine commanders and from the commandos about any problems —anything I can help smooth over."

The next week was a jumble of planning, picking crews, loading stores, and unloading stores. Ben was relieved when they dropped the last line on April 28, 1945, at dawn and moved out.

A day and a half later, the two T-class boats sat on station off the Elbe River. A pair of American destroyers had met them and all checked out the VHF voice radios they carried. The communication was excellent.

Latest reports showed that the first twenty kilometers of the Elbe had been cleared and were in Allied hands. The submarines and destroyers moved upriver and arrived just before dark. At the designated point, the destroyers sat cross channel in a blocking move, and scanned above the surface with radar and underwater with sonar for any evidence of U-boats.

Ben called to the captain of the *Thunder,* and they moved upriver. Both had dropped down far enough that their decks were underwater but part of the conning tower showed.

Ben quickly found that the passage in the dark was much harder than it had been into Brest. The channel was narrower, and he had to check constantly with his charts to stay within deep water. Twice he had to make sudden turns to avoid sandbars.

The *Thunder* trailed them closely. Ben had rigged a small directional light on the stern of his ship to help them follow.

He could see lights along the shore, but in some areas it was totally black. He heard machine-gun fire. It was answered by rifle fire, and then all quieted. A small boat came toward them at high speed. It veered to avoid them at the last minute, and Ben let it go.

"Mr. Bacon, have you ever been shot, or shot at? I mean with a rifle or a pistol or even a machine gun?"

"No, I'm afraid not."

"Good. Let's hope we can keep it that way. Getting shot at up close is no fun, no fun at all."

They kept boring ahead. The river was like a ribbon of steel reflecting the moonlight. The light helped keep them on course, and now all Ben prayed for was that there were no sudden midstream sandbars.

After three hours of dark running, they came to a division in the river. Ben's charts showed he had to swing to the left to get into Hamburg and the pens.

"We're getting close now, Commander," he said. He picked up the radio mike and spoke into it softly.

"*Thunder*?"

The speaker beside him activated at once.

"Ready here, *Thor*."

"A bend here, then about twenty minutes."

"Roger."

Commander Bacon tapped the railing nervously. "It seems so anticlimactic," he said. "We train and

work and prepare and then we simply sail up the river
and we're here."

"The dramatics we can do without, Commander.
Dramatics means somebody gets killed. We just do
our job, we shoot the hell out of all the subs we can
find, we land the commandos and pick them up if we
need to; if we don't, we move out and get our asses
home. No heroics, no wounded, and no letters to write
to mothers and sweethearts of the boys who died."

"Yes, sir. Sorry."

"Live and learn, Commander. If we don't learn
in this business damn fast, we're dead."

They sailed along for five minutes. "You might get
your forward torpedo doors opened, Commander, and
have those eight fish ready to fire."

"Aye, aye, sir."

Bacon spoke into the tube and the crew readied
the bow for firing.

"Shall we open the aft tubes as well, sir?" he asked.

"Good thinking, Mr. Bacon."

It was done.

"Now, damnit, we're ready for you, whoever you
are out there, and wherever you are. We take any
surfaced U-boats stacked in the harbor area first. The
Thunder comes in on our left, Mr. Bacon. We take
any boats on our right, they handle the left. Then
all of our forward tubes except two go into the right
hand half of the sub pens. We want to shoot them
right into those open doors."

They kept working up the river. The current was
sluggish. More lights showed along the shore. Houses,
farms, an occasional taller building. No cars, no traffic.
A soft glow showed farther to the left and ahead.
Ben thought it must be Hamburg.

"Gun crews to stations. Prepare your weapons to
fire. Open ammunition storage. Come to full surface
running."

Ben had not seen pictures of these pens. He had no idea exactly where they were, or how large they were. But they were here and the secret work was here. He would find them.

A machine gun chattered. The noise reminded him of Brest, and his hands tightened on the bridge rail. Then he realized that the sound was from well across the river, two miles from them. He relaxed and stared through his binoculars. He turned and checked the *Thunder*. It was no more than fifty meters behind them. He looked ahead again, waiting to see the docks, the warehouses, the boat works, and the U-boat pens.

"A blinker to the far right, sir."

Ben saw it. It was a navy-type signal. A U-boat would answer it. He couldn't. "Keep it steady as we go, Mr. Bacon. That could be coming from the edge of the pens."

Flare shells. Why didn't he think to bring some flare shells for the four-incher? Ben wasn't sure that they made four-inch flare shells. The signal light came again.

"Give us eight knots forward," Ben barked into the tube. He hit the radio mike switch. "Eight knots, now!"

There was no reply, but the *Thunder* stayed with him.

The river billowed out into a harbor. He wished he could turn off the damn blinker with a round from the twenty-millimeter gun, but not yet. Ben saw the pens looming out of the darkness—huge concrete boxes, like at Brest, slightly ahead and to the left. He hit the radio mike switch.

"Egg basket just forward, you have the left half."

"Roger."

The river wasn't as wide here as he had hoped it

would be. Ben swung the *Thor* away from the target, then turned cross channel and saw the *Thunder* doing the same behind him. Now they both were lined up, and aimed directly at the pens.

There were no submarines lined up outside the pen.

"Mr. Bacon, line her up on the first pen on the right and fire. The current will be moving us slightly sideways downstream, remember."

Bacon had been busy on the target finder. He gave a short command and a torpedo jolted from the *Thor*. They were at point-blank range, not more than a hundred and fifty meters. Bacon began lining up for the second shot when the darkness of the German night was violated with a crackling, stunning roar of TNT. In the brilliant flash, Ben had an image of the pens etched on his brain. He saw a U-boat in the first slot erupting into flames, and guessed that the stern-fired torpedo in the U-boat had exploded as well.

"Fire, gun crews, any target you can find!" he yelled over the noise. Almost at once he heard the four-incher blast from below the bridge.

To the left the *Thunder*'s first torpedo exploded against one of the dividers. Commander Bacon fired again, and another torpedo slanted into the pens. This one took longer to explode, but the blast came from deep inside the slot. They fired four more times, as the boat drifted with the slow current. Ben figured that four of the six torpedoes had hit U-boats. A fire burned brightly at the far end, lighting up much of the harbor. Ben saw a U-boat getting underway near the pens.

"Come to a heading of zero-seven-three, Mr. Bacon. We have a target making way." He followed the jockeying of the big submarine under him, and twenty seconds later the *Thor* fired a torpedo. The U-boat had started to submerge. Ben followed it in the gloom, and just as the control tower started to slip under water, his fish hit, blowing the craft in half, dropping it to the bottom of the bay.

Small-arms fire suddenly came from the roof of the pens. A machine gun fired from the roof, chattering rounds into the bay. High overhead, rifle flares began popping, then larger flares came, and Ben heard heavier guns going off. His own twenty-millimeter gun hammered away, and the four-incher spat out rounds regularly.

Ben got on the radio. "*Thunder*," he called.

"Right, Ben. No way we can land men inside those pens now. We have no platform."

"Right, so we turn around and send our three stern tubes into them."

"Roger, turning now."

It took many precious seconds to maneuver the big submarines in a three-hundred-sixty degree turn in the confines of the small harbor. Ben felt machine-gun fire scraping the *Thor*. One chunk of shrapnel pierced the bridge, but no one was hurt. He took a casualty on the four-incher crew and told them to secure, but he kept the twenty millimeter working.

"You may fire the three stern tubes when ready, Mr. Bacon," he said.

Ben watched with his binoculars. Six more torpedoes from the two submarines blasted into the sub pens at Hamburg, some going inside, some hitting previous wreckage. All went off with devastating effect. Ben checked the level of gunfire from the shore. It was growing stronger.

"Secure front twenty millimeter," he shouted, then sat down on the bridge deck behind the shroud and took the radio mike.

"*Thunder*, let's secure here and move back downstream with as little con showing as possible. Keep your ASDIC man and radar man alert for anything moving on the river."

"Aye, aye. Securing now."

Ben gave the order, and the *Thor* turned and slithered lower in the water and crept away from the smoking, burning hulks in front of the sub pens.

"Mr. Bacon, inspect the boat for damage and report all casualties."

Ben also asked the *Thunder* captain for the same report. He waited. Commander Bacon was ready first.

"One man wounded from rifle fire on the deck-gun crew. No apparent damage to the boat internally. No leaks, all equipment working normally."

"Very good, Mr. Bacon. You may instruct the forward torpedo handlers to reload. Do we still have one forward tube ready to fire?"

"Aye, Captain."

The radio came on.

"Ben, no casualties here. No damage except my skyscope, which is not working, apparently small weapons fire damage. Everything else is shipshape."

"Roger, *Thunder*, we'll go below the port and hold in a blocking position to see if anyone here makes a run for it. If any Twenty-ones are left intact in there I'm guessing they will try to bug out about now."

"Roger, I have you visually, *Thor*, I'll ride your tail."

They went just beyond where the river had forked and set up a small picket line of their own across the Elbe. Their radar searched for submarine snorkels or superstructures, and the ASDIC men checked for any bounce waves that they could find. Within a few minutes a small motorboat came toward them at a high rate of speed from the direction of Hamburg. When it saw them in the pale moonlight, it turned and headed back the way it had come.

The two crews settled down to watching their dials and screens and to waiting.

Chapter 27

After an hour of waiting, they had found no moving craft on the river except the one small boat. For a moment Ben's radar man thought he had a blip, but he couldn't be sure. They asked the *Thunder*'s radar man and he said he wasn't sure either. At last they decided there was a slight bend in the river and he was picking up the reflection of a patch of trees or brush at the edge of the bank.

"Would it be possible for a half-submerged U-boat to be sidled up against the shoreline?" Ben asked the operator. They discussed the possibility but dismissed it.

At 0300 hours they made radio contact with *Thunder* and pulled out. They had the twenty kilometers yet to travel to reach the safe half of the river and the destroyers. They had moved a half a kilometer when the radar man called Ben to his scope.

"It's almost the same pattern, sir. I'm sure it's a ship of some kind. If it's a submarine, they have radar too, and they know where we are and are staying well in back of us."

"Both engines back to two knots," Ben ordered.

"Aye, aye, sir. Two knots."

They watched the blip on the scope. It advanced a little, then slowed and paced them.

"They sure as hell know we're here and have cut

speed and they have matched it," Ben said. "What's the range?"

"Eight hundred meters, the charts show a slight bend in the river about there."

"So she's still hiding. Could we aim well enough to have a chance on that craft with a torpedo? Could we do it with a strictly radar aim off your bearing?"

The radar man looked surprised. "I've never tried that before. What I'm afraid is that there's some land between us and him, some little bend or point."

Ben talked with the other submarine. They had the blip too, and Ben decided to move ahead.

"Come back to six knots, we'll try for him later," Ben said.

An hour later the blip was still behind them. There had been no problems from shore. They had another hour or more to go before they reached the destroyers. It would be daylight in less than two hours. Plenty of time yet.

Ben haunted the radar man. The *Thunder* had moved off to one side in order to be clear of the radar track.

"Is it still there?"

"Yes."

"Do you think he realizes that we know he's tailing us?"

"I'd say he knows we know."

"Then let's throw a pair of fish at him. Are those stern tubes reloaded?"

"Aye, sir, reloaded," Bacon said.

"Open the outer doors, make two parallel tubes ready to fire. Mr. Bacon, adjust our bearing to be exactly one hundred eighty degrees from the bearing on that blip and fire when you are ready."

Bacon hovered over Ben's shoulder. "Range and bearing?"

"Six hundred meters. Bearing, three-two-seven."

There was a thirty-second wait. "Bearing?"

"Continuing at three-two-seven."

Bring our bow to exactly one-four-seven."

"Aye, sir, we're at one-four-seven."

"Fire one and fire two aft," Commander Bacon said. The two torpedoes jolted away. Ben and Commander Bacon hurried topside. The men on the bridge could not follow the wakes or see the target.

"Keep us informed of the range of target," Ben called into the voice tube. The range was shouted up every ten seconds. It varied no more than ten yards.

Ben stared at his first. "That's too long, we missed her." Commander Bacon agreed.

"But we were shooting at a six-foot-wide bow. Any other hit would have slanted off her."

Behind them a flash lighted the sky for a moment, then vanished. There was little sound.

"That was the shore we hit," Ben said.

"Target range?" Ben called.

"Six-four-five."

"We tried," the captain said. "Let's hope he doesn't speak English. We'll suck him along as far as we can and hope the destroyer with its higher radar scan can see him too. Then when we get within a kilometer of the destroyer, we'll ask him to put a dozen rounds on the third blip, six hundred meters behind us. It just might work."

Ben and Commander Bacon looked downstream, kept the *Thor* between the banks, and wished they could make better time.

"Captain, do you think we did much good back there with our fireworks at Hamburg?"

Ben laughed. "Hell yes, we did some good. We must have sent to the bottom twelve to fifteen U-boats. And we hope we blasted some of their secret Twenty-ones. We'll have to wait until after the war ends, then we can get in there and look around to know for sure. But our cost so far was one man wounded. Any good? Hell yes, we did just fine."

"Sir, I have the destroyer on radar, two thousand meters downstream," the radar man said. "The bandit is still hanging in about five hundred meters upstream from us."

Ben took the radio mike to the VHF set.

"Dee One and Two, this is *Thor*. Do you read?"

"Go ahead, *Thor*."

"Estimate two-zero-zero-zero meters from our position to yours. We have a swimming bandit five-zero-zero meters behind our blip, your screen. Can you send twenty rounds on the bandit with radar aiming?"

"When we have him; he's not on our screen yet. Will advise."

Ben waited. It stretched out to five minutes.

"Range to bandit?" he asked.

"Holding at five-zero-zero meters, sir. The destroyers are now at one-five-zero-zero meters."

Ben looked at the speaker. Then it came to life.

"Swimming buddy, we have your bandit on screen. Starting fire now. Do you have him visually?"

"No, Big Dee, no visual."

"Two rounds to register on the way."

A moment later they heard the rounds whisper as the friendly fire flew overhead. The shells went off underwater behind them about five hundred meters, but there was little more than a dull growling. They had exploded underwater.

"Water bursts, Big Dee, my guess. No way we can adjust your fire from here."

"Right, small swimmer. We'll send in twenty on account. Uncle Sam is paying the tab."

Ben heard the rounds go overhead. Most went off in the water or under it with little sound. Two hit the shore and erupted with flashes and a roar that slammed downstream at them.

"What's the bandit's range," Ben asked radar.

"No signal, she must have dived."

"Check the ASDIC."

"Yes, I have her. Range five hundred meters."

By the time the *Thor* came within sight of the two American tin cans, the first streaks of light had snaked into the sky. The enemy U-boat was still behind them, falling farther back but maintaining its underwater position. Ben guessed they were at periscope level and flying by charts until it was light enough to navigate by periscope alone. Then she would try to sneak past the destroyers.

"*Thor*, we lost the bandit on radar," the speaker said. "Did we hit the bandit or did it go underwater?"

"She's dived, Big Dee. She's still following us from down under. Periscope depth I'd guess. Try your sonar."

"You're blocking out the other signals, *Thor*."

"Got any new ideas?"

"Wait her out. She must be trying to get to the sea."

Soon Ben could see the destroyers angled into the slow current with props working to keep them there. They were waiting. Ben's radio sounded again.

"Trouble, *Thor*. I have three more blips coming downriver. And now I get a sonar closer as well. I'd guess we have four U-boats."

"We have no more new blips here."

"Our antenna is higher. Suggest you and the *Thunder* slip past us downstream, and check to see if any of these four get past us."

Ben agreed, and the two British subs passed between the destroyers and slid into calmer water near the shore. They then rode the surface and had both radar and ASDIC working.

"*Thunder*, let's both aim slightly upstream, enough so we will miss each other if we fire a torpedo. Then we can take a shot at any U-boat we see or hear coming down."

Upstream four hundred meters Ben could see the destroyers poised for an attack. The U-boats seemed determined to try to run for it, to break through the destroyer defense. They were playing the odds, hoping one or two could get through. Why were they so desperate? Were these the boats with the loads of loot and top German brass?

Ben watched the destroyers go into action. Simultaneously, they shot out clusters of Squid missiles. One of the subs came to the surface and limped to the shore, where it beached. A second U-boat must have trailed the first and fired a torpedo. It couldn't have traveled fifty meters before it blasted the bow of the destroyer, and the tin can rapidly beached itself and settled into the mud. The second U-boat fell to the attack of the other destroyer.

"Target coming downstream fast!" the ASDIC man shouted. Radar spotted the periscope, and then the *Thunder* skipper called on the radio that they had it, a salvo of two were on the way.

Ben watched. He saw the fish jolt into the river. Then he saw the current catch one and swing it to one side. The other came later, and before the current caught it, the U-boat surged in front of it and a blinding flash erupted in the river into a geyser of water and metal fragments.

"Anything else?" Ben yelled at the ASDIC operator.

"Yes, I have another target, it's receding, going downstream fast."

"Let's haul ass out of here," Ben shouted. Bacon got the boat moving and Ben grabbed the mike. "One got past us somehow, heading downstream," he said. The *Thunder* turned and moved with Ben and the destroyer came surging after them. They made room in the middle of the river, and the sub chaser charged through, slanting too fast down the Elbe after the vanishing U-boat.

The two British subs chased after the destroyer on the surface at over sixteen knots.

"How fast can that new German boat travel underwater?" Bacon asked.

"I don't know. But how did he get past us?"

Bacon lowered his glasses. "She must have been side by side with the one the *Thunder* hit. Two boats that were so close that they sent back one ASDIC signal. I've heard it happening before."

"If they went to that kind of trouble to get out of here, that must be one damn important U-boat," Ben said. "We've got to nail that one."

The radio speaker blared again. "The destroyer should kill that U-boat easily in these waters," the *Thunder* skipper said.

Ben pushed the radio mike switch. "I don't think so, too much shallow water. The sub can slink along the shallows and the destroyer can't even get close. He'll have to rely on his Squid to throw out that circle of twenty-four depth charges."

They rounded a small bend in the river and saw the destroyer stopped ahead. Suddenly, black smoke poured from her stacks and she charged downriver. Two hours later Ben had his last radio communication with the destroyer.

"At mouth of the Elbe, the U-boat is in the North Sea heading north. In pursuit. Our guess here is that the sub may be heading for some secure Nazi positions in southern Norway."

The destroyer captain then sent the radio frequency they used for CW transmissions in Morse code so that it would span many hundreds of miles. They would use it in the clear.

Ben instructed his radio operator to make contact

with the destroyer on the CW frequency and tell them they would be following at fifteen and a half knots, and to keep them informed of any developments or change in general direction.

He relayed the same information to *Thunder.* "Our mission is to destroy those U-boats we found at the pens, but we've let one get away, so let's see where it goes and go get it. We don't have any other pressing mission."

"It might go a thousand kilometers up into the far parts of Norway somewhere," the *Thunder* captain said.

"Then we'll go up there, too. We have plenty of fuel and stores. Inform the commandos that they can relax, get their gear stowed, and start their card games. They have a long cruise ahead of them."

It was a tedious chase. Every four hours Ben checked with the destroyer by radio. A pattern developed. The U-boat could run faster and drop deeper than any the destroyer captain had ever fought, and he was running low on depth charges. Now he was mostly shadowing the sub. It would run underwater at high speeds, then drop into the depths and go silent. The quarry was only twenty kilometers ahead of Ben on the last check.

The fox and hounds game continued.

Forty-four hours later, Ben brought the *Thor* to a stop a hundred meters from the American destroyer and picked up his hand mike.

"Big Dee, where is your little playmate?"

"She slipped inside, and she's all yours. She went into the fjord there, and I'm not going after her. I'd be like a fish in a barrel for her. That's Trondheims Fjord, and the Nazis have some good-sized U-boat pens there that are still solidly in German hands."

"Any E boats included?"

"Don't know, *Thor.*"

"Thanks anyway. You stay outside while I go in and flush him out. *Thunder*, are you there?"

"Ready and waiting."

"Let's divide and conquer here. I'll go into the fjord and the bay and see what I can find. You stay out here with the destroyer and set a trap at the mouth of the fjord. Watch out for those islands down a ways. If we're lucky I can make some noise inside and scare the rat right out of his hole and send him racing out to your net. It's certain now that it is a Twenty-one-class boat in there, and it must tie in with the big Nazi bigwig bug-out plan. I'll go hunting and see what I can find. If I'm not back in six hours, come in with all tubes ready to fire."

"Aye, Ben, take care."

The British submarine *Thor* submerged to periscope level and edged into the fjord. Ben had no charts. Most fjords are outlandishly deep, and he hoped this one was as well. Ben was at the periscope as the craft moved through the channel and inland toward the huge Trondheim bay. The going was slow, and the walls of rock seemed to jolt out at him too quickly. They stopped and Ben edged slowly through a narrow section, and made it without scraping the rust off the bow. Sometime later they came to the opening where a large bay stretched out to the north as far as he could see. Now all Ben had to do was find the city of Trondheim and the pens.

Chapter 28

Commander Wilhelm Fricke waited anxiously in the officers' wardroom at the Trondheim submarine pens. It was much fancier than any other such facility he had seen. The men and officers up in the middle of Norway seemed to have nothing better to do than fix up their living quarters—forcing the Norwegians to do the work, he was sure. What a ridiculous waste of manpower, he thought. All of them should have rifles protecting the Fatherland!

Fricke was still furious and enormously depressed because Germany had lost the war. It was all over now but the final acts. The raid on the Hamburg U-boat pens had been the clincher for him. The Allied raiders had left the base in a total state of destruction. Only four U-boats had been able to leave, and now of the four he was the only one left. There had been four Twenty-one-class U-boats converted for Project Swordfish. Everything was planned, preparations all made. The last two converted boats would leave on the thirtieth to go to Trondheim. They had been one damn day late. One damn day late! What had gone wrong? Hell, almost everything had gone wrong in the past year. First the invasion, then the loss of so many men and so much equipment, and the bombing raids, the incessant, inhuman bombing raids!

He filled the small glass with schnapps and stared at the bottle. This one was a strong gin from Holland. He didn't even like gin.

In Hamburg he had stood and cried when Admiral Doenitz himself told Fricke the plan. That was almost three months ago. It was inevitable, Doenitz had said. The war was lost. It was only a matter of time. Four of the Twenty-one-class submarines were to be gutted of all arms and torpedoes. Quarters were to be built with minimum comfort for eighty persons, civilians, in each of the U-boats. They were to be supplied with food and equipment and fuel suitable for an eighteen-hundred-kilometer trip. They must be ready by April 15. They were.

Now only three such vessels remained. His was the best of the three. One had been destroyed in the Hamburg raid. The other two were already in Trondheim waiting for passengers.

Some high-level German officials were there. Others would arrive by transport aircraft on the small airstrip just in back of the base. The deadline was definite. The U-boats would leave May 2, at the latest, or when all passengers had arrived. There were not as many people as had been planned. Only one U-boat would be going—his. The men at the base had strict instructions to blow up both the other Twenty-one-class boats as soon as Fricke's had cleared the passage into the sea.

Wilhelm Fricke pushed away the glass of gin. He went into the special area in the pens at the end where the steel doors closed off the bay. Yes, he was told the passengers were comfortable, getting used to their surroundings. There were twenty so far. He knew only a few of them by sight. The others had names that were familiar to him when he saw them on his list. They were not the cream of the German intellectuals and military strategists he had been promised.

Fricke had not dared to ask Admiral Doenitz if the top leadership would be leaving. Was that the plan? Or would the top men be sacrificed to the victors? Would they be the scapegoats? He had heard that a stalking horse Führer, an imitation Hitler, would die in the bunker in Berlin. If so, would the real Adolph Hitler be on Fricke's boat? His boat had the only stateroom, a space where twenty bunks could have gone. It had a bed, a rocking chair, a record player, and a small movie screen with projector. Two of Eva Braun's early films had been carefully stored there.

He checked his watch. It was time to go to the airport to pick up the last load of passengers. His boat would sail soon. No more than thirty more persons were expected.

The airport was close by, and the two-engine plane came in low, skimming trees and buildings all the way from Berlin. It landed and taxied to the small main terminal building.

Fricke was at the aircraft's steps welcoming the passengers. Some he knew, most he did not. They were second- and third-level officials, for the most part, who had much to fear from the Allies, and from the occupied countries.

One older man wore a hat pulled low and a scarf around his face. He disembarked last, seemed in ill health, walked with a slight limp, but would not accept assistance. An aide hovered around him.

Fricke's heart pounded. Yes, he was about the right size and the right build. Fricke helped the passengers into a dozen staff cars and ordered them to the sub pens. A truck backed up and unloaded trunks, suitcases, and locked boxes from the aircraft. They were carefully counted and numbers on each checked against a written list, and then Fricke signed for them. He felt sure that if just one of the boxes was missing, he would be executed on the spot.

A half hour later the passengers were on board the submarine. There were forty-five—thirty-five men and ten women. The old man with the covered face had been placed in the large cabin, and none of the crew was permitted to enter. Only one person had the door key. He was a stony-faced colonel, the aide Fricke had seen at the plane. The man was abrupt, overbearing, and contemptuous.

Fricke motioned the colonel into the captain's cabin off the control room. He closed and locked the door, then pulled out his Luger, and put the muzzle against the colonel's right eye.

"Colonel, you need to understand something. I don't need you on this cruise. Rather, you need me. I could blow your brains all over this cabin right now and no one would care, no one would even come to see what happened. I am in complete and total command. Now, you will tell me who the man is in the cabin. I have a right to know."

The thin colonel seemed to age ten years as he nodded.

"I will let you look through the slot in the door, which has a locked cover. I use it from time to time to be sure that he is all right. His health is poor."

They went to the door, and Fricke looked through the slot. He lifted his brows, stared again, then clicked his heels, saluted the aide, and went back to the control room.

Five minutes later they were ready, and Fricke ordered the lines cast off. It was still daylight, but there would be no trouble in the fjord. He would submerge anyway and leave with a pack of four other U-boats. They were told they all were going on a

race back to Hamburg for a final slashing attack at
an invasion force ready to land at the mouth of the
Elbe. They did not know there was an American destroyer at the fjord entrance.

Chapter 29

Ben's hands were relaxed on the grips of the periscope as he turned around. They were in a huge bay, or perhaps a series of finger bays, that ran in both directions from the entrance. The small town of Trondheim was almost due east of the bay entrance and the sub pens were close by.

They moved eastward slowly, at periscope depth. Ben saw no ships in the huge bay and few buildings along the shores. The green hills seemed almost deserted. A rounded hump of green extended into the bay ahead, and Ben swung around it. Just beyond the point of land he saw the town and the concrete gray of the massive submarine pens. Bacon was standing by, and Ben let him take a look."

When Ben took the handles of the scope again, he did a three-hundred-sixty-degree turn just to check, then concentrated on the pens. They were still a kilometer away, but coming up at six knots. Suddenly, Ben shouted.

"My God, there she is! A big U-boat just came out from the last slot in the pens. That has to be a Twenty-one class. Bacon, come take a look."

The first stared at the sub, then agreed it was a Twenty-one.

"Let's try for a hit now, before she can dive. Get your bearings, Mr. Bacon."

Bacon went to work with the bearings and estimated range.

"Shoot a pair, sir?" Bacon asked.

Ben nodded and watched as the officer angled the *Thor* to exactly the heading he wanted. He checked his time and gave the order to fire two rounds.

"Two fish running, Skipper," Commander Bacon said.

"Good, I can't see the wakes, and I hope the lookouts on the Twenty-one over there can't see them either."

Ben was counting the seconds, then he swore as he stared through the periscope.

"She turned! She couldn't have seen us or the fish. She made a damn course change and is coming toward the bay entrance. Our fish will miss her by two hundred meters. Damnit!" he growled.

The torpedoes blasted into the shore across the way and woke up every Nazi within a dozen kilometers.

"She's turned and is coming almost directly at us," Ben said. He stared into the eyepiece again. "Now she's going to submerge, going to periscope depth, I'd guess. Now we don't have a chance in Billy hell of hitting her."

"What action, Skipper?"

"All stop," Ben barked.

"Aye, all stop."

"Maintain trim," he said. The periscope was barely out of the water. There was little chop or wave action in the quiet bay. He stared hard at where the U-boat had vanished, and could see a small feather working toward him.

"No noise, no movement, no transmissions. She should come within fifty or sixty meters of us. But we can't get off a shot. We just wait."

Ben hit the button lowering the scope until water

lapped the lens, then raised it six inches. When the U-boat was within two hundred meters, he would drop the scope underwater.

"Turn off that ASDIC," he shouted.

"It's off, sir. Been off since you said no transmissions."

Ben nodded at the operator, thanking him.

He looked back at the scope, followed the feather of foam from behind the U-boat periscope. It came closer and grew larger. He hit the button and lowered the scope under the water.

"Time it," Ben said. "Two minutes blind."

It was as bad as waiting out a depth charge attack.

"Two minutes, sir," the radioman said.

Ben touched the button, and the scope went up a foot. He saw the water clear the lens then stopped it. He turned it to face the direction the Twenty-one-class U-boat would be. He saw the feather again. It was a hundred meters ahead. Ben did a three-hundred-sixty-degree turn on the periscope looking all ways, then he groaned.

"Trouble, gentlemen. There are four more subs pulling out from the pens. All are VII-C class. All are on the surface, and probably going out as a screen for the big one. Let's get underway. Mr. Bacon, come ahead and swing her around so we can take some bow shots at these ducks if they keep coming. We need about three hundred meters."

The *Thor* moved ahead and turned, then lined up until she was nearly at a ninety-degree angle to the oncoming flotilla.

"I'd say a salvo of six, Mr. Bacon. Space them and see what kind of shooting you can do."

Commander Bacon worked his aiming gear, his fruit machine, and finished his calculations. He used ranges and bearings and then adjusted the bearing of the *Thor* and waited. He checked his calculations again.

"Fire number three tube," he shouted. Ten seconds went by. "Fire number four." He spaced the torpedoes in hope of picking off each of the U-boats like ducks in a shooting gallery.

Ben followed the progress of the first shot. The torpedo closed on a collision course. Suddenly the lead U-boat lifted halfway out of the water. Her bow blew off, and the sound of the blast came surging through the water. A cheer went up.

"Scratch the leader," Ben shouted. Other boats in the line turned rapidly. They waited. "Miss on number two shot," Ben guessed out loud.

A few seconds later the third boat in line swung to the right and connected with a torpedo.

"Whammo! Two down," Ben called. He gave the scope to Mr. Bacon, who saw the ship writhing in its thirty-second death struggle. By that time the other two subs had submerged into the bay and vanished.

"ASDIC report," Ben said.

"Both targets rushing at top underwater speed toward the mouth of the fjord. Range six-zero-zero and increasing."

"Let's follow them, Mr. Bacon. Good shooting. All ahead full. Keep a thirty-second report on those U-boats. Let's herd them into the net."

When Ben was sure that the three German U-boats had entered the channel of the fjord leading out to the North Sea, he had the radioman fire up his CW set and send word to the destroyer that three swimmers were coming at him, one big one and two small ones. They received a reply that the fishnet was ready and waiting.

Ben brought the *Thor* to the surface and ploughed through the Trondheims Fjord at top speed.

He pushed the *Thor* as fast as he could, yet when he came to the mouth of the fjord, neither the destroyer nor the *Thunder* was in sight. He used the voice radio and picked up *Thunder,* who gave him a quick recap.

"They sent out the small subs one at a time, and we sank both of them; but the destroyer was low on depth charges by then, and his Squids were almost gone. The Twenty-one came out so fast and so close to the fjord wall that we missed her. I fired two torpedoes at it and we still missed."

"Where are you?"

He gave the bearing from the fjord mouth. "About six or seven miles south. We've got the sub hurt. One of the Squids did the trick, and the Twenty-one is hiding around a small island. It's looking for some shallow passages where the destroyer can't scrape across."

"Meet you there soon," Ben said, and they charged south along the coast at fifteen knots.

The *Thor* had gone less than three miles on the heading when the ASDIC reported a target moving slowly toward them. The sub was five thousand meters out, and the signal was strange, distorted. Ben cut off the ASDIC and found her with radar. As he suspected, she was surfacing.

"She's on the top whatever she is," he said.

They went to periscope depth and checked on the craft. Ben came up on her slowly, and what he saw surprised him. He had Mr. Bacon take a look to be sure.

"Aye, Skipper. That's the same U-boat we saw in Trondheim bay. She had that paint slash on her con and that same strange mast and snorkel. It's the same boat."

"She's not in trim, Mr. Bacon."

"No, sir. Listing to port. I'd say she has serious damage, and has taken on some extra ballast water she can't pump out."

"And would you say she's heading for Trondheim again?"

"Aye, Skipper, that I would."

Ben got on the radio and checked with the destroyer.

"Are you positive you still have a bandit swimmer there, Big Dee?"

"Not positive, but she went silent and we haven't heard from her. She's here somewhere."

"I don't think so, Big Dee. We have a seriously damaged Twenty-one-class U-boat eleven hundred meters off our bow. Do you want to come confirm before we put a torpedo into her? She's heading back for Trondheim thinking she gave you the slip. Which she must have done."

The skipper of the destroyer was quiet for a moment.

"Our apologies, we lost her, you have her. We have you both on radar. I'll confirm your kill when she goes off radar. Good hunting, *Thor*."

Commander Bacon looked at Ben. "That's more a passenger ship than a man o' war."

"True, but most of those passengers are German criminals, killers and worse, or they wouldn't be on board. You heard about those extermination camps they found in Poland."

Ben and Bacon looked at each other.

"Commander, do we have two forward tubes reloaded?"

"Aye, sir, we do."

"Open the outer doors, Mr. Bacon, and prepare two tubes in the bow for firing."

Bacon sent word forward to flood two tubes, then open the outer doors.

"Two forward torpedoes ready to fire, sir."

Ben moved up to within five hundred meters of the U-boat, saw a frantic attempt to dive the craft, then instructed Mr. Bacon to come to firing position. He quickly calculated, adjusted, then looked up.

"Ready to fire, sir."

"Fire, Mr. Bacon."

"Fire one and two," he said.

They felt the fish expelled by compressed air. Ben watched the big submarine in the scope. One torpedo struck the Twenty-one-class boat near midships. She broke in half. Ben had Commander Bacon confirm the hit. She sank almost at once. There were no survivors.

"Inform the crew of the kill, Mr. Bacon, and then secure the forward tubes and take us back to London. I'll be in my cabin."

Chapter 30

It took them three days to run back to London. They were in no hurry, and by the time they docked and got the commandos offloaded, it was May 4. Ben checked in with Admiral Zilke and gave a complete report. He had a there-hour debriefing with Naval Intelligence and OSS men who had recent information about Hitler's headquarters in Berlin.

Admiral Zilke was expansive.

"We're damned interested in who and what might have been on that U-boat. She got away from Hamburg, which was linked to Berlin that last week. Anyone could have left Berlin, driven to Hamburg, and then got to Trondheim on that U-boat. We know there were some low-flying passenger planes sneaking out of Germany. We shot down at least two and checked them. They were filled with government officials and what looked like stolen gold, jewels, and Allied currency. We guessed at a large-scale bug-out of Hitler's top echelon." The admiral took a phone call, smiled, said a few words, and hung up. He looked around the table at the dozen officers and grinned.

"Gentlemen, let me be the first to tell you. Tonight at 1830 hours, Admiral Hans-Georg von Friedeburg, commander in chief of the *Kriegsmarine*, signed the total and unconditional surrender of Germans in Berlin. The cease fire is set for three days from now on May seventh, 1945. Gentlemen, the war in Europe is over!"

The room erupted with cheers, backslapping, and handshakes. The men milled around for a few minutes laughing, shouting, and clapping.

Then Admiral Zilke asked for their attention. "That's not official until you hear it on the civilian wire services, and it may not be announced until May sixth, but it's happened. We have no need for this meeting. Thank you, gentlemen."

They all jumped to their feet as the admiral and his aide walked out the door.

The rest of the men left at once. Ben found his staff car and drove to his flat as calmly as he could in his excitement. It was nearly nine o'clock. He hoped Betsy was there.

When he came to the door on the second floor, he put his key in the lock, and heard music. He knocked.

The door opened and Betsy stood there with a drink in her hand.

"Ben! Darling, come in, we've been waiting for you!"

The glass in her hand disappeared and Betsy was in his arms and everything was fine. He kissed her a dozen times, then slowly became aware of others. The first face he saw was Moxie Mulford's.

"Moxie!" he bellowed. He grabbed Moxie's hand and whacked him on the back. "Where did you come from?"

"Just dropped in, with Pru."

Ben turned, and Pru was hugging him and kissing him warmly.

"When I tracked you down this time, you were out sailing around again in the North Sea. Today I called, and they said you were coming back. Pru found Betsy, so we came here to wait for you."

Ben looked at them. "You haven't heard, have you?"

"What, Ben?" Betsy asked, suddenly frightened.

"The Germans surrendered at six thirty tonight. Cease-fire in three days. The damn war in Europe is over!"

Moxie looked stunned. "How do you know?"

"A phone call to Admiral Zilke just before our meeting broke up. He told us. Sounds official to me."

The women screamed and cried, Ben and Moxie shook hands and slapped each other on the back. Everyone kissed everyone else. Then the toasts began.

"To the end of the war in Europe!"

"To the end of the killing."

"To sweethearts all over the world who will be reunited."

"In remembrance of all those who died in this one."

"To those of us who lived to tell about it!"

Pru began to cry, and the toasts ended. "I always cry when I'm happy."

They talked about the good times, the old times, all the way back to 1939. Soon it was past midnight.

The girls had made the arrangements. Pru and Moxie would use the bedroom and Ben and Betsy the couch in the living room. When the other two had gone to bed, Ben sat on the couch and Betsy snuggled close to him.

"It's really ended?"

"Yes, it's over. I knew it was close for a couple of months. Some of the OSS men said they think Hitler and Eva Braun are dead, suicides in the bunker in Berlin three or four days ago."

"I can't cry for them."

"I can cry for all the good men and women Hitler killed. It's been in the millions. Betsy, millions!"

"At least this half of it is over."

"This half," Ben said.

"What's next for you, for us?"

"I'm going to try to get transferred to the Pacific before the rush starts."

"But darling, can't you stay here in a nice safe job, where we can be together? You've done more than your share."

"The only ones who did more than their share are dead. No, I want the Pacific, Betsy. I want to fight for my own navy in the boats I trained on. I want a Fleet-class U.S. submarine to command."

"And where does that leave me?"

"It could put you in Honolulu. Hawaii is nice any time of the year."

"I could never get there. Travel restrictions."

"If you went as my wife . . ."

She stared at him. "Not yet, Ben, not yet. I don't think I'm ready for marriage."

"I don't think I am either, Betsy."

He settled back on the couch and closed his eyes. Then he told her about the U-boat they chased for five hundred miles and how they finally sank it, and who they thought might be on board.

They talked quietly. Ben kissed her and held her close. But Ben knew that for him the war was not yet over. It wouldn't be over until the Japanese were pushed back into their island fortress and that bastion was smashed. He was a submariner. He would get a command in the Pacific and fight again.

He kissed Betsy.

"Hold me tight, Ben. I get that old fear that you're about to go off again, to go far away."

He held her and kissed her and tried to make her understand. He was a submariner, and there was still a big job to do. At last she nodded, but he knew that she didn't really understand.

Ben closed his eyes and wondered what he would do in the Pacific, how soon he could get over there, and where his command would be.